P9-DFM-040

RANDOM HOUSE
LARGE PRINT

Also by Luanne Rice
Available from Random House Large Print

The Geometry of Sisters
The Edge of Winter
Last Kiss
Light of the Moon
Sandcastles
Summer of Roses
Summer's Child
What Matters Most

The Deep Blue Sea for Beginners

LUANNE RICE

The Deep Blue Sea for Beginners

[A Novel]

RANDOM HOUSE
LARGE PRINT

This is a work of fiction. Names, characters, places, and incidents either are the product of the author's imagination or are used fictitiously. Any resemblance to actual persons, living or dead, events, or locales is entirely coincidental.

Published in the United States of America by Random House Large Print in association with Bantam Dell, New York.
Distributed by Random House, Inc., New York.

Cover design by Shasti O'Leary Soudant
Cover photograph © Trinette Reed/Getty Images

The Library of Congress has established a Cataloging-in-Publication record for this title.

ISBN: 978-0-7393-2847-7

www.randomhouse.com/largeprint

FIRST LARGE PRINT EDITION

10 9 8 7 6 5 4 3 2 1

This Large Print edition published in accord with the standards of the N.A.V.H.

To Molly Goettsche and Mia Onorato

The Deep Blue Sea for Beginners

Prologue

Lyra Nicholson Davis stood in the olive orchard at the far end of the walled garden overlooking the Bay of Naples. Bees hummed in the bougainvillea, and the morning breeze rustled the fine, silvery leaves overhead. The blue water of Capri was calm and clear, the surface scratched by white wakes of passing ships.

Max had gone to pick up Pell. He'd taken the small yellow boat, left before dawn, to wait at the dock in Sorrento. Pell's flight was on time. Lyra had checked online, had tracked the plane from New York to Rome, watched the tiny airplane graphic as it flew across the Atlantic.

The binoculars felt hot in her hand. What would she see when she looked through them at the boat coming across the water? Would she recognize her daughter? Of course, she told herself. Pell's school pictures were lovely; Lyra had tucked each one away, along with Lucy's, in a corner of her desk drawer.

She looked at her watch: ten a.m. Life was full of changes; every day was a coming together, a casting off. Small things: the white roses were blooming again, the full-moon tide swept a pair of oars off the rocks, you lost your glasses. Big things, too, that took your breath away, altered everything, exploded the course of life.

The joyful ones: she got married, she had two babies. The terrible ones: death, loss. So often the really huge moments came as a shock, a tsunami on a sunny day. It was rare to be given fair notice that the world you've built is about to change.

For Lyra, it would happen within the hour. She held the binoculars, wanting to lift them to her eyes. But she couldn't, not yet. The minute she did, started scanning the horizon for the yellow boat, she would be a mother again.

She would see a girl she barely knew. Brave, amazing child, to have flown all this way, to meet the woman who'd abandoned her and her sister. What kind of young girl would do that? Initiate this visit, get on a plane, come to Capri. What would their first hug be like? Or would Pell push her away?

Lyra couldn't bring herself to raise the binoculars to her eyes. Blue sky and sea surrounded her. Sky, blue sky. Deep, blue deep. Capri. Where she had come to escape herself and all she'd given away.

She wasn't sure she deserved to get any of it back.

One

I'd flown all night. Taking off from New York, banking over the Atlantic, the plane had headed east into the darkness, toward Rome. Stars filled the sky. Once the flight attendants dimmed the cabin lights, I stared out the window at a thousand constellations. I don't think I slept a minute. My thoughts were a web, swinging me from one star to the next.

I was alone. I mean, there were other people on the plane, but I was traveling by myself, without Lucy. You don't take little sisters on missions, especially when you are completely unsure of the outcome. My grandmother insisted I fly first-class. It wasn't even a discussion—once I told her that I was going to Italy to see my mother, as much as she disliked the idea, she put me in touch with the family travel agent, with the words "Pell Davis, you've always loved a lost cause."

Travis drove me from Newport, Rhode Island, to JFK. We didn't speak a lot. We each had too much on our minds. He had to get back to his job, I was thinking about what I'd set out for myself on this trip, and we both were considering the weeks of being apart looming ahead.

There were good reasons for this trip. I knew I didn't have to explain them to Travis. He's my boyfriend, but we have an unusual relationship. He's a football star at our school, and therefore tough, but sensitive in ways that belie outward facts.

He drove me through Connecticut, across the Whitestone Bridge, to the Alitalia terminal at JFK. We got there very early, hours to spare. The June midday sun was hot as we stepped out of the car.

Travis lifted my bags and backpack from the trunk, checked to make sure I had my passport. Twenty-four hours earlier, the maximum allowable span, he had printed out my boarding pass for me. I looked at my watch, calculating the time he would need to drive home to Newport. He had signed on to a fishing boat as deckhand, and they went out at dusk.

We took care of each other, just as we took care of our sisters and, in Travis's case, his mother. Both of our fathers are dead. They died too young, beloved men. We are shaped by the loss of our fathers, and others. Perhaps that's what drew me to Travis in the first place, a sense that he understood love and life's beauty are real, but any assurance they will last forever is a soothing lie.

The flight from New York was smooth. Flying eastward across Long Island at sunset, I looked down and saw the North and South Forks, the curve of Montauk, the dark water of Block Island Sound beneath scratchy white wakes of fishing boats and pleasure craft. Could one of those boats hold Travis? I chose to think yes, I saw him as I left, and he watched my plane pass overhead.

Love is like that. You can see everything. All it takes is the right kind of attention. When my father taught me to play baseball, we'd stand out in the yard until the light died and fireflies came out. He'd throw and I'd catch, or he'd pitch and I'd hit. He'd say, "Don't take your eyes off the ball, sweetheart. No matter what, just keep your eyes on the ball." That's how to see everything with the people you love—keep watching, stay vigilant, watch the ball instead of the fireflies.

So my last sight over the United States was of Travis's boat. He and his family are looking after my sleepwalking sister while I am gone. An ocean later, I landed at Rome, was met by a driver, and taken to Sorrento. Two and a half hours on the road, a chance to think about what I am about to do.

The long drive from Rome to Sorrento, jetlagged, horns blaring, my grandmother's style of driver: uniformed chauffeur. I will be straightforward about something right now, just so you will understand. Gossip columns, before and after she left the country, referred to my mother as "Lyra

Nicholson Davis, heiress." Now they say the same of Lucy and me. Old money, blue bloods, heirs to the Nicholson silver fortune. We ignore what is said. They now say of my mother, "reclusive heiress." We overlook that too.

My grandmother arranged to borrow the chauffeur from her friend Contessa Otavia Migliori, who used to spend summers in Newport, at Stone Lea, the property next door to what used to be the Aitkens', parents of Martha Sharp Crawford, also known as Sunny von Bülow. Another tragic Newport family. I think of Cosima, daughter of Sunny and Claus, her father accused of trying to kill her mother over Christmas holidays by injecting her with insulin, then leaving her in a room with windows open to the frigid sea air. He was convicted, then acquitted.

This is the most terrible thing I ever heard, and it sticks with me over the years, but I once heard my mother crying, shrieking, that something was killing her, killing everything she had inside her. Even as a child, I knew she wasn't talking about a knife or a gun or a drug. She meant her heart and soul. She left us about a week later. And the really unjust, awful thing is, it took a few years, but my father is the one who wound up dying.

Anyway, the contessa's chauffeur drove me to Sorrento, an ancient seaside city filled with dark and crumbling beauty I felt too nervous to notice. Lucy would have—she loves antiquities, ghosts, and architecture. I felt pricked by guilt; perhaps I should have brought my sister. Will Lucy be okay without me this summer? We're very close. For so long, we've been each other's most important person.

But the alternative was to bring her along, without knowing what to expect. What if our mother rejects us all over again? I am strong. I have Travis. But Lucy is my little sister. I want to protect her.

The limousine snaked down the hill to the port. Bright boats lined the docks, reminding me of Newport. I opened the window to smell the sea air. The chauffeur seemed to know just where to go.

He drove along the quay, past shops selling shell jewelry, colorful pareos, and finely woven sun hats. I saw stalls of fresh fish, their glistening bodies packed in seaweed, yellow eyes flat and sightless. The smell of strong coffee hit me as we passed a café. I wanted some, but couldn't bear to stop until I saw if she'd come to meet me.

We drove between a pair of stone pillars, onto a wooden dock. It seemed like a loading zone—fishing boats and small cargo vessels were tied alongside, and trucks filled with supplies for the islands parked along the edge. Metal and wind: halyards clanging against masts, longshoremen swinging big iron hooks. We stopped at the end of the pier. I climbed out. It felt good to stretch my legs, but my chest was in a knot. Had my mother come to meet me? Was I about to see her?

The chauffeur lowered my bags into a yellow wooden boat tied to barnacle-covered pilings. An old man in a blue shirt and rumpled khakis, his face tan and wrinkled and hair pure white, grabbed the bags, stowed them under a varnished wooden seat. I stood on the dock, staring at the man.

"Hello, Pell," the man said in an English accent. "Come along now, and I'll take you to your mother."

"She's not here," I said stupidly.

"No," he said without explanation. I was upset, and he could see. He stared at me with sharp blue eyes. He didn't fill the silence with excuses about a headache, an important phone call, an earthquake, a plague of locusts, any of the many things that could have detained her. Reaching up, he offered to help me down into the boat from the pier.

"Buono viaggio," the chauffeur said to me.

I thanked him. I didn't tip him, knowing my grandmother would have made arrangements with the contessa. Then I took the old man's hand, stepped down from the dock into the yellow boat.

"I'm Max Gardiner," he said.

"Her neighbor," I said. I'd heard the name before, in letters about Capri, the island's expatriate community, all the artists and intellectuals, the fabulous people, the thinkers and writers who so fascinated her, who'd moved to the island from the United States and England, who had become her friends, companions in her desire to insulate herself from the world. From her daughters, Lucy and me. Max owned the land next to hers.

"Yes," he said. "Now sit tight. Prepare for wonder."

Wonder. Had he really said that? I forced a polite smile that hid the pain I felt. I wasn't new to the sea. I'd visited islands before. I'd been on boats every summer of my life. Now I was on the way to force myself in, to spend time with a woman who'd never wanted me, who didn't want me now.

I untied the bowline to be helpful and show him I knew my way around boats, then took my seat as he cast off. The engine sputtered, and we headed out. Bright day, brilliant blue sky, sparkling sea.

It could have been Newport, this atmosphere of the sea, yachts, classic wooden workboats with nets glittering with fish scales; I thought of Travis, in a time zone six hours behind me. He would have returned from a night of fishing; he would be asleep in his family's cottage on the grounds of Newport Academy by now. I hoped my sister was sleeping as well. There was this incident, a dream-state walking-to-Italy kind of thing, that we hope won't repeat itself. I held my backpack tight to my chest. It felt compact, comforting. I had filled it with books, letters, pictures of the people I love.

We puttered out of the channel. I heard a breath come from the water just below the gunwale—a quick, happy intake of air, then a rushed exhalation. Dolphins swimming beside our yellow boat. I glanced over my shoulder at Max. Was this what he'd meant by wonder? He smiled at me, pointed dead ahead.

"You only get this chance once," he said.

"What chance?" I asked.

"To arrive on Capri for the first time. I feel privileged to witness it."

It's an island, I wanted to say. Far from home. A mountain, a harbor. Marine mammals, yes, but no Lucy, no Travis. I faced forward again, my posture stoic as the boat gained speed.

And as I stared ahead, I saw: the white rocks of Monte Solaro, craggy against the sapphire sky, a precipitous drop down to the radiant sea. I smelled lemons, verbena, and pine, their scents carried on the wind. Terraces of olive groves, leaves flashing silver in the sun. Capri rose from the waves, and I realized how often I'd dreamed of this. The island was the most beautiful place I'd ever seen, and not because of the scenery.

Because my mother lived there.

~

Max had left the villa just before dawn. He'd crossed the broad stone terrace, made his way down the steep, winding stairs, through groves of olive and fig trees. The sharply pitched land was terraced, overlooking the Bay of Naples; he used a flashlight, but he could have found his way blindfolded—he was seventy-two, and had lived here over half his life. There was such beauty on Capri; he wanted to shout, wake up the island, tell Lyra, Rafe, all the islanders, to open their eyes. **Love one another, be happy, life is short!**

Two levels down from the villa, he had passed the small white cottage, saw one light burning. Lyra was already awake, keeping vigil. Last night's almost full moon had hung low in the sky, casting silver light across the water, pulling at the tides. Low tide was treacherous twice each month, when the water ebbed under the new and full moons, exposing rocks and stranding sea creatures in tidal pools that wouldn't fill until the lunar cycle came round again.

Now, steering his yellow boat back from Sorrento, he had Pell safe and sound, on her way to Lyra. Max saw his grandson walking the rocky shore, rescuing invertebrates. Capri was a blue mirage, the massif of Monte Solaro floating above the sea. Max looked up, seeking out the whitewashed cottage on the hillside. Sunlight glinted off binoculars held by Lyra, standing among olive trees.

"She's waiting for you," he said.

"My mother," Pell said.

"Yes," Max replied. He slowed the boat down, steered toward the private dock.

"Where?" she asked, shielding her eyes.

"Up there," Max said, pointing.

Pell's expression made his heart catch. He glanced up, wondering if Lyra could catch the full impact of her effect on her daughter through the binoculars. The young girl's head was tilted back, her mouth open. There was joy in hope.

As Max pulled up to the dock, the dolphins leapt and dove, swimming away. Dolphins were emotional creatures, just like people. They were capable of love, great loyalty, staying together for life. If ever they were separated from their children, one ripped from the other, the parents grieved and keened. He'd observed that in dolphins, just as he had in humans.

"Ready?" he asked Pell.

"Ready," she said.

He looked around, wanting help with the lines, but Rafe seemed to have disappeared. So Max climbed up on the wooden dock, and tied the boat fast.

~

Lyra braced her elbows on the wall, to steady them. She finally pressed the binoculars to her eyes. Max docking the boat. And up forward, in the bow, a lovely young girl. Shocking, stunning, take-your-breath-away beauty. Long dark hair tied back, tendrils blowing around her face. Pell stared straight up the hill, as if she could see Lyra behind the stone wall, and maybe she could. Even as a baby she'd had an intense, seeking gaze.

The sight of her daughter made every muscle in Lyra's body jump, as if her skin had memories all its own. She felt pressure on, not in, her chest: a six-pound, seven-ounce weight. Pell, just born, wet and slippery, hot as a coal, bellowing. Lyra had held her daughter. Taylor was right there, standing beside them, but the moment was Lyra and Pell's. It's not every day you have a daughter, and as much as you might love her father, he'll never know the wild electricity you have with her.

Standing in her Italian garden, Lyra Davis stared down at the small yellow boat and thought of that tiny baby. She pictured the six-year-old girl that baby had become. Pell had been six, Lucy four, when Lyra left—ten years since Lyra had seen either of her daughters.

Lyra gazed down, watched Max help Pell onto the deck, hardly able to hold herself back. Her daughter was smart; Lyra knew because she received all her grades, scores, reports from Newport Academy. She had a brilliant mind; several of her teachers said so. But she was so young. At sixteen, she might believe in hope, in redemption, in the possibility of forgiveness. Lyra knew Pell would try to forgive, understand, put herself in her mother's shoes.

But the body remembered. Nothing could be done about that, about all the missed hugs and kisses, the neglected hair-brushing, the times Pell and her sister had needed comfort and their mother hadn't been there to provide it. The cold winters, without Lyra to help them into their snow jackets, and that December day when she had taken Pell to the bridge.

Lyra knew those feelings were lodged in Pell, even if Pell didn't admit them herself. This island was ancient, its mysteries millennia older than anything imaginable in America, and it had taught Lyra some cruel things about time, illusions, and hopeless wishes.

She walked through a break in the wall, onto the stairs. Built centuries ago, they led up to Max's villa, and down to the dock. Thick pines, jasmine, and rosemary covered the steep rocky hillside. Orange blossoms, waxy and fragrant, bloomed behind glossy green leaves.

Lyra hurried down. The steps, chopped roughly into the rocks, formed a precipitous descent. An iron handrail, rusted away in places, provided the only barrier to a sheer abyss. Voices carried up from the water: Max's, low and English-accented, and a girl's.

Pell's.

Lyra broke through the clearing, emerging from pines and vines, and stood at the top of the rock ledge. She saw Rafaele crouched in the shade by the boathouse, frozen in place; she walked right past him, and he ducked out of sight. Max and Pell were hoisting her bags off the boat onto the dock. Lyra hesitated for a second, watching them.

"Pell," she said.

Had she even spoken, made a sound? Everything

seemed lodged in her throat—words, her daughter's name, her heart. Leaves rustled and waves lapped the rocks. Max and Pell looked in her direction.

"Pell," Lyra said again.

Lyra took a slow step toward the dock. Her eyes drank in the young woman standing there, so close now: tall, slim, fine dark hair, creamy pale skin, and mysterious blue eyes. Lyra caught her breath. Raised her arms, held out in front, embracing the air.

Pell's feet pounded down the dock—it seemed impossible that such a delicate girl could make such a racket. She bounded off the pier onto the sea-washed black rock, and only when she stood right there, inches away from Lyra, did she stop.

They stared into each other's eyes, and it wasn't easy, because Lyra's vision was completely blurred with tears. Then, as if remembering what to do from the farthest, most-forgotten past, Pell leaned into her mother's arms, and they held each other for a long time.

Two

In the Nicholson family, all occasions were commemorated with lunch. So, even though I was quivering, literally, from the shock and joy of hugging my mother, and I wanted it to last, and I wanted us to be alone to talk, to just take each other in, she told me that lunch would be served on the villa terrace at one-thirty.

"The villa?" I asked. I couldn't take my eyes off my mother.

I wanted to touch her cheek. She and I had the same coloring—very dark hair and blue eyes. Her hair had a white streak in front, shocking and glamorous. There were lines around her eyes and mouth. The flawless skin I remembered was marred, and that made me love her even more, but then this awful cold wave washed over me—she'd been away from me so long. I had grown from a child into a young woman. What changes did she see in me?

"Yes," she said. "Max's villa, just up the hill. He has kindly offered."

"Are you two . . . ?" I asked, uncharacteristically blunt; I chalk it up to jet lag.

"Oh, no," she said. "Not at all. We're just very good friends. He's kind of a father figure."

That was true. I'd noticed Max's age when we were in the boat. But he had some kind of sparkle one rarely saw—not just in his eyes, but in his very being. As if everything in him, every molecule, was interested in the world around him. He reminded me of someone very young, full of curiosity. Even more, and this is a strange thing to say about a man I'd just met, but it seemed he'd never ever been disappointed by life. He exuded hope and the expectation that all would be well. I liked him.

My mother showed me around. The wonderful, bowled-over expression of, I'll call it love, that she showed on the dock had been put back in its box. Now she was correct, measured, as if we were near-strangers; which, in fact, we were. Speaking carefully, inches of space between us. If this was her default mode, at least with visitors, it reminded me of my grandmother.

"This is my house," she said. "I had an apartment in Capri when I first came to the island, but that only lasted a few months. I've lived here, in Anacapri, since then. The more remote town on the island. Higher up the mountain, harder to get to."

I nodded, saying nothing, but feeling surprised. I knew her address, of course, but until now had no context for what Anacapri was. My mother choosing the town less traveled? That seemed so unlike what my grandmother said about her. When she'd left us, my father, sister, and I, my grandmother said she'd gone straight for "the action." And of course hordes of men.

We walked around the small white house. The walls were thick, the arched windows facing out to sea. A large terrace hung over the precipice, looking straight down the cliff. Six chairs surrounded a table; the cushions were bright blue; I wondered if my mother ate out here a lot, and who joined her. Pots of flowers were everywhere, and vines of japonica, clematis, and bougainvillea clung to the walls. I imagined she must have quite a gardener.

An antique brass telescope, set up on a tripod with spindly legs, faced the bay. The scope drew me over; I stood beside it, wondering why it made me feel strange. She noticed me looking at it; the expression in her eyes made me feel I should back away. Maybe the telescope was really valuable, and she was afraid I'd knock it over.

Inside, the living room had been sponge-painted faded coral pink; it made me feel I was in a seashell. The furniture was covered with white slipcovers. The Nicholson touches, straight from my grandmother, were apparent all through the room: portraits and landscapes in gilded frames, sterling silver everywhere.

A letter opener on the desk, engraved picture frames on the piano, and there, on the sideboard, the familiar, beloved wild-rose tea set with flowers, leaves, and thorns deeply tooled into the heavy silver along with my great-grandmother's monogram. I went straight to it, my heart pounding.

"You remember?" she asked.

"How could I forget?" I picked up the milk pitcher. When I was little, before she left, I used to pretend the pitcher was the teapot, the real pot being too heavy for me to lift. "We had tea parties," I said now.

"With real tea," she said.

"Yes." Other mothers might have given their young children apple or orange juice, but Lucy and I got the real thing, Earl Grey, smoky and delicate. She, Lucy, and I would sit cross-legged on the floor, drinking from translucent Haviland china painted with flowers and butterflies, ladybugs hidden in the blossoms. When my mother left us, we kept that china. But staring at the tea set, I realized my father had shipped her the silver.

"Are you tired from your flight?" she asked as I turned away from the sideboard, composing myself.

"A little," I said.

"The best way to overcome jet lag is to take a

short nap—very brief, less than an hour. More than that, and you're done for. Then you take a long walk . . . we can do that after lunch at Max's."

"Okay," I said.

"Do you . . . are you . . . ," she began, and color drained from her face as she stopped.

"What?" I asked, trying to smile. I felt a gulf opening in my chest.

"I have so many questions," she said. "So much I want to know about you. Are you and Lucy close?"

"The closest," I said. "She's the best sister in the world."

"She was always so sweet and bright," my mother said.

Should I tell her now? How the sweet and bright one has gone rather dark? Over the winter, she tried to contact our father's ghost. He didn't appear to her, of course. She is brave, but I worry she takes it as rejection. Both parents have left her!

That reality has affected her sleep. When her eyes finally close, and dreams come, she climbs out of bed. Her movements are graceful, as if she can see just where she's going. But she can't; she is asleep. She is sleepwalking. There could be worse problems, but lately it seems to be getting more serious. . . .

"Well," my mother said awkwardly, when I didn't say anything more about Lucy. "Would you like to take that rest?"

"Yes," I said. Suddenly I needed air. I walked

onto the terrace. Looking down the stairs toward the cove, I saw the guy again. The one dressed in black, who'd been lurking in the shadows when we came in on the boat, and now he was sitting halfway down the steep stone steps, staring at the bay. He looked not much older than I. "Who's that?" I asked.

"I don't see anyone," my mother said, not even glancing into the thick foliage. The phone rang. She went in to answer it, and when I looked back, the young man in black was gone. I'd gotten barely a look at him but registered danger, furtiveness. I have a good imagination, but also fine instincts. I was sure my mother had seen him, just didn't want to admit it. I wondered if he was her lover.

"That was Max on the phone," my mother said, returning to the terrace. "Lunch is off. . . ."

"Off?" I asked.

"Something came up, and he asked if we would join him for dinner tomorrow night instead."

"Is he okay?" I asked.

"I'm sure he's fine," she said, giving a low laugh that sent shivers down the back of my neck. I knew it so well, and hadn't heard it in ten years. Suddenly I needed to be alone, as much as I'd ever needed anything.

"I'm a little tired," I said, staring at the sea.

"Let me show you your room," she said.

She led me through the loggia, through French doors into a cozy bedroom. The walls were white, the bed covered with a shell-pink silk coverlet and a mountain of pale blue pillows. She had already placed my luggage by the closet. All except for my backpack, which I hadn't set down since arriving.

"Have a good rest," she said. "I'll wake you up in a little while."

I nodded. She left the room. My heart was pounding, or was that the sound of the sea crashing on rocks below? Sun poured through the open doors, scaldingly bright. It hurt my eyes. I wanted darkness, and to crawl under the covers. I pulled the shutters closed, blocking the light. It was all I could do to yank down the silk spread, climb into the soft featherbed.

Tears began to pour down my cheeks. I missed Lucy and Travis, wanted them both, wanted to know Lucy was safe.

Not long ago, one early morning, before the sun came up and the stars were still in the sky, I found Lucy swimming. In the cold water, out past the surf break, in her nightgown.

My sister was fast asleep, and when I led her back to shore, she had no memory of how she got there. Before she woke up, both of us treading water in the bay, she looked straight at me and said, "Mom!" Later she told me she dreamed she had swum to Italy to find our mother.

My mother abandoned us. One day ten years ago she left our house in Grosse Pointe, Michigan, and never came back. That is the single fact that rules my life. Everything else—that I have a sister, that I had a great father, that I love Travis, that I get good grades at school—is by necessity secondary.

Because a mother leaving shapes her daughters in deep and inescapable ways. It is the absence of our mother, the death of our father, that keeps my sister from resting.

Capri felt so far away from Newport. But then the person I really missed, more than anyone, filled my mind. My father. Taylor Davis. His curly brown hair and warm hazel eyes, his sharp cheekbones and great smile. I wanted to take his picture out of my backpack and look at it, but I felt like I was swooning and practically hallucinating with jet lag, and I was crying too hard to move.

"How could you have left us, how could you have left us?" I whispered, weeping, as pathetic as you could possibly get, and the crazy thing was, I'm not sure whether I was talking to my mother or my father.

~

The Villa Andria was a massive, crumbling, secluded repository of history and beauty, love and joy. It sat at the crest of the hill, within sight of the ruins of Tiberius's palace. Built of stone, columns greened and blackened from salt air, the villa was surrounded by lemon groves, olive orchards, walled gardens, and seemed to hang in the air over the Bay of Naples.

The villa's rooms had once seen countless celebrations, soirees, assignations, and salons. They had once welcomed creativity, given Max and his wife a space to make their art. But that time and this place belonged to youth, his and Christina's, and she'd been gone years now. Senile dementia had begun stealing her away three years before she died. Her paintings were gathering dust. And he no longer felt he had a play in him; they'd all been written.

Sitting on the large terrace, shaded by pines clinging to the rock, Max bent over the table. He wrote in a black notebook, the latest in a long line. He ordered them from a stationer in Florence, the son of the man who'd first supplied him. When Max found someone he enjoyed working with, or simply liked, or in any way became attached to, he stuck with that person forever. He prized loyalty above all other qualities. His father had taught him that.

"Well, this is what 'came up'?"

At the sound of Lyra's voice, his heart kicked his ribs. But he merely lifted his fountain pen from the paper and looked up slowly. She stood on the terrace, arms crossed tightly across her chest; but for the white streak in her black hair, she looked like a miffed college girl. He noted with concern her skinniness; she'd been losing weight all spring, as the idea of her daughter's visit became more real.

"Why aren't you with Pell?" he asked.

"She's resting."

"Ah," he said, turning back to his notebook. No more plays, but plenty of thoughts. He wanted to finish the paragraph he'd been writing; oddly, or perhaps not, it concerned Lyra.

"You canceled lunch," she said. "Are you mad at me?"

"Of course not."

"You don't like Pell?" she asked.

The tone in her voice sent a shiver down Max's neck. That's the spirit, he thought, hiding a smile. It pleased him, to hear Lyra defensive on her daughter's behalf.

"On the contrary," he said. "I find her extraordinary."

Lyra sat on the stone bench, her favorite place, as it had been Christina's—she used to sit there for hours, easel set up, painting the bay. Christina had done all of her cloud studies, her oils of the fishing boats, her watercolors of the pines and cypress trees, from that very spot. He felt Lyra's gaze, looked up from the page to meet her eyes.

"Well, you're right, but how can you know she's extraordinary after one boat ride?" Lyra asked.

"I knew it even before meeting her," he said.

"Don't say something sappy," she said. "Like because she's my daughter."

"I wouldn't dream of it," he said. He teased her regularly, and she lapped up their banter as if he were her uncle or an old family friend.

"Then how can you tell?" she asked.

"Because she is here," he said. "She came all this way to see you. She is loyal."

"I don't deserve it," Lyra said.

"I didn't say that," Max said.

"You don't have to," she said, rising. "I'll say it myself. So, why did you really cancel lunch? Are you okay? I had to come up and make sure."

"I'm fine," he said, touched by her concern.

"Does it have to do with Rafaele? I saw him twice today . . . down by the boathouse this morning, when you brought Pell in. And just a few minutes ago, from the terrace. He was still down at the water, just sitting there. Pell saw him too. She asked about him."

"What did you tell her?"

"Nothing." The single word said it all.

Max stared at her. How could he love someone so different from Christina? From him, for that matter? Christina would have embraced Rafaele and his problems, just as Max did. She would have loved and nurtured him, tried to understand him, just as she had when he was a young boy. Rafe had always intrigued her in every way; she would have spent every possible moment with him, drawing close to him and his demons, loving them equally.

"I know he's your grandson," Lyra said, "and I know he just arrived last week. But I don't feel good about him roaming the hillside."

"Roaming," Max said. "Is that what he does? I

would have said 'contemplating.' Because mostly he works on the nets, the boathouse, and the boat."

"Max, you see the good in everyone," Lyra said. "That doesn't mean you're right. Christina always said you were such an innocent. Someone has to protect you from yourself."

"From Rafe, you mean?"

"Max, how can you let him stay with you, after what he did? I don't understand."

"He's my grandson. And Christina's. She would have him stay nowhere but here."

"I can't forget what he did; I don't see how you can either. I'm going to be honest with you—I don't want him around Pell. You did say he wouldn't be at lunch today. . . ."

"When it comes to socializing, you don't have to worry. It's his choice not to join the group," Max said. "As he told me when he arrived, he's in hermit mode."

"Well, is he the reason you canceled lunch?" Lyra asked.

Max gazed at her. Why was she so obtuse? He saw in Lyra Davis all that she could not see in herself. He'd watched her prepare the house for Pell: pull all the family silver out of storage, polish the black tarnish away, obviously hoping Pell would remember their tea parties in Grosse Pointe, their times together. She'd ordered brand-new luxurious bedding in colors Pell had loved as a child—nursery shades of pale pink and blue.

Things won't do it, my darling, Max wanted to say. **Objects are inadequate to the task. Throw the silver off the cliff. Wrap your child in your arms, not linens from Rome.**

"No, it has nothing to do with Rafe," he said, staring into her lovely eyes, bluer than sea or sky, wanting her to get it herself.

"Then why did you cancel?" she asked after a long moment, forcing him to tell her.

"So you and Pell could be alone," he said finally. "So you could spend time with your daughter her first day here."

That did it, as he'd known it would, that she would be ashamed for not realizing. Her face flushed, clearly furious, she turned and walked off the terrace. He watched her go, moving swiftly through the lemon trees toward the stairs to her own house. His heart cracked, knowing her rage wasn't really at him, but at herself.

As he often did, watching Lyra Davis's extreme pain and occasional slow-motion self-destruction with regard to her two daughters, he found himself thinking about Lyra's own mother. Max had met her only once, early in Lyra's stay here on Capri. They'd all had drinks at the Hotel Quisisana, and Christina had left saying Edith Nicholson was a monster. Max had thought her more a caricature of a certain style of American grande dame.

But either way . . .

The base of all pain, the creation of ogres, the

source of all that seemed evil in the world, was a lack of love. It drove people to hate themselves. If only Lyra could know what he saw in her. Christina had seen it first; perhaps it was his wife's devotion to the younger woman that had first opened his eyes to her.

Watching how Lyra had tended Christina in her decline, loved her even as everything slipped away, had caused Max's feelings to grow. He closed his notebook, capped his fountain pen, and for the second time that day went down the steep, narrow stairs to the cove.

~

Here he was on Capri, no escape. The whole island had once been Rafaele Gardiner's playground, first when his parents would take him around, and then, after his mother's death, when he grew up fast and basically owned the place himself, in the lawless days when he had no rules.

He knew everyone. The locals, the fishermen, and the socialite summer people, the kids from wherever, he'd partied with them all on the waterfront, and in the caves, and on the mule tracks, and the hill paths, and in the Piazzetta right in front of their parents.

Being the grandson of Max and Christina Gardiner opened every door on Capri, and he'd taken advantage of that. Not that he cared about social life, hanging with the glitterati douche bags or getting invited onto Prince Whoever's yacht. He'd enjoyed the parties and the entrée because he'd liked getting fucked up.

Those days were over. He was nineteen. The jury was in: he had wrecked his life and others'. Two years ago he'd gotten arrested in New York, kicked out of school. He'd come back here to do more damage, then spent over a year in rehab—his third, this one in Malibu. He'd been out for three weeks now.

Rafe missed a girl he'd never see again, and now all he wanted to do was make everything up to his grandfather. Nicolas had torn some fishing nets, and it was Rafe's job to repair them.

The work was slow and took concentration. That was good, because it kept him busy, out of trouble. It kept him from feeling so empty, longing for Monica and wondering why she had disappeared the way she did, whether she was okay. She'd told him to pray to his grandmother to keep him clean, and he tried, but it was easier to ask for help for others, for Monica.

Peering at the bay, he saw one of the tourist boats, hired to take people into the Grotta Azzurra. Low to the water to fit through the small rock opening, the wooden boat looked like a thin red line on the waves. Arturo drove it in a circle; Rafe ducked, but it was too late. The boat was empty; Arturo tied up at the dock and walked across the rock ledge.

"Ciao," Arturo said. "I thought it was you."

"It's not me," Rafe said. "Let's just say it's not the same me you knew."

"You owe me money."

"I'll pay you." Rafe sat still, stayed calm.

"It's been over a year," Arturo said. "You have an outstanding debt. Do you think I don't keep records?"

Rafe stared into Arturo's brown eyes. Wow, back only a week and his past had tracked him down. Still, he stayed cool, giving nothing away. He saw Arturo register the fact he couldn't push him around.

"You're clean?" Arturo asked.

Rafe nodded.

"I lost a good customer."

"Yeah."

"You'll be back," Arturo said.

"No," Rafe said. He thought of Monica. "I won't."

Arturo shrugged as if he knew better. "They still talk about you on this island. You see your grandmother's face, don't you?" he asked. "I'll give you something to chase it right out of your head."

"Get your boat off our dock," Rafe said, standing. Arturo was big, but Rafe was younger and stronger. One thing about rehab, it had started him eating again, putting on muscle. The goodness of those talks with Monica had stayed with him. Working out helped him stay clean, and the idea of whatever they were saying about him made him want to kill Arturo.

"Portando il nero," Arturo said, backing away. "That's good, to wear black. Because you made people mourn. Christina was beloved on Capri. That's what everyone says."

Rafe couldn't even argue with that. He just stood there, watching his old drug dealer climb into his crummy little boat and putter away. He stared at the wake, white ripples dissolving into nothing.

"What did he want?" his grandfather asked, coming down the stairs behind him. Rafe didn't want to turn around, have his grandfather see his face. But he stood out of respect and love.

"Nothing, Grandpa," Rafe said.

"Is he giving you trouble?"

"No, not really."

"Because if he is, I'll talk to the police, and—"

"That would make it worse for me," Rafe said. "Okay, please? You have to trust me."

"I want to," his grandfather said.

"I know," Rafe said. They stared at each other a few seconds, tense but trying to get past it.

"How are the nets?" his grandfather asked, looking at the pile.

"Pretty much got them mended," Rafe said. "Nicolas can fish tonight."

"Would you like to go with us?"

Rafe heard the "us," looked at his grandfather with surprise. "You got up at the crack of dawn, to go to Sorrento," he said. "I thought you'd want to be asleep early tonight."

"Life is short," his grandfather said. "The less time I spend sleeping, the better."

Rafe smiled; he knew his grandfather's embrace-life philosophy.

"You could have come with me," his grandfather said. "To pick up Pell."

"I, uh, slept late," Rafe said. He didn't want to go into the fact he knew Lyra Davis hated him, wouldn't want him anywhere near her daughter. Or reveal that he'd been mending nets in the shadows when his grandfather and the girl had arrived, seen her step off the boat.

Pell had long dark hair, blue eyes; Monica had a black pixie cut, green eyes. But this girl's beauty and radiance, an intelligent sorrow she wore like a shawl, reminded him so much of the girl he knew he'd never see again. His grandfather was a strange, uncanny mind reader, and Rafe looked away so he wouldn't show too much.

Rafe happened to glance up, not at the villa, but the other way, toward Lyra's cottage. And he saw the girl, Pell, looking down at him, over the terrace wall. Their eyes locked for a minute; he deliberately turned away.

"I thought you invited them for lunch," Rafe said. "Lyra and her daughter."

"Dinner tomorrow instead," his grandfather said. "I thought the traveler might need some rest, and to spend time with her mother. And you're invited too, of course."

"Looks as if she's not resting," Rafe said, glancing up and meeting her curious gaze again. He felt a shiver go through his bones. He had felt his last chance slipping away. Life, sobriety, hope; Monica had given him the feeling he wanted to live again, to grab onto this opportunity. With her gone, he'd been so alone.

"Ah," his grandfather said, following Rafe's gaze. He saw Pell, smiled and gave her a big wave.

"She's like you," Rafe said. "Likes to be awake."

"Life is a gift," his grandfather said. "Every moment we are here. Fresh, beautiful. **Siete buono come il mare.**" Good as the sea.

"Right," Rafe said, looking up at the pretty girl. He had the feeling she was standing on the brink; that coming here was her own sort of last chance. His heart cracked open, knowing what that was like. In that moment, in honor of another girl who'd helped him, he knew he wanted to be a friend to Pell. She waved at his grandfather, as if they were lifelong friends, as if she had heard his words and agreed completely with his assessment of life.

Good as the sea.

That was something Rafe's grandmother used to say. His throat ached. He had so much to make up for. If he could help someone else, maybe he could get through.

And maybe Pell could too.

Pell was really here. Lyra could hardly believe it; she had started burying her feelings years ago, but how impossible. She had worked hard to stop being a mother—as if it were a switch she could throw. Walking through the olive orchard, she tried to breathe as emotions stormed through her.

The light changed, diffusing the water from aquamarine to cobalt blue. The sky's color deepened. She walked through the garden, trying to calm down. As she did, she thought of Grosse Pointe, the garden she'd kept at home, the statue of Hermes she'd set in the shady corner of the backyard.

The marble statue of the god had originally come from Capri; Lyra had shipped him home the summer of her Grand Tour after college graduation. The trip, and relics from every city in Europe, had been her mother's graduation gift.

Edith Nicholson had mapped out Lyra's life: debut, college, Europe, board membership at the Bellevue Garden Society, marriage. Lyra would be expected to marry someone who would summer in Newport, own an estate near the Nicholsons' on Bellevue Avenue or on Ocean Drive, have the cabana beside her mother's at Bailey's Beach.

Lyra had no doubt that her mother wished that while traveling she'd meet the heir to a British mining fortune, or an Italian manufacturing fortune, a titled-someone with a villa in Tuscany or a château in the Dordogne. But there could be no exotic European love, because there was Taylor Davis. Lyra knew her mother hoped she'd forget him that summer—not because he wasn't kind, intelligent, or wealthy. Just because, in the eyes of Edith Nicholson, he wasn't **enough.**

Her mother had arranged for Lyra to be fitted for a Chanel suit in Paris, riding boots in Milan. She'd sent her to a glassblower on Murano, told her to choose the most exquisite chandelier in the studio, for her future home. Lyra had felt she was being trained to buy, to fill her heart with **things** instead of nature, spirit, poetry, ineffable beauty. She felt strangely unmoved by the whole trip—until secretly meeting Taylor in Rome.

She had first met him during their prep school years; it was hard to pinpoint the exact moment they spotted each other. She went to Miss Porter's, he to Newport Academy. She'd see him when she went home; they had mutual friends, and they would hang out at dances, parties, football games. He always seemed to be around, until the first time she noticed he wasn't. That was the crazy thing about Taylor; she never really paid attention to him until he wasn't there.

Taylor. His face filled her mind now: angular features, sharp jaw, deep-set, thoughtful hazel eyes, warm smile. His light brown hair curled when he swam in salt water. He was a serious boy with an easy laugh; everyone said he'd be a lawyer like his father. Lyra liked him a lot, especially the way he seemed so uninterested in her family's name or money. He talked about his parents as if he really enjoyed them, cared about them. Lyra noticed that.

Midway through Taylor's senior year of college, his parents died in a car accident. Lyra and several friends from Vassar had headed up to Brown University in Providence, Rhode Island, for the Princeton game. Without even admitting it to herself, Lyra was hoping to see Taylor. He was the quarterback, but he didn't play that day. She heard the news about his parents—driving home late at night, wet leaves, a spinout into oncoming traffic, both killed instantly.

The next day she flew to Detroit. She spent the night in Grosse Pointe, with the parents of a friend from Farmington. On Monday she went to the funeral, at an Anglican church that looked as if it belonged in the English countryside—built of stone, covered with ivy, cool light slanting through blue stained-glass windows.

When Taylor saw her, he seemed surprised, but not half as shocked as Lyra herself was. She had never done anything like that in her life, but something had made her want to be present for him. She knew, deep down, even though they'd never been very close, that he would have done it for her.

Seeing Taylor walk down the aisle behind his parents' coffins, she'd wept and felt his loss as if it were her own.

"Thank you for coming," he said to her after the blessing at the graveside.

"You're welcome. I'm so sorry."

"We were close," he said, looking over at the grave. "I was so lucky to have them as parents."

"They must have been wonderful people," she said.

He nodded, choked up. She saw that he couldn't speak. He was filled with grief so penetrating it seemed to come from his bones, and the sight of it made her cry.

She and Taylor had never dated, never even taken a walk alone together. But she'd seen something of his goodness already: kindness when a friend of theirs was sick in the hospital, care for a teammate who broke his wrist in a game. She had been drawn to him for his warmth, something she'd never gotten at home. Now, on the worst day of his life, he was tender to her.

"I shouldn't cry," she said, taking his handkerchief. "I just wanted to come and be here with you."

"I'll never forget it," he said. "You don't know what it means to me."

They began to see each other. On weekends he made her pancakes with raspberry jam instead of maple syrup. She took him into the middle of the football field one night and showed him Capella and the Pleiades. He read the comics on Sunday, loved Calvin and Hobbes, wanted her to love it too. She did her best.

Commitment came slowly. Her parents were divorced; she wasn't sure she believed in marriage, because she'd never seen a way of loving that lasted. Taylor worked as a paralegal, wanting to be sure the law was for him. If so, there'd be law school, then the bar exam. Her mother thought he seemed nice, but she couldn't comprehend Lyra even contemplating life in Michigan.

On the summer trip after college graduation, Lyra and Taylor planned a rendezvous in Rome. He and his best friends had family money, but they were taking this trip on their own: backpacking, staying in hostels. She didn't tell her mother and met Taylor in Trastevere, in a romantic old **ostello** overlooking the square. They'd lived on his budget—the hostel, spaghetti, cheap bars, long walks, and lots of espresso—instead of hers: the Hotel Hassler, dinner at La Rosetta, shopping on the Via Veneto.

Her mother's life felt soulless to Lyra. She swore she'd ditch the fancy ways as soon as she could leave home. Visiting Capri after parting from Taylor, she vowed to have a one-year plan: she'd go home, let Taylor figure out whether the law was right for him or not, then move out of Newport, join him in Michigan.

Her mother wanted one thing, Taylor another. But what about Lyra? On that trip, Capri's bright sunlight and morning mists surrounded and enchanted her, made her moods swing wildly, made her feel so alive and at home. The Italian island grabbed her, captivated her as no place on earth ever had. The wild beauty, the damp sea haze, the dazzling blue sea, the riotous flowers, and the English and American émigrés both soothed her soul and fed a strange sense of melancholy. This place was hers alone. She could imagine never leaving, avoiding all strife. She'd stood on a cliff not far from where she now lived, and the way she felt outside matched the way she felt inside.

Staring out at the intense blue sea, into the unfathomable depths, she'd felt both sad and peaceful. Pure nature, far from her mother's expectations. The lonely apartness touched her soul. For the first time in her entire life, Lyra felt as if she belonged, and as if she knew who she was.

She found the statue of Hermes—chipped, darkened with moss and time—at an antiques dealer near the Piazzetta. The piece wasn't rare or valuable, except to her; she had it shipped home, a souvenir of Italy, and a reminder of the way Capri had made her feel. Time went by. She became more involved with the garden society, and Taylor threw himself into the law.

They broke up. It seemed inevitable. Lyra tried things her mother's way. Living in Newport, she dated the sons of society mavens. Alexander Baker, a playboy with a year-round tan, a house in Newport and one in Palm Beach, asked her to marry him. In that moment, she realized how crazy it was, living someone else's life. She'd felt despair closing in.

She shipped Hermes to Taylor with a letter telling him she'd bought the statue during their Italian summer, dreamed of putting it in their garden. She said she knew she'd missed her chance with him but wanted him to have Hermes anyway. Deep inside, she had the sense of taking care of her affairs, tying up loose ends.

Taylor showed up on her doorstep in Newport shortly after he'd received the statue. Sent Alexander packing, looked Lyra in the eye.

"You sent me a statue for the garden," he said, "but there's no garden without you. There never was. Please come home with me, Lyra. Marry me."

And she did, in one of the biggest weddings Newport had ever seen. Taylor might not have been her mother's first choice, but if Edith's only daughter was getting married, the wedding would be something the town would never forget. Lyra had felt so bleak with Alexander; she prayed that **he** was the reason, that Newport was the problem, that marrying Taylor would fix everything.

Taylor and Lyra honeymooned in Bermuda, and then they began their life. Lyra had expected love to heal everything, to make her feel as if she was all right. They placed Hermes in their backyard, and Lyra made great plans to cultivate beautiful gardens all around him.

It didn't quite work out that way.

Vines and dampness and her own demons took over. As time went on, the children were born, and the statue scared Pell. It was as tall as she, covered with moss. The marble god had a distant, yearning look in his eyes. Pell called him "that gone man." When Lyra asked what she meant, Pell said, "It looks as if he's gone. He's not really here."

Sensitive, prescient child. Did Pell see the same look in her mother's eyes? Because by that night ten years ago, when she took Pell into the backyard to look through the telescope at the stars, Lyra knew she was leaving the next day.

Leaving home, her husband, her two daughters.

She'd made her choice, and closed the door behind her. More than that: she'd locked and sealed it, thrown away the key. What kind of mother stays in touch with her children only through Christmas and birthday cards, occasional letters? Lyra had tried to save her own skin, thought she could protect everyone from the worst of herself. She had told herself it was better for everyone.

What had she done?

Three

~

The next morning, Lyra dressed in a sweater, khakis, and garden clogs and went outside at dawn. She paused for a minute, watching the moon set. Mist hovered over the sea, as if rising from the salt water. She had looked in on Pell a few minutes before and felt shocked to realize her daughter was really here, sleeping in her house. Lyra needed to clear her head, put her hands in the earth, connect with Christina's good advice.

Dew coated the grass; small cobwebs stretched between green blades. Back in Grosse Pointe, the girls had called them "fairy tablecloths." Lyra remembered telling Christina about that one day when they were planting rosebushes. Her friend had knelt there in the dirt, listening. This was where Lyra had let herself think about her daughters most: outdoors, in the garden. For some reason, she could bear it here in a way she couldn't in the house.

Lyra pushed her wheelbarrow through a white

gate set between stone posts. She had planted many flower beds on her property.

"That's how you'll learn," Christina once said. "Hibiscus and roses overwhelm each other; lark-spur and delphinium are rich and delicate blue; use orange blossoms for scent, lavender for comfort. Finding out what pleases you will help when you start designing gardens for others."

Her landscape design business had started right here, during conversations with Christina.

Lyra set a small suede cushion on the wet grass; it had been her friend's, and made her feel close to her now. Kneeling, she used small clippers to cut through a tangle of overgrown coreopsis. She felt cool dew on the tough stems, smelled the freshness of early summer, tasted salt in the morning mist, heard finches singing wildly in the trees. The yel-low flowers soothed her spirit. Every color in the garden came with a feeling that touched her soul.

Working intently now, she didn't hear the foot-steps until Pell was standing right beside her.

"Good morning, Mom," Pell said.

"Hi, Pell," Lyra said. "You found me."

"Followed your footsteps in the dew. You're gardening?"

"Yes," Lyra said.

"I thought you had a gardener."

"No, I do it all myself. I garden for others, as well. . . ."

"You mean you work?"

Lyra nodded. She saw the shock in Pell's face.

"People do work," Lyra said.

"Well, I know I'm going to," Pell said. "It's just that I thought you . . ."

"Were a spoiled socialite?" Lyra asked.

A slow smile came to Pell's face. "I didn't say that," she said.

"I guess there are a few things we have to learn about each other," Lyra said.

"Yes, there are," Pell said.

Lyra pushed herself off her knees, stood beside her daughter.

Christina had been Lyra's mentor; she'd mothered her in ways her own mother never had. Max was a love, endlessly supportive, but her relationship with him was different. Lyra had gotten pure, hands-on maternal care from her wonderful, beloved neighbor Christina; she missed her friend so much, and felt she needed her right now, to guide her with Pell.

"Who is C.G.?" Pell asked, gesturing at the initials on the worn suede pillow.

"Christina, Max's wife."

"She lets you use it?"

"Well, she gave it to me," Lyra said. "Before she died."

Pell watched Lyra with solemn eyes, registering the still-present grief.

"I'm sorry," Pell said. She reached for her mother's hand, held it warmly. Lyra teared up—

she didn't back away; she let the feeling of closeness grow and knew it was because Christina had taught her how.

"Thank you," Lyra said. "She was a wonderful friend. I wish you could have known her. She heard a lot about you."

"You talked about us?" Pell asked.

"I did," Lyra said.

"When did she die?" Pell asked.

"Two years ago," Lyra said. "She developed Alzheimer's . . . her mind started going, and it was really hard to watch. She was such an amazing woman."

At that, Pell pulled her hand away. Sharply, and with a sudden, cold look in her eyes. She stared down at the pile of clippings, stems and brown leaves, as if the garden had disappeared and all that was left was detritus, dead flowers.

"What's the matter?" Lyra asked, reaching for her.

"It was like that with Dad," Pell said. "After the brain tumor. He'd ask for a glass of sunshine when he meant water. He forgot our names."

"Oh, Pell . . ."

"Couldn't remember my name was Pell, and Lucy's was Lucy, just couldn't bring them into his mind. He cried because he'd lost our names."

Pell's eyes filled, as if remembering her father's tears.

"I'm so sorry," Lyra said.

"You said Lucy was so sweet and bright," Pell said. "She's not only that, you know. She's . . . a wreck. She lost it after Dad died. We both did. We can't stand that he's gone."

"Oh, Pell," Lyra said, reaching out.

But Pell didn't take her hand. She turned fast, strode back through the garden toward the house. Lyra knew Christina would have told her to go after her, but she couldn't move. She thought of Taylor, the best father in the world, forgetting their daughters' names. She sank onto the wet grass and covered her eyes.

~

I couldn't get away from my mother fast enough. The place is strange, with a crazy, dangerous beauty. Cliffs everywhere. My mother's house is open but cozy, filled with things I remember from childhood. Comforting, but a reminder of how goodness gets yanked away. And my feelings are out of control.

The grounds are magical, and to find out my mother cares for the gardens herself, instead of hiring someone—an expert, a horticulturist, the Miss Miller of flowers—was the hugest, most wonderful surprise. Then to have her talk about this neighbor Christina, her good friend, an "amazing woman," with such love and respect, turned me into a snarling beast. I could have ripped out her throat.

I wanted to leave. The island, I mean. True, I'd been there only one full day. Get back to Lucy, my little sister, my other half. Already my emotions had run the gamut. I'd been feeling strong, happy to be with my mother, compassionate about her path in life, the one that had led her away from us and into her expatriate existence. But talking about Christina's diminished mental capacity made me think of my dad, and I went straight back to being thirteen.

Thirteen, the world's worst age. Especially when your mother's gone and your father, whom you loved more than anyone, has just died. I don't want you to feel sorry for me. It's just that I'd like you to have the whole picture. Our dad had to be both father and mother to me and Lucy. And he did it so well; he never made us feel it was hard on him, or that he'd rather be doing anything else.

My mother left ten years ago, June of the year I turned six. When fathers leave, it's bad, but society just calls them "deadbeat dads." When mothers leave, people act as if it's a crime against nature. There are no words. People don't talk about it, because it's so disturbing: not just to the kids, but to anyone who hears about it.

That first year Lucy and I missed her so much. We couldn't eat or sleep, we developed weird tics. I pulled out my eyelashes and a circle of hair on the top of my head, gave myself a half-dollar-sized bald spot. Lucy sucked her thumb all the time, even at school. She scratched her face. Kids made fun of us both, but we barely noticed. We were too crazed, missing our mother.

Our nanny, Miss Miller, loved our mother, having raised her herself, and must have been brokenhearted in her own way. She told us everything was lovely, our mother was on a wonderful trip. If we cried, she told us to stop, that it would hurt our mother if she could see us. Once I said that was silly, our mother couldn't see us because she wasn't there anymore, she'd left us, she didn't love us. Miss Miller slapped me, then instantly grabbed me in a huge hug, weeping and saying she was sorry but she couldn't let me say such things about my mother, who loved us more than anything.

Poor Nanny. Talk about a rock and a hard place. The truth was, we knew nothing. My mother never said a definite goodbye. She told my father that she was going to Newport for a week to see my grandmother. I think my father was relieved at first.

See, my mother had had a breakdown that winter. Lying in bed one night, I'd heard her shrieking, "This is killing me!" Death of the soul, don't you know? A severe depression that had required hospitalization. Months at McLean, in Massachusetts, one of the best places. She finally came out of the hospital, but she wasn't herself.

That's what Nanny told us. "Your mother's not herself."

Our grandmother pretended it hadn't happened. She would have preferred to send my mother on a yacht through the Greek Islands than to a locked ward where she might actually get help. I think that's where the adultery rumor started: it was easier for my grandmother to imagine my mother was in love with another man than to think the marriage was falling apart because of mental problems.

We'd been worried about her all that spring; our father tried to ease our fears, saying it took time, but she was healing. She left for Newport in June; we expected her back by the Fourth of July, but she never came. Panic filled our dreams; Lucy would wake up sobbing for her. And one day at the end of July, my father sat the two of us on his knees.

His eyes: hazel, green, and gold. Filled with more sadness than I've ever seen on this earth. Even forgetting our names seemed easier than the day he told us about our mother. How had he decided when to have the talk with us? He must have weighed the benefits of truth against those of letting us continue to hope. Because our anxiety was exploding.

"She loves you both," he said. "But she has to go away for a while."

"Go away? She just got home," I said. She'd been in the hospital for some of the winter and all of the spring. "Is she sick again?"

"No, Pell," he said. "She's better. But we want

her to stay that way. So she's going to take care of herself. . . ."

"We'll take care of her," I said, feeling stubborn and starting to panic.

"We can't, not the way she needs," he said. "She's going to a special place to live, and we'll be staying here at home."

"We live with you, and we live with her," Lucy said, nervous but still almost-happy, the truth not dawning. "We live with you both!"

"That's how it's been," he said.

"How it **is**," Lucy said stubbornly, wanting him to get it right.

"What special place?" I asked.

"Italy," he said.

"Who says she has to go there?" I asked.

"The grownups talked about it," he said. "And decided it was the best idea."

The grownups! Who **were** these people?

"She's not coming back," I said. I shook, quivering uncontrollably. I felt the truth in my fingers, toes, the top of my head, the way I imagine a diviner must sense water. I stared at my father, watching his eyes. All he had to do was contradict me. Just say I was wrong. But he couldn't. He didn't have to.

"She has to come home now, right now," Lucy said, immediately starting to sob. "I want her! I miss her!"

"Lucy, she loves you. She told me—"

"I love her, I need her, get her for me!" Lucy shrieked, a four-year-old with the ferocity of a bobcat.

She tried to squirm off his lap, and I tried to grab her, but my father took care of it. He held us both, so tightly, letting us scream our lungs out, our throats raw and sore. Lucy raked her own face, and I tore at my hair. Our father held us, rocked us, tried to keep us from hurting ourselves more. When he set us down, much later, his shirt was streaked with our blood.

He gave us baths, washed us off. We sat on the back porch and felt a cool breeze coming through the screens. Lucy cried softly, sucking her thumb. The sound of crickets was loud in the trees. That night he tucked us in and slept on the floor of our room, between our twin beds.

He didn't give us any more details that night. They trickled in, over time, with her letters. By September, she was in Italy. She lived in a place that reminded her of Newport. She could see the ocean from her house. There were gray mists on the shore. We were shocked, beside ourselves in a whole new way. Our mother had moved to Europe, a different continent. An ocean separated us from her. Our longing made us sick. We had fevers, we threw up.

When my father was at work, Miss Miller tried to smooth everything out. She defended our mother, saying she had her reasons for leaving, and that we would understand when we were older. Finally, one afternoon she promised our mother was coming back, would definitely be on her way home soon, and that she would bring us lovely presents. Lucy and I bolted ourselves to the front steps.

Was there any reality to the rumor? Had Miss Miller talked to her, was my mother having misgivings? Lucy sucked her thumb so hard, she drew blood. Miss Miller painted it with iodine to make it taste bad. Lucy didn't care, just sat on the steps beside me, sucking her poor sore thumb while I twirled my hair out, both of us staring down the street for someone who wasn't coming. When my father got home, after dark, we were still sitting there.

My father fired Miss Miller and took us to therapy. Ah, the joys. He found two highly recommended clinical psychologists. I had Dr. Robertson, Lucy had Dr. Milhauser, and we had individual sessions, then group sessions, each of us alone, then with our father, then all three of us, with both doctors.

We let it all out, believe me, and nobody medicated us. No Ritalin, no antidepressants. Just being heard, allowed to weep over things that hurt, that are terrible, beyond comprehension—and, with Miss Miller gone, not being told everything was okay, no lies that our mother would come back. There were no panaceas, no empty promises. That's how our father and the doctors helped us survive losing her.

The only reason I'm here right now is because I was allowed to hate her. The irony is, being permitted such dark feelings kept me from having them. I've never hated my mother. I grieve what she did, even though I know she—supposedly—had her reasons. Miss Miller wasn't wrong about that.

We are fine, Lucy and I. We are strong. She's had setbacks, the sleeping stuff. She once asked me how people know the difference between sleep and death. I told her they didn't have to—their bodies took care of it for them. Being her older sister has made me grow up fast. Sometimes I sound off with such weird wisdom, I wonder where it comes from.

While my father was sick, he tried to tell me something. I was thirteen, and suddenly he was talking to me as if I was an adult.

"It was my fault, Pell. She never wanted—" He stopped himself.

"Wanted what, Dad?" I asked.

"She didn't mean to hurt you."

By leaving us? Was he kidding? He was on heavy pain medication. Radiation, chemo, the aftereffects, and then the tumor came back anyway. He was getting morphine; it took him away, he'd fall asleep in the middle of a sentence. And it made him think crazy things. I sat by his bed that day, waiting for him to wake up and finish his thoughts.

When he opened his eyes, he started right in again.

"She left you," he said.

"Mom."

He nodded. "River. Stars," he said.

Was this like seahorse, starfish, sunshine in a glass?

"You could have died," he said.

"Dad?" I said, scared. Did he know who I was?

"I told her," he said, and then he began to cry. He was so upset, I wanted to call for the nurse, to give him more medicine, but he grabbed my wrist, looked into my eyes in a pleading way. "Sweetheart. At the river, I want you to know, she never would have done it. Never."

If only I could translate what he was trying to say to me. Tears rolled down my cheeks as I tried to guess and get it right. "It's okay, Dad," I said, trying to calm him.

"Your mother," he said.

"What about her, Dad?"

He was trying to tell me something; he must have thought I was thirteen, ready to know. It had to do with my mother, and if only I could unlock my father's language, the way at the end his words became like secret code, maybe I could understand. I never did; he died soon after that.

Learning the details of why she left is sort of beside the point, although I admit there are times I would like to know. The truth is, I am on Capri because I want my mother to come home. Time is running out. Of course it always has been, life being so short and uncertain and all. But this is different, and it's real. The timetable will become more acute in September.

That's when I become a senior at Newport Academy, my father's alma mater. It's a boarding school, and now Lucy attends as well. Our rooms are side-by-side. My grandmother, Edith Nicholson, lives in Newport; we spend holidays and, except for this one, summers with her.

But trust me when I tell you, my grandmother is not the sweet, kindly grandma you might be picturing. She lives on the society page. Literally. She goes to the best parties, moves in the swankiest circles, and first thing every morning she looks online for Google alerts about herself. High society in the Internet age.

In September I start applying to colleges. Next year I'm off to who knows where. I do well at school; I'm a National Merit Scholar. I want to be a psychologist, and my advisor thinks I should apply to Harvard. I'm leaning toward Berkeley, where Dr. Robertson went. It's far from Newport and Lucy, all the way across the country. But once I leave for college, no matter where the campus is located, Lucy will be alone.

Lucy and I have been together since the day she was born. We've had nights, weekends, even weeks apart. Sleepovers, camp, things like that. But these are real emotional problems that my little sister suffers.

My sister and Beck, Travis's sister, talked to ghosts, attempted a mathematical connection to the spirit world. My sister is very smart and creative, brilliant in math. But can you imagine how that made me worry? She craves nothing more than connection. She has it with me, but she needs more than that. She cries in a way I don't—high, wild, keening, helpless, and despairing. I don't know what to do.

I've felt almost like her mother, and sometimes it's too much. I am her person here on earth. She comes to me, leans on me, for everything. I love that, and want it to continue. But it's more than I can handle. She needs someone else too.

Is there a strain of despair that will grip me and Lucy the way it did our mother? What if I'm like my mother? I'm in love with Travis Shaw; we're young, but he's wonderful, and we really know and get each other. What if we have children, make a life, and I realize I can't stay?

Is there a name for the disorder that drove our mother away from us? I want to understand, but that's not the primary reason I'm here. It's simple: Lucy and I want our mother in our lives. I've come to ask her to come home, so the three of us can have this year before I go to college. Lucy needs a mother, a real one. We both do.

After leaving the garden, I went back to the house. It was six a.m. Italian time, which made it midnight in Newport. I thought about calling Travis, but I figured he was fishing in the middle of Block Island Sound. Besides, the person I really wanted to talk to was Lucy. I have an international plan on my iPhone, so I dialed her number, and she answered.

"Seahorse!" she said, obviously seeing my number on the screen.

"Starfish!" I said.

We basked in silence, just knowing the other was on the line. Peace, the ultimate connection, being together.

"How is it there?" she asked finally.

"It's quite beautiful," I said. Brave, stoic me.

"How is **she**? Is she completely crazy?"

"She doesn't seem to be."

"That's a relief. How are the playboys?"

The men my grandmother had always alluded to, as if my mother lived on a mad, never-ending treadmill of dating the rich and famous.

"I haven't seen one yet."

"Well, the summer is young," my sister said.

"Here's something," I said. "She **gardens.** . . ."

"You mean, in the **dirt**?" Lucy asked, giggling with delight.

"Yep."

"What you're saying is she deadheads the marigolds," Lucy said. "Right? She wears Chanel garden gloves and pays some poor Capri person to hold the perfect Martha Stewart basket while she goes snip, snip, and the flower heads fall oh-so-quaintly into the basket, and it's going to be a feature story in Italian **Vogue**?"

I laughed because Lucy is droll and hilarious and because I could just picture the look on her face as she imitated our grandmother's manufactured idea of our mother.

"Shades of Edie," Lucy went on, again referring to our grandmother. "Like mother, like daughter, right? Is Lyra exactly the same as Edie?"

"Surprisingly, not very much at all," I said.

"I knew it!" she said, sounding more delighted than before. "Tell me more!"

"Well, for one thing, she works. She actually does garden—that's her job. Her own garden is beautiful, and she does it for other people too."

"Holy shit," Lucy said. "Employment!"

"Yes," I said, feeling proud. "Our mother."

"What's her house like? Did she blow through the trust fund? Does she have manic episodes where she gives everything away? Is she strapped financially? Was one of the playboys a con-man gigolo who drained her accounts? Did she have to pawn the silver?"

"Doesn't look it," I said, glancing onto the terrace at the brass telescope, around the living room at the mahogany tables, the cashmere throws, a marble bust, a bronze monkey, a Meissen bowl in the Thousand and One Nights pattern, the oil paintings, the silver tea set. "She still has the wild rose teapot. Do you remember?"

"Mmm," Lucy said, and fell silent.

That's the thing with us sisters. We remember everything. We have Velcro brains. I could just imagine Lucy spinning back, all the way to when she was three and I was five, having a tea party with our mother on the floor of our sunroom in Grosse Pointe. Back when we were all together, before the winter when she fell apart.

"Are you glad you're there?" Lucy asked.

"I think so," I said.

"Hmm," she said. "Do you love her?"

"What do you think?"

"Yeah, you do."

"And you?"

"More than anything," Lucy said.

The sands and dust, powerful feelings, began to swirl. The sirocco. It came up sometimes when we talked about our mother. We were silent a moment, getting the lumps out of our throats. We had to face facts, the person we loved most in the world, now that our dad was dead, was the woman who'd walked out on us.

"Are you okay?" I asked.

"I just miss you," she said. "It's hard with you away. But . . ."

"Tell me."

"I want you to be there," she said, choking up. "For her."

"For her?"

"If I feel this way," she said, "think of how she feels. We all need each other. Does she have anyone? A good friend, anything like that?"

"She has Max. He's her neighbor, and he picked me up in Sorrento yesterday, and he's a dream and if it weren't for Travis I might consider falling in love with him myself. But he's pretty old, and she was best friends with his wife, who died of Alzheimer's."

"God bless," Lucy said, because we both have a tender spot for anyone with any kind of dementia.

I was still thinking of Max, and I drifted over to the doorway, carrying the phone out onto the terrace. The sun hadn't yet crested over Monte Solaro, and the rocks and tide pools down below were deep in shadow. The Bay of Naples was layered with morning haze, a film of white gauze over dark blue. In the cliff's shadow I saw a figure, walking along the rocks above the tide line, bending down, picking something up, and flinging it into the sea.

"Are you sleeping?" I asked, keeping my eyes on the person.

"Sort of. I'm staying at Beck's."

"Good," I said. I'd told Travis everything, so he and his mother would be looking out for her. "How's the sleepwalking?"

"I don't think I've done any," she said. "Pell, can I speak to her?"

"She's not here this second, but yes, of course. Why don't you get some sleep now, and we'll call you in the morning?"

"Listen," Lucy said. "I'm not really tired. What I'll do is lie down right now, get some shut-eye, and call you there in one hour."

"Lucy, tomorrow."

"No," she said stubbornly. "I'm calling you back in one hour. I need to, okay?"

"Okay. I love you," I said.

"I love you," Lucy said.

That's how we always said goodbye. Now it was Lucy's night and my morning. We kissed each other through the phone line, hung up. I stood on the terrace, staring down at the rocks. The sun inched around the mountain, casting bright yellow light, and suddenly I saw more clearly. It was that young man from yesterday, the one I'd seen talking to Max.

He was scouring the rocks, just above the waves' reach, intent on searching the rocks and wrack and tidal pools. I watched as he'd find what he was looking for, pick it up, and throw it into the water.

This happened over and over. I couldn't see what he was throwing, but I swear it looked like starfish.

I tore into the walled garden, through the pine trees, and down the steep stairs that led to the rock beach, compelled to see what he was doing, but I knew I had to be back in an hour. For Lucy's call.

I hoped my mother would be too.

Four

Mornings were good. Yesterday Rafe had told his grandfather that he slept late, but that wasn't true. He just hadn't been up for a discussion about Pell, why he hadn't wanted to go pick her up. His grandfather wanted so badly for him to do well, to have a nice, normal nineteen-year-old life. He was trying to show Rafe that he'd moved on, moved past, so Rafe would too.

Rafe had been doing his best. Since arriving on Capri, he lived in the boathouse, instead of up in the villa. If he had to be on the island at all, it was better that he not spend time in the flat shadows of his worst moments. Besides, the boathouse was good. No heat, no electricity. A hard cot. But windows open to the sky, and the constant sound and feel of waves.

He walked along the rocks, staring down. He and his dad used to take tide walks. Right now the tide was far out, as low as it ever got. Above the tide line, he found a tiny octopus hiding in an abandoned cockleshell. Its skin was already drying out. He carried it to the water's edge, lowered it down, watched the cephalopod jet away. Then back to the top of the rocks, where the suffering was greatest.

There, a starfish stranded on a rock that wouldn't be underwater again until the new moon. He peeled it off, winged it as far as he could into the deep water. He wondered whether any of this was worth it; the things he saved would die eventually anyway.

"Way to be negative," he said out loud to himself. It was called stinking thinking, and no one did it better.

At rehab they told him he had choices. Every thought he had, every act he took, was leading him either toward or away from relapse. He'd thought he was doing well, getting up early, meditating, working on his college admissions package, trying to be disciplined, but seeing Arturo yesterday was messing him up. The desire for chemical relief had come flooding back along with the negativity. He spotted another doomed starfish, held it in his hand, and prepared to throw.

"Buongiorno."

He recognized the voice from yesterday. Stopping mid-throw, he turned and saw Pell Davis.

"Good morning," he said.

"You speak English," she said. "Does everyone on Capri? I haven't met an Italian yet."

"You're in expat central. Didn't your mother tell you?"

"You know my mother?"

He nodded. Did this mean Lyra hadn't warned her about him? "Yeah," he said. "I'm Rafaele Gardiner. Max's grandson."

"Pell Davis," she said. "Pleased to meet you. I know Max is English, but you sound American."

"Born in London, grew up in New York. My father's job . . ." he said, and shrugged.

"Ah," she said, as if she understood overseas posting, British companies with Manhattan offices. "But your first name is Italian."

"It is. My mother was born in Naples, came here to work. My parents met at the marina. I'm called 'Rafe,' mostly. It went over better in New York than 'Rafaele.' "

She laughed. "Do you mind if I ask what you were doing just now?"

"Walking the beach," he said.

"No, I mean with that. It's a starfish, isn't it?"

"Yeah," he said, holding his hand out, as she seemed to want to see. She bent close, touching one spiny arm with her finger. Morning light glinted on her ebony hair. When she glanced up, he saw electric blue eyes.

"What are you doing with it?"

"Saving its life," he said, flinging the starfish as hard as he could into the deep water.

"Why do you have to?" she asked. "Won't it take care of itself?"

He glared at her. Was she kidding? "I guess you

don't hang around the sea much. There are these things called tides. They come in and go out every six hours. Starfish can usually make it between normal tides if seagulls don't get them, if the sun doesn't dry them out."

"But the moon's full, so the tides are more extreme, and the starfish get stranded. I get it."

She sounded so nice, calm, even in spite of his nasty sarcasm. In rehab he'd learned that his character defects came out full-force when he felt like using. He gave her an apologetic look.

"Sorry for being a jerk."

"Sorry you're having a bad day," she said. She gave him a smile tinged with irony, then started walking away.

"You came all the way down to make sure I wasn't doing something evil to the starfish?"

"I kind of have a thing for them," she said. "Seahorses too. Are there any of those around?"

"Not on Capri, but nearby," he said. "A whole colony on the Faraglioni."

"Where's that?"

"You don't know?" he asked. "Wow."

"I just got here," she said.

"Man. The Faraglioni. Limestone colossi, cool islands off the other side of Capri. They're on every other postcard."

"Seahorses are there, really?"

He nodded.

"I would love to see them," she said, sounding

wistful. He glanced at the boat tied at the end of the dock. He could take her himself, but her mother would probably kill him when they returned.

"Lots to see around here," he said, steering away from the idea.

"I know," she said. "Tiberius's Leap, the Villa Jovis, Rock of the Sirens. I've been reading guidebooks about Capri my whole life."

"You left out the Grotta Azzurra," he said.

"Of course, how could I? The Blue Grotto."

"I was kidding. You know it's a tourist trap, right? There are better, unspoiled caves all along the coast. We have some right here on the property."

"I live in Newport, Rhode Island. We invented tourist places."

"Newport?" he asked. "Do you know Ty Cooper?"

"He goes to my school," she said. "Plays football with my boyfriend."

"Weird," Rafe said. "He lived in my building in the city. So, you grew up in Newport."

"I grew up in Michigan, but I've lived in Newport the last few years," she said. "Look, another starfish."

"Good eyes," he said, crouching down. Then he turned to her. "Why don't you take care of this one?"

"Okay," she said.

He watched her bend down, carefully remove

the starfish from the black rock. She walked to the water's edge, wound up, and gave a really respectable throw. The starfish landed between waves with a light splash.

"Starfish and seahorses," he said, giving her a quizzical look.

"It's a long story," she said. "You?"

"Also a long story."

"Hmm," she said, gazing at him. For a minute he thought of asking her to sit on the dock, so they could exchange personal tales about sea creatures. But again he thought of Lyra, didn't feel like rocking that boat.

"I'd better go," Pell said. "My sister is calling soon."

"Okay," he said.

They said goodbye, and Rafe watched her walk slowly along the shore. He turned to continue his quest. He didn't want to see her head up the stairs; he liked having her on the beach.

As he walked along, he found himself moving faster. He threw the starfish farther, and had more hope that they wouldn't strand again, that they wouldn't meet up with a predator, that they'd live awhile longer. He also noticed he didn't feel like using anymore. The desire to get high had left him.

He glanced back, feeling a strange impulse to thank Pell, but she had already disappeared up the stairs.

~

Lucy Davis lay in bed, thinking, watching the clock, wishing the time would pass faster. Her heart was skittering with excitement and anxiety. She hadn't spoken to her mother in a long time. Years had added up.

People—Lucy's grandmother—criticized her mother unmercifully. Said she was selfish, uncaring, asked what kind of woman could leave her children. Those comments hurt Lucy. She always wanted to defend her mother—sometimes felt a physical desire to strike whoever talked against her—because no one understood her. No one except Lucy and Pell. Lucy didn't know what had made her mother leave, but she was sure of one thing—her mother had had a good reason.

Lucy knew love. Pell and she had it in their bones for each other, for their father. And for their mother. And Lucy was sure their mother had it for them too. Love that powerful was the only explanation for their mother's long silence. For as completely as love could bond and heal, so could it tear people apart. Lucy was sure her mother hadn't gone to that mental hospital for the fun of it. No, she'd been in some kind of terrible trouble. And it had driven her away.

Pell was hoping to convince their mother to come home. Lucy was sure of it. Even though Pell hadn't spelled it out, this had all started last winter, after Beck and Travis's sister, Carrie, returned to the family, with her baby daughter. Split families were familiar to the Davis girls. They knew it was hard for some people to stay, for reasons all their own.

A squawk sounded from down the hall—Carrie's daughter Gracie having a dream. Lucy pushed back the covers, tiptoed through the Shaws' house—a newer, larger faculty house than the small cottage they'd first moved in to when Mrs. Shaw began teaching at Newport Academy. Lucy felt glad for the distraction, ready to lean over Gracie's crib rail and whisper to her.

She met Carrie in the hallway, rubbing sleep from her eyes as she left her daughter's room.

"Hi, Lucy," Carrie said. "Everything okay?"

"Just thought I'd check on Gracie," Lucy said.

"That's sweet of you," Carrie said, trying to hide a yawn. "She's fine. I think she knows it's going to be a beach day tomorrow, and she was dreaming of playing in the sand."

"Did she tell you?" Lucy asked.

Carrie just smiled. Gracie didn't really talk yet. But Lucy stood there, wanting the young mother's secret to understanding and communication with her child. How had Carrie understood what Gracie was dreaming? Had Lucy's mother known Lucy's dreams?

"Did she tell you?" Lucy asked again.

"She can't talk yet," Carrie said, touching her shoulder. "I was just imagining."

Lucy nodded, checked her watch. Still not time to call.

"Want some milk?" Carrie asked. "I was just going to fix Gracie a bottle."

"That's okay," Lucy said. She had to hug herself. A bottle; her mother used to heat up warm milk for her. Lucy knew her mother had often looked in on her and Pell and tried to soothe them back to sleep. Had she ever imagined their dreams, like Carrie did with Gracie?

Of course she had.

"Carrie?" Lucy whispered, stopping suddenly.

"Yes?"

Lucy stared down the dimly lit hall. What would it take for Carrie to leave Gracie? Lucy saw them together all the time; it was hard for Carrie to go to work at the library, even knowing Gracie was being well looked after by Mrs. Shaw, or Beck and Lucy, or Travis.

Carrie herself had run away, the day her father died. She had left her family—brother, sister, mother who loved her. She had left a hole in their lives, made them worry about her. Lucy understood that. See, when a parent died or left, all bets were off. Carrie had gone daughter-crazy. There's a sort of madness all children who've lost a parent understand. Their lives are divided into before and after; the "after" part is not pretty.

"Are you okay?" Carrie asked, still standing in the near-dark hall.

Lucy kept staring at her. She knew her late nights, the times she sleepwalked, caused people to worry. She wanted to tell Carrie not to, that this was different. The reality was hitting her: she was about to hear her mother's voice. Knowing she was about to speak to her mother after so many years made Lucy's stomach flip.

"I'm fine," Lucy said, and she started to beam. "Good night."

"Good night," Carrie said.

Lucy walked into her room, closed the door behind her. One a.m. Newport time was close, and then it was here, and then, her fingers trembling, Lucy picked up her cell phone and dialed.

"Hello?" came Pell's voice.

"Hi," Lucy said. "Am I on time?"

"Yes, perfectly."

"Oh, good," Lucy said, her heart kicking like mad. "Is she there? With you now?"

"I'm giving the phone to her," Pell said.

Silence for three seconds. Then, "Lucy?"

Yikes. Tears in Lucy's eyes. Her mother's voice, for real, right now in the middle of the night.

"Yep, it's me," Lucy said.

"Oh, my gosh," her mother said. "Oh, my gosh."

Lucy held the phone.

"It's so late in Newport," her mother said.

"That's okay," Lucy said.

"I wish you were here," her mother said. "With us."

"You do? You wish I were there?"

"Oh, Lucy, I do. There's so much to say."

"There is," Lucy said, and she beamed even harder as the words tumbled out. "Pell said she's so happy to be with you, you live by the sea, you like to garden!"

Five

Talking to Lucy with my mother, how to begin?

It was like the best, weirdest, most troubling yet wonderful reunion. I wished Lucy were there to see what her voice did to our mother: her eyes shone, her mouth trembled, and then she smiled and cried.

The combination of all three of us on the phone was like Miracle-Gro on my emotions. When we hung up from Lucy, I walked through a portal into the past and went straight to the brass telescope set up on my mother's terrace.

"That was amazing," my mother said. "She sounds so grown up."

"She's fourteen now," I said.

"She didn't want to come with you?"

"I wouldn't say that," I said. "I just thought . . ."

"You weren't sure what you'd find here?"

I pressed my eye to the telescope lens, suddenly

knowing that I'd done it before. The sun was blindingly bright, the scope trained straight into the sky.

"What are you looking at?" my mother asked.

"I'm not sure," I said. I'd expected the line of sight to be directed toward the water, yachts and fishing boats.

"You can adjust it if you'd like," she said.

But the thing was, I didn't want to. I can't explain why, but it felt right, gazing up at the sky. I stood there for a few minutes, looking into the cloudless blue. Something sparkled—a plane, a satellite, a planet, I wasn't sure.

"Do you remember the telescope?" she asked.

"I don't know," I said. "Should I?" She didn't reply. I moved my face away from the eyepiece, noticed engraving on the telescope's brass tube. It said **Vega-Capella-Pollux**. "What's that?" I asked.

"An imaginary constellation," she said. "Made up of stars that are nowhere near one another."

"Who thought of it?" I asked.

"I did," she said.

"You like stars?"

She nodded. "When I was little, my father said I was lucky there was both day and night. Because I loved the flowers by day and the stars by night."

I loved that, and it surprised me. I didn't associate soul or poetry with the Nicholson side of the family.

"I used to want to be an astronomer when I was little. Before I wanted to be a gardener," she said.

New information. I leaned on the stone balustrade, waiting for her to say more. But she didn't, so I had to press.

"Why didn't you?"

"One didn't," she said.

The phrase was straight out of my grandmother's mouth. One doesn't go to such places, one doesn't associate with such people, one didn't attend graduate school, one didn't follow one's dreams when one already had a trust fund. Here, I'll conjugate it for you: one doesn't, one didn't, one never shall.

"What about after you married Dad? Wouldn't he have been happy for you to become an astronomer? Or whatever you wanted?"

"I think the moment had passed," she said. "I was a mother by then. I had you and Lucy."

I gave her a sharp look, unable to help myself. Did having children mean you had to give up your life? There was no such thing as a woman who was both a mother and a scientist? I could have said, but didn't want to be contentious, **What about after you left us?** She must have felt it herself, because she blushed. She looked down, her white-streaked dark hair falling across her eyes.

"Did we have the telescope in Michigan?" I asked.

"Yes," she said, looking grateful that I'd let her off the hook. "You loved it when you were little. I'd pick you up and you'd hold on tight, look through the lens, and we'd pretend we were explorers."

"It's so odd," I said. "I remember everything, but not that."

"Everything?" she asked.

I nodded solemnly. It was a curse, really, having Velcro brain. There are so many memories I'd like to wipe out. My mother is the exception: I want to remember more about her, but can't. The ones I have get fuzzy and sometimes slip away. This sounded like one I would have loved, a scene of mother-daughter happiness.

"Tell me one thing," she said.

"That I remember?"

She nodded.

"About you?"

"About us," she said.

Oh, the possibilities. I had this secret trove of memories of my mother. I'd stored them away, just as if my mind were an attic. A place to put clothes that didn't fit anymore, broken toys, old furniture—stuff you never used anymore, but weren't quite ready to toss. I never went up there. But I did now, opened the door, and the rooms were overflowing.

"You taught me how to do somersaults," I said. "Out in the backyard while Lucy took her nap. She was in her playpen under the crabapple tree, and we were on the grass, and I got stuck on my head.

You helped me over. I can still feel your hand on my back. And oncc that happened, I got it."

"And you kept going, all across the yard," she said.

"You did too," I said. "Together, side by side, somersaulting to the fence and back. We laughed . . . and Lucy woke up."

"And you wanted to show her how, but I told you she was too young."

"A baby," I said. "You told me she could have hurt her soft spot. Then you showed me, and I kissed the top of her head."

"You were a good big sister," she said.

I still am, I wanted to say. My eyes welled up and I stared at her, wondering what she thought of my tears. They were a combination of remembering the mother I'd loved so much and the worst hurt in the world. How could she have left me? Left us? I was fine—but did she have any idea what this had done to Lucy? Sometimes it seemed to me that my sister had been rent asunder; the phrase came to me, oddly, from earth science class: "galaxies rent asunder in a gigantic cosmic collision."

"Tell me another," she said.

Another memory? I didn't feel like it, think I could. I shook my head. The feelings coursing through me were wild and powerful. I sat down at the other end of the settee. Six feet separated us, an unbridgeable gulf. Being in the same house, on the same terrace, was in some ways harder than living a continent and ocean apart.

"What about you?" she said after a few minutes.

I looked at her, not getting it.

"I told you I wanted to be an astronomer when I was young."

"And now you garden," I said.

"Yes. So will you tell me what you want to do?"

"When I grow up?" I asked.

"You seem very grown up now," she said. "But yes. When you finish high school. Have you decided on a college? Do you know what you want to study?"

"Berkeley," I said, deciding in that very moment. "And I want to be a psychologist."

"Oh," she said. Nothing more. Just a long stare out over the water as the color rushed into her face again. Had my career choice scathed her? I obviously had spent plenty of time in therapy; no need to clue her in there. We stared into each other's blue eyes; it was really strange, because I saw myself in the future, how I'll appear in twenty-five years. We look so much alike, it felt scary.

I read a lot of psychology. Winnicott, Schore, Van der Kolk. Mainly because of Lucy. But I also read self-help books. It's not that cool in high school to read things that appeal mainly to people who've been divorced, widowed, brokenhearted, or conned, but I've never met a self-help book I didn't like.

Grief and bereavement, abandonment issues, birth order, dream analysis, codependency, sexuality, parenting, body image, women's health—I can't get enough. My self needs help, that's for sure. But looking at my mother, seeing the brokenness in her eyes, I realized hers did too.

"What did we pretend we were exploring?" I asked. "When we looked through the telescope back in Michigan."

"We had a make-believe country," she said.

"Dorset," I said, remembering that part as if it were yesterday. Our country shared its name with our street; we'd lived at 640 Dorset Road. Suddenly I could see the map we drew when I was six; sitting at the kitchen table, we'd spread out a large sheet of paper.

With a green crayon, my mother drew a big wobbly circle. I'd colored it green. My mother had helped me add cities and towns, mountain ranges and bodies of water. Rivers, ponds, lakes, and the ocean.

"But we live in Michigan," she'd said. "There's no ocean near here."

"Our country has an ocean," I'd said firmly. I'd been to Newport, to visit her family, and been astonished by the Atlantic. Beach, shells, seaweed, rocks. The mystery of where waves came from and where they went, the endlessness of it all.

"If you say so," she'd said.

"I do," I'd said. "It's our country, we can have whatever we want."

"And you want the sea."

"Yes!"

Staring at her now, I remembered all that. But I still couldn't bring back the telescope, and her holding me in her arms while we explored . . . our yard? Our imaginary country? All I recalled was the map. I'd let Lucy paste tiny foil stars all around the edges, to symbolize the sky. I pictured her now, tiny little girl working so hard to make the sky bright.

And when our father came home from work that night, he'd studied it, and I'd wondered why he seemed so sad. I thought maybe he felt left out, because my mother and Lucy and I had created a country without him. Families were supposed to be together. That night I felt bad, afraid we'd hurt his feelings. The next day, my mother left.

"The map," she said now. "You did such an amazing job."

"I loved it," I said.

"Do you . . . ," she began. She trailed off, then went for it. "Do you still have it?"

I shook my head. "We got rid of everything," I said. "When we sold the house after Dad died."

She nodded, as if I were any old stranger talking about the sale of real estate. She seemed to accept it. Maybe she knew how it went: you give the listing to an agent, and your family lawyer gets in touch with an auction house, to dispose of the contents of your family home. Because Lucy and I were so young, all this was handled by my grandmother's lawyers. My father's parents were dead, so even though he wasn't Edith Nicholson's kid, she saw to it for our sake, mine and Lucy's. Suddenly I felt kind of terrible.

"Are you okay?" she asked.

"Yes," I said. Another lie. I wasn't okay. My stomach was churning, head spinning, with a general sense of despair rising up.

Lucy and I shared this feeling quite often; I called it the sirocco, the hot, vicious wind that blows off the Sahara. Ironically, it was also the name of our grandmother's yacht; I thought if I gave Lucy a name for the terrible feelings inside, it could help her. But it kind of backfired. She told me it reminded her that people and things we loved have been swept off this earth.

"Well, I want to show you around the island, but maybe you should take it easy today," she said. "Jet lag and all. We don't have to be at Max's till seven-thirty tonight."

"Will Rafe be there?" I asked.

The color literally drained from her face. "How do you know about Rafaele?"

"I met him on the rocks," I said. "When I went for a walk before."

"Pell," she said. "He's very troubled. I know I can't tell you what to do, but I think you should stay away from him."

"What do you mean, 'troubled'?" I asked. If only she knew my friends back home: Travis and his sisters were good examples. Their family had been ripped apart; his older sister had had a baby at sixteen. She'd seen her father drown. Their younger sister, Beck, Lucy's best friend, stole things. People who were lost and wounded found their ways to one another.

"Rafaele's had a lot of problems, including with the law," she said.

"He seemed nice," I said. "He was rescuing starfish."

She narrowed her eyes. "Believe me, he's not a rescuer." Whatever the truth about Rafe, I could see that she believed what she was saying. It didn't really matter; I was here for a specific reason, not to make new friends.

"I think I'll go read in my room," I said, standing up.

"Have a good rest," she said.

Pausing, I looked through the telescope. I loosened the knob, swung the scope to watch clouds move across the white face of Monte Solaro. A raptor circled a crevasse. Angling down, I saw the yellow boat heading out from the dock, into the bay. Max was at the wheel, Rafe in the bow, a third man in the stern with piles of fishing nets. I watched for a few moments, wondering what Rafe had done.

Without the telescope, the boat looked tiny—a yellow speck with a white wake. Sunlight bounced off the endless blue ocean, ripples of silver, broken glass, spread out from Capri as far as I could see.

The sight of water always soothed me, no matter how upset I felt. Maybe that's why I wanted so much of it on the map of Dorset, the country my mother and I had invented. I could almost picture it, the carefully colored green countryside, the rivers, tributaries, coves, bays, and all of it, the green contours of Dorset, surrounded by an ocean. I could see it so perfectly because my other lie, the first one of the conversation, was that I'd thrown out the map. Of course I hadn't.

I never could.

~

Lyra pulled out her sketchpad, incorporating two memories into her design, a garden for Amanda and Renata, two friends who lived near Sirens' Rock. She drew white flowers that would glow under the light of a full moon. The summer after college, Lyra had seen a **jardin de la lune** in Paris, a moon garden full of white flowers. Later, on their honeymoon, she and Taylor had seen a moon gate.

Honeymoon.

The memory made Lyra close her eyes. Bermuda, Martin Cottages Resort, private pink-sand beach, white cottages with blue shutters. She and Taylor had spent two weeks in bathing suits and bare feet. They had made it through the huge wedding; her mother had tried to get them to go to her friend's palazzo in Portofino, but Taylor had stood up to her.

He'd found the cottages in a guidebook, the way normal people traveled, the antithesis of Alexander Baker, and Lyra had felt so grateful. But their first night in Bermuda, in bed, Lyra had an allergic reaction. She was itchy and embarrassed; she couldn't stop scratching. She was sensitive to certain products, so the next day Taylor asked the manager if the laundry could try something else. Second night, new detergent, same rash. It was mostly terrible, but slightly hilarious—she was spending their honeymoon in hives.

Taylor rinsed the sheets himself, in cool, clear well water, hanging them over the fence to dry. That night Lyra was fine. They'd held each other, making love over and over. She loved his mind, and his kindness, and his athletic body. He'd played football, then worked out all through law school. But that day she was moved by the sight of her big, strong husband sloshing sheets around the tub, wringing them out just for her. She couldn't even start to imagine her parents doing that for each other, even in the early days.

A white fence lined the property; the private

beach entrance was through a moon gate, a perfect half-circle made of stone, arching over the path. Everyone said that when a newly married couple held hands and walked through, they would have eternal love and happiness. Lyra and Taylor hit the moon gate many times each day. Each time, Lyra touched stone.

In Newport, back when she and Taylor were apart, her mother had arranged an appointment to the board of the Bellevue Garden Society. The position was unpaid, but prestigious enough for the daughter of Edith Nicholson. Lyra had toured the historical mansion grounds with landscape designers, world-famous gardeners.

Lyra had had to vet the designers' credentials and references, oversee their designs. As they walked through rose bowers, topiary mazes, English country gardens, formal French **jardins,** Lyra longed to drop her notebook and pick up a shovel, dig and plant, get her hands dirty. She felt thwarted in her own desires. They started eating her up inside, like cancer. Some days she couldn't get up, and she called in sick.

As soon as Lyra and Taylor returned from their honeymoon, she started right at home: clearing land, planting flower and vegetable beds. Finding a place for Hermes. Then she got pregnant.

One of every ten women suffers major depression during pregnancy; Lyra was that one. She read a checklist of symptoms some women had part of the time. She had all of them all of the time—sadness, constant sleeping, despair.

She'd tried to blame the feelings on pregnancy, but the truth was, she'd had them for years. In Newport, with Alexander, she'd imagined that life with Taylor would change her. Before that, in Europe, she'd felt oppressed and bleak, overwhelmed by the meaningless of everything—until Capri.

This place had opened her mind, given her a strange, magical hope. She'd been able to imagine herself living here, on the rocky shore, free of everyone else's expectations for her. But pregnancy sent her crashing. Medication was risky for the baby, so she didn't take it. And things got worse.

Sketching now, Lyra drew the moon gate. Symbols were so important to a garden. She'd seen Pell's mood change when they talked about Dorset, their pretend country. Her clear blue eyes, so bright when she'd looked at the telescope, had filled with darkness, sorrow.

What was coming back to Pell? Did she remember all of it, or just the last part, after Lyra had finally gone to the hospital? Dorset was part of all that. It had come to be the week Lyra came home from McLean. She had planted the made-up place in Pell's mind, so her daughter would have a place to go to, a place where she could always find Lyra, no matter what happened.

"Mommy, will we always live here?" her six-year-old had asked.

"I don't know," Lyra had said.

The uncertain answer had bothered Pell. She'd looked up, frowning, from the kitchen table where she'd been coloring a picture of their house.

"Where else would we go?" Pell had asked.

Lyra was aware of Henrietta Miller listening behind them. She'd been especially vigilant about Lyra since wintertime, since the bridge and the hospital.

"Sometimes people move," Lyra had said.

Pell laughed, shook her head. "No, Mommy. We're staying here. I like our house."

"What made you ask if we'll always stay?" Lyra asked.

" 'Cause you were in the hospital," Pell said. "You were gone for so long."

Lyra pictured Pell on the bridge. Sitting at the kitchen table, Lyra watched her daughter color and broke into a cold sweat. Miss Miller hovered close by in the laundry, washing the children's clothes.

"Are you better now?" Pell pressed.

"Yes, honey," Lyra said.

"Because I missed you so much."

Lyra reached for the crayons. She poked through the box, picking out the colors she liked best, her eyes stinging. She thought of Taylor, the talk they'd had in the car on their way home from the airport, after she'd flown home from the hospital in Massachusetts.

"I missed **you,**" Lyra said, clutching Pell's hands.

Miss Miller walked over to the table. She wore a white uniform, stretched tightly across her large bosom. Her brown hair was permed, the exact style of Queen Elizabeth's. Lyra looked up at the woman who had raised her. Henrietta Miller knew Lyra better than her own mother. She understood what was going on; Lyra had explained to her the night before.

"Shall I take Pell outside for a walk?" Henrietta asked as the washing machine chugged. But Pell hadn't wanted her mother out of her sight since she'd come home from the hospital. As if she felt the ground shifting, the seismic change coming, she grabbed Lyra's wrist.

"No," she said. "I'm staying to color with Mommy."

"Pell, you need sunshine," Miss Miller said. "We shall walk to the park, and—"

"Coloring with Mommy," Pell said dangerously, and even Miss Miller knew to back off.

That's when Dorset began. Miss Miller went down the hall, to tidy up the nursery. Lyra had her crayons ready. Pell whipped a new sheet of paper off the pad. Lyra, using the green crayon, drew the outline.

"What's that?" Pell asked.

"A beautiful country, just for us, where we'll always be happy."

"And always be together!" Pell said, leaning over with a different, darker green crayon.

"What will we call it?" Lyra asked.

"Dorset," Pell said. She'd learned her address and phone number, to tell the police in case she ever got lost. Her street was foremost in her mind, the place she lived, her family's home.

The map took three days to finish. During that time, Lyra would take Pell and Lucy through the yard on expeditions of Dorset. Their private country was filled with beauty and discoveries: purple flowers in the myrtle, a white-throated sparrow singing in a maple tree, an old stone walkway nearly covered over with grass.

They'd take the telescope with them. Lyra had brought it with them to the bridge that frozen night; if Pell remembered, she didn't let on. Walking in the yard with her mother and Lucy, they would take turns pressing their eyes to the lens, looking up at the ship's weathervane, the bluebird house Taylor had nailed high up in the oak tree, a robin's nest in the crook of a white pine.

Lyra's last night at home, there was a meteor shower. While Lucy slept, she took Pell outside at midnight, set up the telescope. They'd watched the shooting stars, and then Lyra had pointed out the constellations that had always inspired her.

Pell felt everything her mother felt; sometimes it seemed they shared the same heart. She listened to Lyra's story about the sky, spilled out one of her own.

"They are for us, those stars," Pell said. "They have our names on them. We see them fall, and where do they go?" Lyra opened her mouth to speak, but Pell went on. "They fly through the night, the longest journey any stars have ever made, and they are scared. The sky is so big, and what if they lose one another? And they do . . ."

"Lose one another?" Lyra asked.

Pell nodded, staring rapt at the sky. "They go apart. And they fall in different places. Other countries. And they go into the water, down under the sea. And I keep them."

"How do you keep them, Pell?"

"In Dorset. On our map. The stars Lucy pasted to the paper. Those are the falling stars that lost one another in the sky."

"You have them?"

Pell nodded, and Lyra saw tears glinting in the darkness. "I keep the lost stars, so when they're ready to find one another again, they'll know where to look. They're on our map. I have them in Dorset."

Lyra had knelt on the ground to hug her. Pell had buried her face in her neck. Lyra had felt her daughter's breath on her skin. She'd thought of that moment so many times after she left. She'd carried the feeling all this way, all these years. And somehow it had comforted her to think of Pell and Lucy with the map they'd made of their country, of Dorset; the map that held the lost stars.

The map that no longer existed.

Six

The Villa Andria was set a step up the mountain from Lyra's house, on a lush plateau overlooking the Bay of Naples. A loggia of columns, some dating back to Tiberius, were thickly overgrown with ivy and honeysuckle, and led to an airy white house, open to the sea and gardens, to the sky and clouds. Tonight it sparkled with candlelight and good conversation.

Max had invited old friends from the island to dinner, to meet Pell. He seated Lyra at the far end of the table; seeing her with her daughter made him feel emotional, and he wanted to keep his feelings in check. He was a fool, and he knew it. He just wanted to be sure no one else did.

Bella and Alonzo, the couple who had worked for him and Christina for many years, had prepared a meal of pasta, zucchini, and the bass Max, Rafaele, and Nicolas had caught earlier that day: **ravioli alla caprese, zucchini sautéed, spigola cotta con rosmarino**.

As he looked around the table, Max felt the contentment that dinner with old friends and family always brought. Especially because, to his great surprise, Rafaele had decided to join the party. Bella filled the glasses with Fiano di Avellino, the good white wine of southern Italy. Max tried not to be too vigilant about Rafe, but he was quietly pleased to see his grandson ask Bella for sparkling water instead.

"How lovely to have your daughter with us, Lyra," said Amanda Drake, an American artist who had studied with Christina and had a studio in an old brick stable near the Piazzetta.

"Yes," Lyra said, gazing at Pell. "It's wonderful."

Pell smiled. "Thank you for inviting me, Max. And for picking me up in Sorrento."

"Max makes the trip himself only for the most important visitors," said Giovanni Restelli, a sculptor.

"It was my pleasure," Max said. "Your mother has thought of nothing else since she learned you were coming. It was the best gift of the entire winter, hearing of your plans."

"Well, a summer with her daughter," said Renata Woodwell, Amanda's partner, a poet and essayist also from the States. "No wonder!"

"Ah, was it a surprise?" asked John Harriman, a British novelist who'd once worked in government service at 12 Downing Street and wanted everything in life to be a spy thriller.

"I'd hoped to come last Christmas," Pell said. "But I realized there wouldn't be enough time. So I waited until summer vacation."

"And we have the whole summer together!" Lyra said.

"You've kept your daughter away from us," John said, scolding Lyra.

"Pell," Max said, "your mother talks about you and Lucy every day."

"Max, you're like an old priest," John said. "Hearing confessions."

"He's the dearest friend," Lyra said.

"That sounds about as boring as an old priest," John said, but his eyes were glinting, as if he'd seen straight into Max's heart and clumsy desires.

"How are you enjoying your first visit to Capri, my dear?" asked Stefan Corelli, a stage director based in Rome.

"I've never seen such a magical place," Pell said.

"What do you love most so far?" Amanda asked.

"Well, the cove," Pell said. "The clear water, beautiful rocks, and starfish all around." She gave Rafe a dazzling smile, and Max was pleased to see his grandson's expression lighten.

"'Nature never did betray the heart that loved her,'" Max said.

"Wordsworth," Renata said, nodding.

"Capri brings all kinds together," John said, and Max wasn't sure whether he was talking about the teenagers or something else. "But it's not all outdoor activities, is it? There's a world of the higher mind. Artists and intellectual misfits gravitate to our paradise. Turns one into a philosopher, doesn't it? And let's not forget Eros. One god who has definitely smiled on our island."

"I agree with Pell," Stefan said. "Nature is so beautiful here. The sensations of being in the sea air, the water all around, sensuous and primal. If ever I were to stage **The Tempest,** I would imagine it set on Capri. Shakespeare must have traveled to our island to write the play. And he must have met you, Max."

"I'm old, but not that old!" Max said.

"But you **are** Prospero," Lyra said, affection in her eyes.

"A weary, washed-up magician," Max said, gazing at her.

"I didn't mean that," she said. "Certainly not the 'weary and washed-up' part."

"We need a new play from you, Gardiner," John said. "Perhaps you've been lacking material. That's what you need—a big shake-up, so you can write your last masterpiece."

"Don't say 'last,'" Lyra said sharply. "He has plenty of time ahead of him."

"Listen to the lady," John said, pouring more wine into Max's glass, a glint in his eye. "Get moving. I sense the muse is here tonight."

"The muse?" Pell asked.

"Yes," John said. "Max's muse. She's right here, isn't she, Gardiner?"

"In the air," Max said. "On the night wind. My muse is a generous spirit." He looked up, as if thanking the sky, hoping that John would shut the hell up.

"Pell, your visit is just beginning," said Amanda. "Just wait until Capri begins to reveal her secrets to you."

"Romans discovered Capri, you know," Stefan said. "Caesar Augustus, no less. But it was his successor, Tiberius, who made Capri his home and sanctuary, his gloomy hermitage by the azure sea, to contemplate his tormented reign."

"Do you suppose Tiberius examined anything?" John said. "He came to indulge his pleasures. Orgies at the Blue Grotto, young participants slaughtered. He threw enemies off the cliff. Tiberius's Leap, it's called, Pell."

"The dark side of Capri," Lyra said.

"I don't believe in Tiberius's supposedly heinous acts," Rafe said.

Everyone at the table turned to look at him.

"Why do you say that?" John asked.

"Not just me," Rafe said. "There are books that say Tiberius was a moral person, misunderstood."

"Sentimentalists say that," John said, reaching

for the wine, refilling glasses of those around him. Max watched Rafe cover his glass.

"People make up stories," Rafe said. "When they don't understand someone. People like to think the worst of one another."

"Some accusations are valid," John said. "Not everyone in life has pure intentions, much less actions."

"He made plenty of mistakes," Rafe said, his eyes hot as he stared at John, "and he came here to ponder them."

"A good place to reflect," Stefan agreed.

Max nodded. He watched his grandson drain his glass of Pellegrino, saw Lyra staring at Rafe. Max loved them both, two people with shattered hearts and tortured consciences, and he thought it ironic and unspeakably sad that they couldn't stand each other.

Out the arched window, the sky turned purple and filled with stars. They blazed over the sea, cast Monte Solaro in deep silhouette.

"Max, when did you come here?" Pell asked.

"I arrived on Capri in 1966, when I was twenty-eight. I'd never found anyplace more inspiring."

"I can see why," Pell said, smiling.

"Max used that inspiration in all his plays," Stefan said. "He's one of the most brilliant playwrights of our time. I should know. I've directed his work, and they've all been hits."

"So you moved here to write?"

"Yes," Max said. "I came first, when I was young. I loved it so much, I wrote to Christina, an art student I'd met in London."

"She followed you here?" Pell asked.

"Yes. She was a painter; we both loved the sun, and were fortunate to have freedom in our work. I built her a studio facing Monte Solaro; the view was so magnificent, I put my desk in there, beside her easel. We worked side by side for all those years. We sent our son to Eton, then Cambridge, but he'd always come back to the island. Capri captured all of our hearts."

"Your father?" Pell asked, turning to Rafe.

Rafe nodded.

"Yes, David. He married Violetta, a beautiful young woman who worked at Marina Piccola," Max said.

"One of the harbors on Capri," Amanda explained to Pell. "Near Renata's and my house, next to Scoglio delle Sirene . . . Sirens' Rock."

"I would love to see that," Pell said, then turned to Rafe. "So your parents met here; do they still live in New York?"

"My father does," Rafe said.

"Do they come here for the summer?"

"It's been some time," Max said, answering for him. "Rafe's mother died when he was young, and his father hasn't been back. . . ."

"For the last two summers," Rafe said, looking around the table, as if daring anyone to comment.

"I'm sorry about your mother," Pell said. "And grandmother."

Rafe didn't reply. Max saw his grandson glowering at the mountain. No one else said a word.

"David—Rafe's father—will return here," Max said. "Of that I am sure."

"I saw you fishing earlier," Pell said, gesturing at the platter of **spigola,** as if sensing the subject needed changing. "Is this your day's catch?"

"It is, thanks to Rafe and Nicolas," Max said.

"I have been fishing with Max for thirty years," Nicolas said, raising his glass of wine. His gold tooth flashed in a wide smile. "Every day I have off, I go out on the water with Max. He always brings me luck!"

"This time Rafe brought the luck," Max said, reaching across the table to clink with his grandson.

The table fell silent again; perhaps it was the notion of "luck" in the same thought as "Rafe."

"He brought luck to the starfish, that's for sure," Pell said.

"Ah, yes," Max said. "Rafe, the **lanciatore della stella.** The star-thrower."

"I can't take credit," Rafe said. "My dad taught me to save them."

"Nevertheless. **Lanciatore della stella,**" Max said again, pushing back his chair. "The young man who throws stars. Shall we go outdoors, take our coffee on the terrace? Gaze upon the real stars and make wishes?"

"Wishes sound good to me," Pell said, rising along with Max. He glanced at Lyra, hoping she would join them. Then he linked his arms with Pell, and together they walked out the door, into the brilliant night.

~

Dinner parties are strange. Life with my grandmother has trained me for the peculiar hostility that can occur at a seemingly friendly table. Perhaps it's an "upper-class" emotion, and I say that with quotation marks and irony.

I wished Travis were with me. My boyfriend is sensitive, sweet, and funny. We'd be standing out here on Max's terrace, trying to figure it all out. He would have enjoyed Nicolas: salt-of-the-earth, weathered from a life on the sea, a true fisherman. He has a gold tooth right in front; from that and his frayed collar, and by shaking his rough hand, I can tell he's a workman. It makes me respect Max all the more, to think of him including Nicolas with all the fancy expatriate types.

We all gathered on the terrace, where Bella served espresso and pastries. My mother pointed out the different types to me.

"That one's delicious," my mother said. "Made from figs that grow right here at the villa. Oh, and that one is stuffed with pine nuts and wild thyme honey, bought from the market, and the lemon zest came from fruit in my orchard . . ."

I tasted the lemon tart; it was so delicious, both sweet and tart, bittersweet to think of her tending an orchard while Lucy and I went on without her. We sipped coffee; Bella came around with anisette; we both passed. John and Stefan seemed to be doing it up, after-dinner-drink-wise. They were arguing about a **Times** of London review of some friend's memoirs, Stefan saying the criticism was unwarranted and John railing that the reviewer let the author off easy.

"John seems a little full of himself," I said to my mother.

"Perhaps a bit," she said, smiling like a conspirator.

We laughed, and it was nice. The sky was ink-dark, glittering with stars. I thought of her telescope, her invented constellation, and nearly asked her to show me Vega, Capella, and Pollux. But I couldn't give her that. I felt bad about it, but my heart was very tight with her. I knew it would make her too happy to share a star-watching moment, and I guess I wasn't ready for it.

"Lyra," Amanda said, walking over with Renata. "We love your sketches for the moon garden! So dreamy and wonderful. Pell, your mother's the island's best gardener."

"That's right," Renata said. "Learned from the

master. Will you plant us an herb garden too? How did you and Christina manage the **giardino di erbe** in that shady section behind the villa?"

I saw my mother hesitate; she could talk gardens with Amanda and Renata, or continue our bonding moment. She must have registered the tension in my shoulders—I felt them hike up to my ears—at the mention of Christina's name. Christina, who'd gardened with my mother, given her the suede kneeling pillow, lost her mental faculties while my mother mourned. She'd probably been a wonderful person, but she was a gigantic thorn in my motherless side. I grabbed a pastry and left my mother talking to the women.

Stepping off the main terrace, I strolled through the vine-draped loggia. I ate the pastry, tiny seeds crunching, the good flavor filling me with comfort. There's something about eating food that's been grown within sight that made me feel as if all, or almost all, would eventually be okay.

I smelled cigarette smoke, and saw the glow. Someone was sitting on a rock, close to the precipice just beneath the villa's overhanging terrace. I headed over; even before I could see his face, I knew it was Rafe.

"Hi," I said.

"Hi," he said.

"Mind if I join you?"

He thought I meant I wanted a cigarette and started to tap one out of his pack. I shook my head and sat on the rock next to him. We stared down at the water, sparkling under the stars and reflecting the lights of Capri.

"It's beautiful," I said.

"Yeah," he said.

"I didn't think I'd see you here tonight," I said.

He glanced at me. "You didn't think my grandfather would invite me to his dinner party?"

"I didn't think dinner parties were your kind of thing."

"You're right about that. Especially this crowd."

"Older people?"

"Assholes," he said. He gave me a wry smile. "My grandfather, Nicolas, and present company excepted."

"My mother?"

"No comment."

I let that hang in the air. I'd been feeling conflicted about her, but hearing him clump her with the others made my back go up. Nobody talks about my family. How would he feel if I attacked his parents? I focused on boats down below, their running lights red and green, forced myself to breathe, and thought of Travis on a trawler out of Newport. Thoughts of Travis always soothed my spirit and made me feel more reasonable.

"I noticed you didn't have wine tonight," I said, changing the subject.

"Nope," he said.

"You don't drink?"

"I used to," he said. "I used to do a lot of things I don't anymore."

"Is that why my mother doesn't like you? Drinking and other assorted bad behaviors?"

"Part of it," he said.

"You're that terrible," I said.

"Don't joke about what you don't understand," he said.

"You know, I defended you earlier," I said, and almost immediately felt bad, for opening my mother up to Rafe: letting him know that she had said something about him that had required defending.

"Thanks," he said, taking a drag and exhaling a long, angry plume of smoke. Then he calmed down. "What'd you say?"

"That you really couldn't be that bad, considering you look after the sea creatures the way you do."

He nodded. "Well, again—thank you. Not that Lyra would listen."

That might be true; I'd seen the look in her eyes. "What did you do that's so awful?"

He didn't reply; he stared into the sea so intently, he might not even have heard the question. Then he looked at me. "Want to see the seahorses?" he asked. "You asked about them. I could take you out on the boat, over to the Faraglioni, if you'd like."

"I'd love to," I said. "When?"

"How about Monday? There won't be so many tourists then."

"Okay, good," I said. I heard the party breaking up, decided I'd better get back before my mother began to worry. Standing, I brushed off the back of my white pants. I started walking up the short gravel path to the loggia.

"Maybe you should know something before you decide for sure," he said. "Whether or not you head out in the boat with me. Your mother has her reasons for not wanting you near me."

I felt like telling him I'd lived ten years without my mother's participation, but I didn't want to seem to be siding with him against her. I also wanted to ask about his mother—how long he'd lived without her—but didn't feel the question would be welcome. So I just stared at him. "I don't need her permission to go in your boat," I said.

"You asked me before why your mother hates me."

"No, I asked what you did that was so awful."

"Same thing," he said.

"Okay," I said. "What is it?"

"I let my grandmother die," he said.

The words sizzled in the air. Electricity crackled all around as if he'd stripped a live wire of its insulation. Crickets rasped in the bushes, cicadas hummed overhead in the olive trees. I felt a slight breeze on my skin, and I saw Rafe stub his cigarette out on the rock. He stared up at me, his eyes filled with sorrow and self-hating, waiting for the next question.

I didn't have any. Something made me put my hand on his shoulder. In comfort, with pity, I'm not sure. I knew it's what Travis would have done. I didn't have anything else to ask or even say. So I left him sitting there.

~

Something about the dinner party: Lyra's first time in public with Pell since she'd left home. Watching her nearly grown-up child, Lyra saw traces of herself and, especially, flashes of Taylor. Pell had extraordinary bearing: the seriousness of purpose, the gravity, just like her father.

Lyra sat alone on the balcony. She heard Pell let herself into the house, go straight to her room. Lyra was glad for the chance to be alone. She closed her eyes and thought of Taylor.

Months after they'd broken up, he'd flown to Newport to see her. Her mother had arranged a season of parties, excursions for the garden society, even the New York Yacht Club cruise aboard **Sirocco.** She'd spent weeks dating Alexander, feeling as if he was impeccably right for her, and insufferably boring. Taylor showed up one rainy day, came straight from the airport, found Lyra on the porch of her mother's house.

She sat in a white wicker rocking chair, dressed

in a coral sundress, waiting for her ride to the Vanderbilt tea. Staring at the rented Ford, she wondered what had happened to Alexander's Bentley. And then Taylor had climbed out.

The short walk from the driveway to the curved porch drenched him. He stood on the stone path, gazing up at her, waiting for her to say something. She felt frozen, seeing him there.

"Taylor," she said.

"This isn't what you want," he said. Rain drove out of the east, rattling leaves and soaking every inch of him. His brown hair hung in his face, dripping into his eyes; he didn't bother brushing it away.

"Come out of the rain," she said.

He did. He climbed the curved white steps, his jaw set, his expression serious—not angry, hurt, none of the emotions Lyra had expected him to feel. She sat there, staring up at him, noticing he kept his distance; she felt herself quivering, and wanted to hold him.

"Thank you for the statue," he said. "Hermes."

She almost laughed. "You came all the way to say that?"

"No," he said. "I came all the way to tell you I love you."

"Taylor, I'm with someone else now."

"No, you're not," he said. "I know you, Lyra. You're trying your best to do it your mother's way. Whoever the guy is, I'm sure he's perfect."

Lyra pictured Alexander's tan, his car, his gold

crest ring. She thought of his Christmas in Gstaad, his New Year's at Palm Beach. His memberships in the Reading Room and Bailey's Beach. She stared at Taylor's salt-marsh hazel eyes, his dripping hair, the frayed collar on his blue shirt.

"Yeah," Lyra said. "He is. Perfect."

"Honey, you don't want that," Taylor said.

Her eyes filled with tears, and she shook her head. "No. I don't."

Something about the storm enclosed them and made it impossible to lie. Her mother's wishes for wealth and status and the right kind of lineage suddenly seemed both funny and sad, like a very old novel with characters quaint and antiquated.

Lyra stood, faced him. The wind was blowing hard, but it felt warm—tropical air, up from the islands. She knew there'd be whitecaps in the harbor, and huge breakers at the beach, and she was glad Taylor's flight had made it in before the airport was shut down.

"What can we do?" she asked.

"Do?" he asked, smiling as if the answer was so obvious. But to Lyra it wasn't—this was her dilemma, and always had been. She wondered why she didn't feel she could really exist with this man she still loved. Her true feelings seemed impossible to support; it would be easier to construct a life from her mother's specifications than to follow her own heart.

"I'm afraid it won't last," she said.

"But you don't know that," he said. "You can't know if you don't try."

"Why would you want me?" she asked.

"You're an idiot to even ask."

He hadn't touched her yet. There was a foot of air between them. That gravity in his eyes—it pulled her straight toward him, as if she were a falling leaf and he was the earth. She crushed into him, soaking her coral silk sundress. They kissed, surrounded by hurricane energy. Raindrops tapped the roof and the leaves on all the trees, and the wind swirled through the porch.

Alexander's tires crunched on the driveway. Lyra heard, and couldn't look. She buried her face in Taylor's shirt.

"Lyra?" Alexander asked.

"I'm sorry," she said, turning finally. He hadn't gotten out of his car; he sat in the driver's seat, window rolled down, staring up at her and Taylor.

Not another word. All the anger she might have once expected to see in Taylor's face showed up in Alexander's as he shifted into reverse and backed out of the driveway. Lyra wondered why she didn't feel triumphant, joyous—she was with the man she loved, not her mother's Mr. Right.

"You sent me a statue for the garden," he said. "But there's no garden without you. There never was. Please come home with me, Lyra. Marry me."

"What if it goes wrong?" she asked, looking up at Taylor.

"And what if it doesn't?" he asked, kissing her again.

Now, sitting on the balcony of her house on Capri, she pictured Pell. The expression she'd seen in her eyes last night, that extraordinary seriousness, had come straight from Taylor. Two people who trusted themselves, who took charge of life, who knew a little rough weather couldn't keep them from what needed to be done.

Lyra stared at the stars over the Bay of Naples, closed her eyes, saw Taylor gazing back at her. In the end, he'd been the one to flinch. His steadiness hadn't held. Everyone had a breaking point, even someone filled with as much love as Taylor Davis.

Seven

~

Sitting outside for breakfast, Lyra served fresh-squeezed orange juice to Pell. They both drank espresso. Lyra watched her daughter butter her toast, add some wild strawberry jam, take the first bite. It felt so simple and regular, so everyday, nothing momentous, but somehow the best summer morning Lyra had had in over ten years.

"Did you have a good time last night?" Lyra asked.

"It was great. I love Max," Pell said.

Pell finished her coffee, and Lyra went inside to make some more. She paused in the living room, watching Pell as she thought herself unobserved: sitting in the shade, staring out at the water, lost in a dream.

"May I ask you something?" Pell asked when Lyra walked out, refilled their cups.

"Of course," Lyra said.

"Is the reason you hate Rafe," Pell asked, "because of how you felt about Christina?"

"I don't hate him," Lyra said.

"He told me what happened," Pell said. "He said he let his grandmother die. What did he mean by that?"

Lyra set down her coffee cup. A pair of hummingbirds darted into the bougainvillea cascading down the terrace wall. She watched them hover and feed. The morning had been so sweet; she didn't want to upset it with this.

"Max left him with Christina one day," Lyra said. "Rafe was supposed to watch her, keep her safe. But he didn't, and she wandered away."

"Where?"

"Just into the yard," Lyra said. She closed her eyes, remembering the day. "She was so frail. She fell in the garden, and broke her hip. And she never recovered. The doctor said the fall shortened her life."

"What was he doing when she fell?" Pell asked, her voice soft with shock.

"He was high," she said.

"On what?"

"Her medication, among other things. But other drugs too. He bought them from someone down at the marina. He'd been kicked out of school. That's how he wound up here—his father couldn't handle him anymore. David thought if he got out of New York, away from his friends there, things might get better."

Pell seemed to take that in. Lyra had a bucking feeling inside, just saying the words: **his father couldn't handle him anymore.** Was Pell thinking of herself, that Lyra had done the same to her as Rafe's father had to him? Lyra knew that was one reason she couldn't stand even seeing the boy. He reminded her so much of her own failure.

"What's his father like?" Pell asked.

"He's got a very demanding job," Lyra said. "High finance, Bank of Kensington, that kind of thing. He runs the New York office, flies back and forth to London a lot. Other countries too. He's a director of the bank, and they have offices around the world."

Pell stared at her, so many things going on in her eyes. Lyra wished she could read her mind.

"And Rafe's mother died when he was young?"

"Yes," Lyra said. "I know how hard that must have been for him. But David did his best; he certainly made sure Rafe had everything he needed."

"He had his own Miss Miller?"

"He had a governess, yes. But David loved him. He would bring Rafe here each summer, and they'd spend a month together. I'd see them swimming and boating, playing on the beach, picking up shells, identifying sea creatures. Max and Christina would dote on Rafe . . . he was such a sweet young boy."

Pell stood up, walked across the terrace. Lyra

watched her look down at the beach. She knew Rafe was down there, scouring the rocks as he always did.

"I feel bad for him," Pell said.

"He was being selfish," Lyra said. "Not looking after someone so vulnerable."

"I'm sure he's punishing himself now," Pell said. "Is that why he spends all his time alone?"

"I wouldn't give him that much credit," Lyra said, and Pell shot her a look.

"People suffer, Mom," Pell said. "They stay alone, they sleepwalk, there are lots of ways."

Lyra sensed her daughter's great heart, but she wanted to set her straight. "Pell, I found Christina after she fell," Lyra said.

"That must have been terrible," Pell said.

Lyra nodded. "She was a wonderful woman. So strong when I first knew her, but by then, so frail and dependent. Max was completely devoted to her, never left her alone. He had stepped out for just a short while; he left Rafe with her, thinking he could trust him."

"What did Rafe say happened?"

Lyra stared at Pell. "What does it matter? It's what he did, and didn't do, that counts."

The day had been clear and bright. Lyra had been standing right here, on the terrace. She'd heard a cry; at first she'd thought it was a seagull. But the crying continued, and she ran in search of the sound. She found Christina crumpled on the ground.

"I ran to her," Lyra said. "I wanted to pick her up, carry her back upstairs. She was in a lot of pain."

"But you couldn't?"

"They took her to the hospital."

"How long had she been sick?" Pell asked. "Before she fell?"

"Three years," Lyra said.

"Sometimes you can't hold on to a person," Pell said. "No matter how much you want to."

"I wasn't ready to lose her," Lyra said.

"I wasn't ready to lose **you,**" Pell said, and Lyra saw her trembling.

"Pell, I'm so sorry."

"I hated when you left," Pell said. "I know you were depressed, but we loved you. We could have helped you."

"Oh, Pell," Lyra said.

"I've never forgotten what Dad told us—that 'the grownups decided.' You, your doctors, Grandmother, who? Why did you let them decide your life—**our** lives—that way?"

Lyra felt Pell's eyes on her, waiting for answers. She stiffened, looking away; she wanted Pell to stop. From the time she'd known Pell was coming, she'd dreaded this conversation.

"You won't talk about it," Pell said.

"It's in the past. You're here now," Lyra said.

"I'd like to understand what happened," Pell said. "Can you imagine what it was like for us—for Dad—to have you leave? He had to do everything."

"Pell, your father was incredibly good. He put up with a lot, my illness. I know they've told you that I was depressed."

"They didn't have to. I saw," Pell said. "I remember what it was like."

Lyra took that in: so Pell did recall. "I'm sorry, Pell. I wish you didn't."

No answer to that. Pell just stared.

"You were six," Lyra said. "I wasn't sure what you saw and knew. But it took me over, wiped me out. I felt as if a tidal wave had hit me. Everything in me destroyed. I loved you and Lucy, and your father. I wanted to be strong again. So I had to go away and build myself back up."

"That's what the hospital was for," Pell said. "You went to McLean, and came home, and you were fine."

"I wasn't fine," she said. "You might have thought so, because I was so happy to see you. To spend time with you and Lucy again. I'd missed you more than you'll ever know while I was away."

"So your solution was to leave us? This time for good?" Pell asked, pacing the terrace.

Lyra watched her, thinking back to the week between returning from the hospital and leaving her husband and children. She saw herself in the car, having the conversation that would change all of their lives forever. One short car ride, the end of life as she'd known it, dreamed of it.

"You've lived here all this time," Pell said. "Honestly, when I came, I wasn't sure what to expect. I pictured you going to parties, wearing gowns, diamonds. But your life here isn't so different from how it would have been at home. Only there you'd have been with us, instead of wonderful Christina."

"She was never a stand-in for you," Lyra said sharply. "Pell, I have one family. You and Lucy."

"You don't know what it's like for her."

"Lucy?" Lyra asked, but Pell ignored her.

"You never divorced him," Pell said. "In all that time. So you must have been thinking of returning at some point. You stayed married."

Lyra stared at her, shocked. Pell didn't know; Taylor hadn't told her?

"We didn't stay married," Lyra said carefully.

"What are you talking about? He'd have told me if you divorced him."

"I didn't."

"Then what?" Pell asked. They stared at each other, across the stone terrace. Two tiny lizards skittered up the wall, out of the bright sun, into the bougainvillea. Lyra saw Pell watch them. The truth hit Pell hard, suddenly. She turned red, as if she'd been slapped. Without another word she started to walk away, and Lyra grabbed her arm.

"Pell," she said.

"No," Pell said.

"He divorced me," Lyra said, and Pell stared for a long time before turning away, walking off the terrace, disappearing down the path.

~

In Newport, Rhode Island, worlds collided on the waterfront. The wharf was shaped like a U, with fishing boats tied up along one pier jutting into the harbor, yachts on the other. Fishermen wore oilskins and rubber boots and hosed the fish scales off their battered decks, while the yacht owners wore fashionable clothes and barely seemed to notice the industry just across the way from their bright white boats.

Travis Shaw had been fishing overnight, and by eight a.m. was heading home. They'd had a good haul of cod, and the captain had given him his pay for the week. Now, with his first day off, he was looking forward to calling Pell. He wasn't the jealous type, but she'd been mentioning some mysterious kid over in Capri, and Travis wanted to know what that was about. Heading down the dock, he crossed the cobblestones of Bowen's Wharf, and ran straight into Pell's grandmother.

"Mrs. Nicholson," he said, stopping short. His work clothes smelled of cod, salt coated his brown hair, and he needed a shower. She was imposing as ever, pageboy-style silver-blonde hair turned slightly under, dressed all in white except for a diamond and coral necklace; carrying a canvas bag, she was obviously on her way from her mansion to her yacht. She wrinkled her nose and took half a step back, and Travis wasn't sure her distaste had anything to do with the smell of fish.

"Hello, Travis," she said.

"How's your summer so far?" he asked.

"Lovely. And yours?"

"Working hard," he said. "I'm saving up for tuition."

"That's not necessary," she said. "The endowment provides for scholarship students."

"Thank you for the last two semesters, but as I told you, I'm paying my own way for senior year."

They stared at each other. Travis knew she disapproved of Pell seeing him. Mrs. Nicholson was on the board of Newport Academy. When his mother had started teaching there last year, she'd been told that her children could attend for free. He and his younger sister, Beck, had jumped right into classes—he as a high school junior, Beck as a freshman; later, at a football game, Mrs. Nicholson had found a way to make them feel ashamed for accepting the school's charity. Travis had decided to shut that right down, and took the job fishing.

"There's no need for pride, young man," she said now.

"I'm my father's son," he said.

"Well, as you wish."

Travis nodded. His father had died two summers ago. He missed him every day, always asked himself what his father would do in given situations. That's why he wanted to be responsible for himself. The work was hard, but it paid well. He wished he could go to Italy to support Pell, but he needed every penny for school.

Mrs. Nicholson shifted under the weight of her canvas bag. Travis hesitated, then reached for it.

"Could I help you carry that to the boat?"

"Well," she said, seeming to give the offer due consideration. "Yes. That would be very helpful."

They headed out to the dock, the opposite arm of the U from the fishing fleet. A couple of the guys spotted Travis, and gave him some whistles and catcalls. "Way to move up in the world!" Jake Keating called.

"They think you've gone to the dark side," Mrs. Nicholson said, sounding amused.

He glanced at her, surprised. The blue-blood old lady had a sense of humor? Her yacht was **Sirocco,** sleek with a teak deck and mahogany brightwork. They stopped on the dock; one glance at Travis's dirty boots let him know he wasn't to step aboard. She stood still, facing him. As he handed her the canvas bag, he noticed that it was filled with books on art, painting, and drawing.

"Thank you," she said. He nodded, about to leave, but she grabbed his wrist.

"Did you want me to carry the bag on board for you?" he asked, confused. "I figured with my boots, and your nice teak deck and all . . ."

"What do you hear from her?" she asked.

"Her?" he asked. "You mean Pell?"

She nodded. Her face was impassive, but some indefinable emotion clouded her eyes. "Yes. Has she contacted you?"

"Of course," he said. "We email and call each other."

"Does she say how she is?"

"Pell is fine. She says that Capri is beautiful, and—"

"How is her mother?"

Again, Travis felt shocked by the conversation. The fact that Mrs. Nicholson was talking to him, that she would come out and ask him anything, was surprising.

"Pell said they're enjoying time together," Travis said, careful not to divulge too much of what Pell had told him. It was up to her, if she wanted to confide in her grandmother.

"Her mother is not the person Pell wishes her to be," Mrs. Nicholson said. As he watched, the old woman's eyes turned sad and bitter.

"No, but she's still her mother," Travis said.

"Do you think that's enough?" Mrs. Nicholson asked.

"For Pell it is," Travis said.

"She insisted on taking this trip," Mrs. Nicholson said. "Against my advice. She will be disappointed."

Travis wanted to tell her that she didn't know Pell, but he held back. He watched her step on board **Sirocco.** Then he turned and jogged up Memorial Boulevard to Newport Academy. Huge old trees shaded the grounds; like many other Newport mansions, the grand and imposing main building was set on Cliff Walk, overlooking the ocean.

Travis's family had recently moved to a slightly bigger house, with a bedroom for Carrie and Gracie, in a wooded grove behind the academic buildings. Opening the screen door, he felt exhaustion overtaking him. His arms ached from pulling nets, and he couldn't stop yawning. The smell of coffee came from the kitchen; he walked in, found his mother at the table, reading the paper.

"You're home!" she said as he bent to give her a kiss.

"Where's everyone?" he asked.

"Carrie had to be at the library by nine, and Beck and Lucy already took Gracie to the beach," she said.

"Is Lucy okay?"

"I'm keeping an eye on her," his mother said. "She misses Pell."

Travis worked long, strange hours, and on nights Lucy slept over, he'd find her pacing the house, or sitting in the living room, staring at TV with the sound off. Sometimes even with the picture dark, just a black screen. Travis was used to traumatized young girls—his sister Beck had gone through a massive stealing phase after their father died.

"Pell's kind of worried about her," Travis said.

"Sounds as if you are too."

"She's not sleeping much."

"I know, honey," his mother said. "But I think it gave her a huge lift to talk to her mother. They're trying to work it all out."

Travis sat across from his mother, feeling lucky. His family had been through a tough year. Moving to Newport, coming to grips with his father's death, his sister's absence, watching his mother try to get her life together. That had included reuniting with Carrie's father—J. D. Blackstone, his mother's old boyfriend from a Newport summer long ago.

The Shaws were getting through it. Mainly because his mom, no matter what mistakes anyone made, including herself, reminded them that they were a family, that's what counted. They talked, argued, took time for themselves, but always eventually worked it out. For most people, there were no guarantees in life or love.

"I have the feeling Lucy will be fine," his mother said. "I hope she's relaxing this morning, down at the beach. There's nothing more soothing than sun and salt water."

Travis hoped she was right. Pell and Lucy had held themselves together all this time. Everyone had secret ways of getting through.

~

Lucy and Beck took Gracie down the hill from Newport Academy to Easton's Beach. It was really early, so they had the whole strand to themselves. The waves rolled to shore in long, silvery frills, trailing white foam behind. Beck dug a huge hole by the water's edge, and Lucy held Gracie, dipping her little feet into the chilly, shallow wave wash, making her laugh each time.

"Almost ready," Beck called as she dug deeper and deeper, throwing sand aside.

Gracie wriggled, wanting to be free, and toddled over to the big pile of wet sand. She buried her hands, and made Lucy find them. Lucy pretended to be surprised each time, gasping with shock, making them all laugh. It was strange, playing on this beach. Most of Lucy's best young memories were of her dad; like when she'd ride her tricycle in their Grosse Pointe driveway, and he'd watch her going up and down as long as she wanted, until her legs got tired. Or when he brought home her first baseball glove and played catch with her in the backyard until after dark, when fireflies would appear in the bushes and tall grass.

But the beach belonged to her mother. When Lucy and Pell were very young, the year before their mother left, they had come to Newport to stay. All four of them, for their father's vacation. He'd gone fishing with his old school friends—three men like uncles to Lucy and Pell: J. D. Blackstone, Stephen Campbell, and Ted Shannon. And Lucy and Pell and their mother had come to the beach.

Perhaps it had been this very stretch. Lucy remembered wearing a pink bathing suit; Pell's had been light blue. Their mother had worn a navy one-piece, sleek and beautiful, and sunglasses and a big straw hat. They'd spread out their blanket, weighting down the corners with rocks.

Their mother had seemed happy, as if just being at the beach, by the sea, made her better.

"You're smiling so much," Pell had asked, a five-year-old trying to figure out the magic formula of why things seemed different. Lucy had tuned in too, wanting their mother's happiness to last.

"I love salt water," their mother had said. "And I love seeing my girls on the beach. . . ."

They'd built sandcastles, and gone swimming, and picked up clamshells all along the tide line. Bubbles poured from tiny holes in the hard sand, and their mother told the girls if they dug fast, they'd find quahogs. They tried, but never were quick enough. Their mother had found bits of brown and green seaweed, and they'd draped the pieces on their arms and hair and pretended to be mermaids.

"Look, Gracie," Lucy said now, finding a long cord of sargassum weed, brown and glistening, dotted with glossy round air pockets, remembering how she and Pell had loved to pop them. Gracie reached for the seaweed, smiling and feeling the smooth, wet surface. Lucy draped it around Beck's neck.

"Gracie, want a mermaid bracelet?" Beck asked, getting into the spirit and smoothing a slippery band of pale green sea lettuce around Gracie's tiny wrist, making her squeal with delight.

Lucy watched Beck and her niece. They dunked into the big hole Beck had dug, which was filling up as the incoming tide pushed the water higher up the beach. Everyone laughed, and Lucy felt hope sweeping over her. It came from seeing family together. Lucy had a weak spot for family. She thought of her sister in Capri, and she thought of the sound of her mother's voice.

Lucy wasn't sure how long she could wait. She had a feeling of wildness, deep in her center, that seemed to be getting bigger. It felt as if her heartbeat was pushing hope outward, into her ribs, her muscles, her skin.

Beck looked over; Lucy felt as if she was sprouting wings.

"What is it?" Beck asked.

"I want to fly there myself."

"Like a bird?"

Lucy laughed. "Yes. A homing pigeon who knows her way to Italy."

"Flying's better than swimming."

"Hey, I only tried to do that once!"

Beck held her hand. "You can stay right here with us," she said. "Pell is going to bring her back."

"Do you really think so?"

Beck nodded, ferociously. Lucy felt both buoyed up and held tight by her best friend. Her back itched, right on her shoulder blades, as if wings really were trying to grow there.

"I love salt water," Lucy said out loud, because her mother had said it once, and it had made her happy. "I love the beach."

Beck gave her a huge smile, because she was her best friend, and because she got it, and because she understood Lucy wanted more than anything to fly away to her mother and Pell.

Eight

~

Max sat at Café Figaro in the Piazzetta, face tipped toward the sun, black notebook opened on the small marble table. Aurelia, the waitress, brought him a short macchiato, and he sipped it, savoring the milk foam.

Tables close together, multicolored umbrellas touching overhead. The clock tower, with its rounded Moorish cupola, shaded the square. Max thought about the play that had come to him last night.

Four characters: a boy and a girl, a woman and an older man. All had lost the most important people in their lives, come together on an island: Capri. An epic storm blows up. A modern-day **Tempest**. He made notes, imagining the characters.

How do people find their way back to life? How does love heal? How does forgiveness take place? Redemption was an overused word and theme, yet the only one that mattered to Max. He had just written the words **where is love to be found?** when he heard someone clear his throat.

John Harriman stood over him, newspaper tucked under his arm.

"The world comes to the Piazzetta!" he said. "Drawing room of Capri."

"Hello, John."

"So glad to see you here. Last night was ever so interesting. Thank you for a lovely evening. May I . . . ?"

Max nodded, gesturing for him to take a seat. He covered his page, closed his notebook, but not quite in time.

"Ah, I was right!" John said. "The muse is speaking to you."

"She's never far away," Max said.

"Of course not," John said. "She lives in your back garden."

"Harriman," Max said warningly.

"Oh, stop. You're very taken with Lyra."

Max began to disavow the statement, but he found he couldn't speak. It was as if the truth had become as much a part of him as his eyes. He tapped his pen on the marble tabletop.

"We're old friends, Max," John said. "If you can't reveal yourself to me, who's left? I've known you since Cambridge. I've seen it all."

"Enough, John," Max said.

"I loved Christina," John said, ignoring Max's

raised hand. "You two had an epic marriage, one of the great ones. Christina was the sun—all warmth and light, no two ways about it. What happened in her last years was tragic, beyond words, to see her mind go . . ."

"John," Max said sharply.

"And Lyra loved her too. That was quite obvious. She soaked up Christina's goodness and care, as we all did. That last year, you and Lyra were completely devoted to Christina. It was touching to see, for all of us who know you well."

Aurelia delivered coffees. Max stirred the foam with a tiny silver spoon, thinking of that last year. John was right: Lyra had been by Christina's side. She had fed her, by hand when necessary. She had sat with her in the garden, tending the flower beds as Christina had taught her. Many days Lyra read to her, from Christina's favorite books and new ones Lyra thought she might like.

That's when Max's feelings for Lyra had started to shift. He had always been fond of her, but thought of her as a troubled, spoiled, somewhat flighty American woman with endless money and a trail of wreckage left behind. Christina had gotten close to her, come home to Max with wrenching stories about Lyra's lonely childhood and, worse, how devastated she was about leaving her own children.

Seeing her minister to Christina, reading to her with such patience, tilling the garden and planting flowers with her looking on, had filled Max with peace. Later, as Christina declined even further, Lyra took care of her in a different way. She would wipe her chin during meals; she would change her soiled clothes. She'd changed her diaper. There were nurses as well, but they were professionals. Lyra's actions were borne of love.

"Why don't you tell her?" John asked now.

"Don't be foolish," Max said.

"Don't be cowardly."

"I'm old enough to be—"

"Don't say it!"

"Her father."

"Max, you're only as young as you feel. You go up and down those steps to the dock how many times a day? You give young Rafe a run for his money, although maybe that's not so remarkable considering what he's done to his body."

"Stop it," Max said, so sharply this time John had no choice but to take heed.

"Sorry," John said.

"Just leave Rafe alone. He burned too brightly, hit rock bottom. He's overcome his problems, he's getting his life back."

"Perhaps a romance will bloom between him and Pell. Summer love? Lyra's daughter is lovely."

"Yes, she is," Max said.

John chuckled. "You and Lyra, Rafe and Pell."

"You've gone round the bend, Harriman," Max said, pushing back his chair.

"I'm an old romantic," John said.

"Old fool, more like it," Max said.

Max paid for his coffee, then stood up. He shook John's hand, walked away. He strolled through the Belvedere, a loggia of white columns with a spectacular view of the Neapolitan Gulf from Ischia to Vesuvius. John Harriman was one of his oldest friends. He had figured out Max's secret, the old spy.

It was with that thought in mind that he walked to the Belvedere, for fresh breezes and an open view of the water, and came face-to-face with Pell. The elder daughter of his heart's desire.

~

My father divorced her? Was my mother lying or just crazy? Everything feels wrong. I feel sliced to ribbons. How can I tell her Lucy and I need her when I don't trust her? Coming here was a mistake. I ran away from my mother's terrace as fast as I could, headed toward town. The Piazzetta. On the way, I called Travis.

"I miss you," I said.

"Same for me," he said. "It's driving me crazy."

"Me too. Four thousand miles between us." And I felt every one of them.

"How's everything going?" he asked.

"I don't know," I said.

"You don't know?" he asked, giving a little laugh. For some reason, his laugh felt like a slap. We were so close; couldn't he tell when something was really wrong? I felt myself shut down.

"I saw your grandmother this morning," Travis went on. "She asked about you—and your mother."

"That's surprising," I said. "I think she wrote my mother off long ago."

"Maybe not. She was definitely curious about how things are going. So am I, Pell. Did I say the wrong thing?"

"It's just that things are tense here right now. We're just getting to know each other. I don't even know what to hope for."

"A relationship with her," he said.

I said nothing. Did he think that hadn't occurred to me? What was happening, going wrong with me? I felt sensitive to everything Travis said. I'd felt so together when I flew over, able to handle my life and Lucy's, at least temporarily. I'd thought I would act calmly and rationally, explain to my mother my concerns. But it was as if all Capri's mountains and cliffs stood between me and what I needed to do, to say. I couldn't get there from here.

"Why are you mad at me?" he asked.

"I'm not. I'm sorry, I'm just in a weird mood."

"Are you hanging out with anyone over there?" he asked finally.

"No."

"What about the mystery man on the beach?"

"It turns out he's Max's grandson, and what my mother calls 'troubled.' "

"What does that mean?"

"I don't know," I said. "Family problems, I guess." This is odd, but I found myself not wanting to tell Travis about Rafe. Travis picked up on it, and he went silent. Nothing was going right. Travis and I had always been great. So why couldn't I talk to him?

"Travis. I'm sorry. . . ."

"Don't keep saying that, okay?" he requested.

"Okay."

"It's just, I wish you'd tell me what's going on."

"Nothing's going on! Maybe I shouldn't have come here."

He was silent for a few seconds. A lesser man might have agreed with me, suggested I return home. Not Travis. "You're there to get to know your mother," he said.

"If that's possible," I said, still not wanting to believe what she had told me about my father. Everything was swirling around—my parents, Lucy, the terrible fact that I didn't feel like talking to Travis. I started to sweat; the sun was hot. "I'd better go," I said. We said goodbye.

Walking down the Phoenician Steps, I lost count at seven hundred. I was a zombie, an unhappy sleepwalker. I'd told Travis that Rafe was troubled, but maybe I'd been talking about myself instead. Suddenly I was in Capri town; that had to be the Piazzetta, café tables everywhere. I glimpsed John Harriman, his tan face tilted to the sun; thankful he didn't see me, I ducked down an alley, began walking toward the blue: breathtaking, shocking sea and sky. The beauty began to calm my spirit and soul, but also made me feel like crying.

"Hello, Pell . . ."

I looked up, and guess who was taking in the same view? Max. An angel out of nowhere.

"Hi, Max," I said. I saw him staring at my red eyes. He smiled gently. I loved how he didn't ask me what was wrong. I had the oddest idea that he didn't have to, that he knew. He knew my mother; he understood something of our family pitfalls.

We stood on the Belvedere, gazing out at the endless blue bay. Down below, boats thronged the harbor, white wakes splashing behind. The Marina Grande was bustling. Even from here, it reminded me of Newport—of Travis. That gave me a pang of guilt.

"Another beautiful view," I said, feeling miserable.

"Yes, Capri has many lovely overlooks," he said.

"Nothing could be better than the one from your terrace."

"Or your mother's," he agreed. "We are very lucky. Although she's luckiest to have you. A wise daughter willing to come all this way to make things right."

"You know that's what I'm doing?" I asked.

He nodded. There was such wisdom in his blue eyes. Once again, I saw the spark of youth there—

eternal energy and hope. It made me think of my father; my eyes stung with more quick tears of missing him, and anger over what my mother had told me, and everything. Max saw again.

"Shall we walk?" he asked.

I nodded, my throat too tight to speak. We strolled across the piazza, and he pointed out the spot where Greeks built their acropolis in the fifth century B.C. He showed me the ruins of ancient tombs from that period. We admired the clock tower, which once had been bell tower to the now-gone cathedral, and Max pointed out the tower's eastern influences, Moroccan tiles. Bougainvillea seemed to cascade over every wall, and humming-birds thronged.

I found comfort in his knowledge, in the way he showed me around, pointing out structures centuries old. We saw Town Hall, former home to the bishop, then the Church of St. Stephen, a brilliant white seventeenth-century building designed by Picchiatti. Lucy would have loved it, baroque with a Byzantine rounded cupola, built on the site of the ancient monastery. I stopped and stared.

"My sister would love to see this," I said.

"Lucy," he said.

I nodded. Suddenly tears spilled out, and this time they couldn't be stopped. "I miss her," I said. "She's my little sister, my responsibility. Last year, in school, she became obsessed with contacting our father's ghost. When he didn't come, she felt so let down. She doesn't sleep enough. And sometimes when she does, she sleepwalks. . . ."

We walked, entering the medieval district, a maze of lanes and alleys. Small white houses stood close together, some first floors filled with shops and workshops, the passageways narrow, tilting up the hill, then a set of steps, a twist in the lane, a covered alley, a flash of brilliant blue sky, stone arches, more bright blue, an overhang of lush greenery and red trumpet flowers, sunlight splashing at our feet. When we came to another impossibly steep and narrow stone staircase, Max turned and gave me his hand to help me down.

"How did Lucy try to contact your father's ghost?" Max asked.

"Through mathematical formulas," I said. " 'Ghosts of departed quantities,' she called it. Lucy's very smart. But also so sensitive . . . she idolized my father. We both did."

"He must have been a wonderful man."

"He was," I said. And then I turned to face Max. "Did my mother ever tell you they were divorced?"

He nodded, gazing at me with sadness and compassion, as if he knew the whole story, felt sorry we'd gone through so much.

"It was **his** idea?" I asked.

"I believe so," Max said.

"Why?"

"He must have needed to let her go, so he could live his life. And perhaps it was a kindness to her, as well. Allowing her to live hers."

I thought that over. It would be so like my father to be thinking of her, setting her free so she could get better, do whatever it was she'd needed to accomplish by leaving us. Yes, that was my father all over. I felt just a tiny bit better. I gave Max a look of gratitude, for helping me to see the situation this way.

I thought of asking him if we could take the funicular down to the Marina Grande—I wanted to walk the docks, feel the buzz of the waterfront, the connection to Newport and Travis, let the salt water wash away the shocks of this day and return me to feeling close to my boyfriend. But something stopped me in my tracks. Straight ahead: the Grand Hotel Quisisana, old, elegant, and venerable. I recognized it immediately; Lucy and I had received a postcard of it.

"My grandmother stayed here," I said, staring at the façade.

"Yes," he said. "I met her when she came. She visited your mother only once."

"They never got along," I said.

"I believe your grandmother had certain ideas about how your mother should live her life."

"Lots of mothers and daughters disagree," I said.

"Christina took note of your mother's great talent," Max said. "She loves the garden, and exhibits true artistry. It became obvious quickly that all forms of self-expression were stifled from a young age. When I met your grandmother, I mentioned your mother's love of flowers. And Edith said—"

"Let me guess," I said. "'That's why we have gardeners.'"

"You know her well."

"I guess I do," I said.

"She told Christina that she wanted to be an artist when she was a young girl."

"My **grandmother**?" I asked.

Max nodded. "She told Christina her mother said that art was for bohemians. Christina could have been insulted, but chose not to be; she heard great wistfulness in your grandmother's voice."

"My grandmother isn't known for being wistful," I said.

"No," Max said. "It was a fleeting moment. But enough to see that her dreams had been thwarted. Instead of gaining insight, and nurturing your mother's talent, Edith passed on her own parents' lessons."

"Ghosts of the nursery," I said, using a phrase I'd read in a psychology text.

"Pell," Max said, "you're very young. And you and Lucy have been through so much. I find the fact you want to understand and forgive your mother to be touching beyond words. But do you really want to understand?" he asked.

"Of course," I said, shocked by the question.

"Then, as you spend time here this summer, notice her life and ask yourself what it must have been like for her at home, as a young woman, being held back, imprisoned by her mother's ideas of how life should be lived."

"My grandmother didn't force my mother to leave us," I said. "Leave our home in Michigan."

"No," Max said, sadly and with deep love in his eyes. "She didn't believe your mother should have gone to Michigan in the first place. Your grandmother devalued her own daughter. Lyra came here, came alive through her garden."

"Her garden," I said.

"It brings her solace," Max said.

"Solace?" I asked. Not only because the word is odd and old-fashioned, but because of the way Max said it: I'd swear his voice was filled with longing. For my mother? I felt stunned by what I saw in his eyes.

"We all need it," he said. "And search for it. Your sister, through math and a connection with your father's ghost. You, by coming here to Capri, rightly wanting more from your mother. My grandson, walking the tide line as he did long ago with his father."

"Rafe," I said.

"Yes," Max said. "I wish I could help him more."

"I think you're the reason he gets up in the morning," I said. "Walks the beach, and saves the starfish."

"Because I want him to keep busy?"

"No," I said. "Because you love him and you're saving **him**."

Max gave me a long look, as if I'd shown him a new way to see something. He smiled. We walked along a little farther, then came to an ice-cream shop. We went inside, and he bought me a cone, one scoop of dark chocolate. I ate it slowly as we continued our walk.

Solace.

Nine

Lyra got up early the next morning, looked in on Pell. She slept on her side. Long hair covered her face. Lyra sat on the edge of the bed, stared at her for a long time. Dawn light slanted through the east window, clear and bright. It fell on Pell's open backpack. Books were spilling out. A photograph. Lyra reached for it.

Her wedding photo. Lyra looked at herself and Taylor. He looked so happy and protective; she looked elusive. She wore the famous Nicholson family veil, two hundred years old. She remembered her mother saying "Don't rip it" perhaps ten times through the wedding day, as if the fabric of the veil were more important than that of the marriage.

Lyra's gaze drifted from the picture to her daughter. Why was Pell carrying it with her? The idea of a happy family had never left her. But formal photographs are funny things. They capture a moment, and not necessarily a real one, but an arrangement directed by a photographer to create a mood.

Lyra and Taylor had had the wedding of the year; it was literally called that by the style editor at the **New York Times.** Four hundred guests, high nuptial mass at church, Pachelbel's Canon and the Prince of Denmark's March, limousines home to the Nicholson estate on Bellevue Avenue, a candlelit path to the tent—the candles in hurricane lamps to protect against the fresh sea breeze, vintage Krug champagne, Lyra in her white gown and family's heirloom veil.

A storybook wedding. The wedding guests included the governor of Rhode Island, two senators, European royalty, all friends of her mother. Sitting in the limousine with Taylor as they arrived at the reception, she'd stared at the sprawling house she'd grown up in and had had a panic attack. She'd been unable to breathe. Taylor's hand on the back of her neck, easing her head down, his calm voice telling her everything was wonderful, they were married now, about to start their lives together.

"I'll tell the driver to just keep going," he'd joked. "We'll skip out on the party and go straight to Bermuda."

"Could we?" she'd asked, not kidding.

Lyra stared at the photo another minute. She replaced it in the backpack, returned to the edge of Pell's bed. She touched her daughter's shoulder.

Fine-boned, vulnerable. She felt a lump in her throat. Ten years missing.

"Pell?" she said.

"Mmm."

The last time she'd done this, Pell had been a little girl. But she slept the same way: facing the wall, fists drawn up beneath her chin, hair tangled over her face. Lyra shook with emotion. After all these years, her daughter was right here, sleeping in her house.

"Could you get up? I'd like you to come with me."

And Pell did, without question. She rolled out of bed, washed her face, threw on jeans and a sleeveless shirt. Together they walked through the garden, down to the driveway she shared with the villa. Glancing up, Pell saw Max sitting on his terrace, writing. He waved, and looked so happy to see Lyra and Pell together, it hit her in the heart.

They drove to the market, shopped for white flowers. Lyra watched Pell walk up and down the rows of long tables, choosing the best flats of white impatiens and geraniums. She was beautiful, caught the attention of the shopkeepers. Lyra introduced her as her daughter.

"I didn't know you had a daughter!" some of them said.

"You've kept her hidden away!"

"She has your eyes. . . ."

Lyra felt proud. They loaded the plants and

flowers into Lyra's old Alfa, pulled out of the parking lot, and drove toward Amanda and Renata's house. White flowers, fragrant herbs, lush greenery, an archway, a curved gate.

"Lyra!"

She waved at Gregorio Dante, a stonemason she'd hired. He stood by a half-built structure, piles of concrete and white rock beside him, two columns rising on either side of the four-foot-wide garden path. Curly dark hair, deep tan, muscles bulging in his T-shirt. He came toward her, teeth gleaming in a wide smile.

"Ciao, Lyra," he said, kissing her on both cheeks.

"Ciao, Gregorio," she said.

"It's a beautiful day," he said. "Always, when I see you. And who is this lovely girl?"

"My daughter, Pell," Lyra said.

"How do you do?" Pell asked.

"Pleased to meet you," he said, smiling.

"Pell," Lyra said, "Gregorio is building a moon gate for Renata and Amanda's garden."

"Very romantic," Gregorio said. "To capture the moon as it rises in the east."

"I've seen pictures of one," Pell said.

Lyra tingled; this was why she'd wanted Pell to come to the job site. "From our honeymoon," she said. "Your father's and mine."

"Yes," Pell said. "I still have your wedding album."

"I saw the photo you brought," Lyra said.

Pell didn't answer. She walked back to the car, started unloading the garden tools. Lyra watched her carry them to the flower bed she'd staked out.

"It was right there, in your room," Lyra said. "I didn't go through your things."

"I didn't think you had," Pell said. "I'm just surprised you mentioned it. I don't know what you think about him—about your marriage. I had no idea you were divorced."

"I didn't know it would make that much difference to you," Lyra said.

"It does," Pell said.

"Then will it also make a difference to know that when I think of love, I think of your father?" Lyra asked. "Renata and Amanda wanted their garden to reflect their love. I gave that a lot of thought, and came up with the moon gate. It honors your father's memory, and also the dreams we once had."

"Dreams?" Pell asked.

"Yes," Lyra said. "Your father and I had dreams."

"What were they?" Pell asked.

"Let's work first. Then I'll tell you."

They began to dig. When they came to deeply embedded rocks, bits of calcareous stone, they heaved them toward Gregorio, and he washed and set them into the white columns. The ground gave way, and they got into a rhythm. Sun beat down on their heads; ribbons of sweat ran down Lyra's back.

"There's a problem," Gregorio said, walking over

to Lyra and Pell. "The sides of the gate are coming along. But the arch, overhead. I need more information."

"What kind of information?" Pell asked.

"It needs to be a half-circle. But I don't have the proper calculations. Let me take a break, see what I can figure out." He walked away, sat in the shade of an olive tree, started making notations on the back of an envelope while the fine silver-green leaves rustled in the breeze overhead.

"Will you tell me now?" Pell asked. "About your dreams?"

"I will. You saw pictures of the moon gate in our wedding album. Do you know the story?" Lyra asked.

"No," Pell said.

"In 1860, in Bermuda, a sea captain brought the idea back from a voyage to China. He had one built of island stone; the simple arch symbolized peace, joy, and long life. When a couple passed through holding hands, their future would be blessed."

"Yours wasn't," Pell said.

"It was for a while," Lyra said.

Pell stopped, looking at her.

"We had you," Lyra said. "You and Lucy. You were our dreams."

"We were **real,**" Pell said quietly. "Not dreams. We're flesh and blood. We needed you, but you left."

"I know that, Pell. This is hard for me to say. I wanted to be a great mother. I loved you—there was no shortage of love. But I wasn't good at what I'd set out to do."

"You weren't good at being a mother?" Pell asked. Her eyes flashed with anger and skepticism. "You are **wrong**."

Lyra stared at her; she could see Pell believed what she was saying. But Pell was still so young—sixteen. Her own life had barely started unfolding yet. What if she discovered things about herself that made her take a path she couldn't see yet?

"I talked to Max yesterday," Pell said.

"What about?" Lyra asked, surprised.

"You. The divorce. Grandmother. Lucy. Talking to him, I can be so rational and kind. I want to understand you. But being here—sitting with you . . . it makes me feel crazy. You have no idea what it's been like. And not so much for me—for Lucy."

"Tell me," Lyra said.

"I'm worried about her. She's so restless. She doesn't sleep well, sometimes she sleepwalks. I'm supposed to go to college next year, but how can I leave her? She's relied on me all this time. But she really needs you."

Lyra stared at Pell. How could she explain how this made her feel? She felt she'd abdicated the right to be needed by her kids. There was a sacredness about being a mother. Everyone expected devotion and sacrifice. A woman leaving her family shocked people more than if she committed murder for them. If she became a prostitute to take care of them, it would be more acceptable.

She remembered being held in Grosse Pointe for a psych evaluation, before going to McLean. One of the women on her unit had dealt drugs to afford a house for her and her two children. She'd sold crack and heroin, slept with her supplier to pay him. One day she had to go to Detroit to pick up supplies; her three-year-old daughter was home from preschool with a fever. The woman left her in the car while she went inside to have sex and get the drugs. When she came out, there were two men trying to break in to her car, to get her daughter.

The woman had gone crazy, literally lost it. She'd grabbed a baseball bat off the porch, come off swinging. She cracked the skull of one man, broke teeth and the nose of the other. She'd jumped into her car, grabbed her shrieking daughter. She'd been arrested, sent for psychiatric help; her children taken by the state until she completed her sentence. Lyra thought of her now—a madwoman wielding a baseball bat to protect her kids.

The idea of Lucy suffering ripped Lyra apart. She'd done nothing to help her girls; she'd walked away from them instead. She saw Pell staring at her. The hostility drained from Pell's eyes.

"Do you know why I want to become a psychologist?" Pell asked.

"Because I've caused so much damage?"

"No," Pell said. "Because of this, right here." She tapped her forehead just above her right eyebrow. Then she reached across the dirt and touched the same spot on Lyra's head.

"Is that the site of craziness?" Lyra asked.

"No," Pell said, shaking her head. "It's the right frontal cortex," she said. "And something happened there, for both me and Lucy, when we were four months old."

"What?" Lyra asked. She had never dropped her, never shaken her. She felt stunned by the idea of an injury. Could she have forgotten, blocked out an incident? Is this why Lucy couldn't sleep?

"At that age, a baby's need for her mother becomes so intense—not just for survival, as it is right after birth—but for emotional connection. The baby needs her mother to show her the way."

"And I didn't do that," Lyra said. "I didn't show you the way."

"Oh, you did," Pell said. "That's why it made me so mad, when you said you weren't good at being a mother."

"But, Pell—" Lyra started.

Pell talked right over her. "You and I were so connected. I felt you with me every second. I remember how it felt to have you hold me, sing to me, whisper stories to me as I fell asleep. You rocked me when I cried. When I was teething, you rubbed my gums with your finger."

"But your . . . head . . . What happened, did I hurt you, did . . ."

Pell shook her head. "No. You didn't hurt me—the opposite. You were there, and that's all that mattered. See, things happen in a baby's brain, all having to do with her mother. Neurons firing, synapses sparking, just as if there's lightning flashing between mother and child. It's so real, and so energized, the baby's brain literally grows toward the mother's."

"And the mother's?" Lyra asked.

"Grows toward the child's. It's the realest connection there is. I felt myself being part of you, and you part of me. It's how I made sense of the world. Lucy too."

"As babies?" Lyra asked.

"Always," Pell said.

"Even after . . ."

Pell nodded. "Even after you left."

Lyra dug her hands into the dirt. She felt the ground's heat. Pell stared at her; Lucy couldn't sleep. Lyra tried to hold tight, as if she could keep from flying off the planet.

"This is how it works," Pell said. "The way mothers and children navigate life together."

"And it all happened when you were four months old?" Lyra asked.

"Not all," Pell said. "It continues until the child is twenty-five."

"'It?'" Lyra asked.

"Activity in the right frontal cortex. The child looking to her mother to show her the way. Their brains growing toward each other's."

Lyra nodded. She felt a zinging sensation in her head, just above her right eyebrow. The feeling was familiar; she'd had it all along. She just hadn't realized it was her brain not just yearning for her daughters, but actually reaching for them. It was biological.

"So much time has gone by," Lyra said.

"It doesn't matter," Pell said. "We have until Lucy and I turn twenty-five." She smiled.

"You've taken such good care of Lucy," Lyra said. "She must miss you now."

"She's staying with the Shaws," Pell said. "My boyfriend's family. His sister Beck is Lucy's best friend. Their mother is . . . kind of like a mom to Lucy."

It killed Lyra, hearing that. She hated thinking of another woman being like a mom to her daughter.

"Lyra," Gregorio called. "Will you come see? What do I do? The plans are not coming together; I can't figure out the arch."

"Just a second," she said. Lyra wiped her eyes and went over.

"Look at this," Gregorio said, tugging her hand. He wanted her to stand close, look at his drawing, but she kept her distance. She wore overalls and a white peasant blouse, garden clogs and a blue sun visor: her uniform, baggy clothes that hid her body. She wanted Pell to know there'd never been anyone but her father—the flaw had been with her, not with his love.

"I am not an engineer. I should have asked you before I started," Gregorio said. "Do you think less of me?"

Lyra didn't answer. She looked at the white columns, going nowhere. Thinking of what Pell had said about Lucy, the garden suddenly seemed meaningless. Lyra spun back over ten years. Being depressed, she'd wanted to sleep all the time. But then it had changed: she'd stopped sleeping altogether. That's when the crisis began.

"Mom!" Pell called. She had her cell phone out.

"Yes?" Lyra said, walking over. Her heart was pounding, wondering if Lucy was in the same kind of emotional danger she had been.

"I knew Lucy wouldn't be asleep," Pell said. "So I called her. She's on the line now. . . ."

Lyra took the phone.

~

Two in the morning, Lucy's witching hour, the most haunted zone of the night, when Lucy felt the most alone, when she was most afraid to sleep.

The hour her father had died.

Back home in Grosse Pointe, his heart had stopped, he'd drawn his last breath, at 2:01 a.m. Now Lucy paced the Shaws' house, wanting the time to pass. She could fall asleep once the clock ticked past that time, but until then, she felt tied up in knots. When her cell phone went off, buzzing because she had it on vibrate, for a minute she thought it was her father calling.

But it was Pell and her mother, making Lucy melt with joy.

"Hello?" she said.

"Lucy," Pell said, "Mom needs you."

"Needs **me**?" Lucy asked. No words had ever meant more.

"Yes. Hold on," Pell said.

And then their mother's voice: "Lucy?"

"Hi, Mom. What can I do to help?"

"Lucy, it's so late over there. Are we disturbing you? Can't you sleep?"

"Not really," Lucy said. "I'm used to it, though."

"I wish I could sing you to sleep," her mother said.

Sing her to sleep? Lucy took those words in. They felt like a blanket, hot milk, and a hug. Her mother was thinking of her, enough to be worried. Lucy's mouth wobbled, not sure whether to smile. How could someone's concern make her feel both so happy and so much like crying?

"I'm really okay," Lucy said. "Pell can tell you, I'm just a night owl. That's all. . . ."

"Hmm," her mother said, as if she was trying to believe her.

"You need my help?" Lucy asked.

"Oh. Yes, that's right," her mother said. "See, I'm having this moon gate built for a garden I'm designing. I want it to be about six and a half feet tall at its highest point. Six feet wide, and curved in the shape of the full moon."

"It sounds beautiful," Lucy said, her mind starting to work. "Well, it's easy. Circumference divided by diameter is 3.14159. Just figure out the diameter you want, multiply that by 3.14159, and that gives you the inside circumference. Then add the thickness and get the outside. Then subtract the inside circumference from the outside one and divide that by the number of stones."

There was a brief pause. Then: "I'm so impressed," her mother said.

"It's the only thing I'm good at," Lucy said. "Math."

Her mother was silent for so long, Lucy thought maybe she'd hung up. But then she heard her mother clear her throat.

"I'm sure there are many things, Lucy," her mother said. "Many things you are good at, my darling. I would like us to talk, so I can find out much more about you."

"Talk? Us? You and me?" Lucy asked.

"Oh, yes," her mother said. "You and me. Now, Lucy . . . will you do something for me?"

"Anything," Lucy said.

"I'd like you to climb into bed. Get under the covers," her mother said. "Close your eyes, and think of something beautiful. Like a field of flowers, or a wonderful beach . . . something you love."

"I can do that," Lucy said.

"And let it fill your mind, and just drift off," her mother said, and she began to sing. Very softly, a song Lucy remembered from her childhood:

"White coral bells upon a slender stalk, lilies of the valley deck my garden walk. . . ."

Lucy heard the music, and she smiled and felt everything bad melt away.

She wished they'd never hang up, but finally they did. And she kept her promise. She went into the room she shared with Beck, climbed into her bed. She could almost hear her mother's voice: **Get under the covers . . . close your eyes . . . think of something beautiful. . . .**

Lucy did think of something beautiful. And it wasn't a garden of flowers, or a magical beach, or even the song. It was her mother's voice saying the words "you and me."

"You and me," Lucy whispered in bed, eyes closed. "You and me, you and me, you and me . . . you said I am your darling, and we will talk, you and me, you and me."

~

I could see what Max had said: that gardening brought my mother solace. There at the site, working for Amanda and Renata, I could see the glow. She was tan, sweaty, tired in the good way. I knew her muscles were aching; her face and arms were streaked with dirt. That guy was flirting with her, but she didn't care. She loved the garden. And—I have to say this—she loved being with me, and calling Lucy. I felt it.

It seemed like the greatest gift, calling Lucy, having the three of us on the phone again. And I could tell Lucy was overjoyed. My mother too. It was the three of us together, just like old times. To hear my mother taking care of Lucy—over the phone, soothing her, singing her to sleep—made me think of all the ways we've needed and missed one another.

Being here, especially after the call with Lucy, all my early love for my mother came flooding back. My head's been throbbing, practically lighting up. Ever since reading Allan Schore's book on the neurobiology of emotional development, recommended reading by Dr. Robertson, a few more puzzle pieces have fallen into place. That feeling—that physical longing for my mother—started to make sense. She is part of me.

And I am part of her. I came out of her body. And our hearts and minds are hardwired for each other. As she spoke to Lucy, I watched her face. I saw the years of love and the decade of pain. We were everything to each other. Everything! And then she went away.

Waking up with her sitting on my bed did something to me. This is how it could have been! My dad used to wake me up for school. I hold on to that, trying to understand why he'd held back the fact he'd divorced her. It shimmers, like the azure water around the island, the idea that if he hadn't, if she'd remained legally bound, she might have had more reason to return to us. But I tell myself that's not real.

It's just foolish, wishful thinking. My mother was troubled—the word that came so easily to her, describing Rafe. She was damaged. Screwed up by her mother. My grandmother isn't a bad person, but you wouldn't want her as your mother. She is cold, in ways my mother never could be. But you know what's sad? I am sure that she, too, suffered as a child. **Her** mother probably didn't show her enough love.

Talking to Max, I had realized the weight of my family history even more. Standing with him in front of the Hotel Quisisana, remembering my grandmother's postcard, thinking of her visit here, I had been faced again with her warped notion of what life for women should be all about. The goal was to become the wife of a rich man; if you failed in that, you might as well not bother.

"What happened when Edith visited you here?" I asked my mother now. We had both taken showers and were relaxing on the terrace after hours of gardening.

"That was years ago," my mother said.

"I know. She only came once?"

My mother nodded. "Yes. She hoped she'd find me among the smart set, the yachting crowd. Instead, I was living in this little house, on the quiet side of the island. I hadn't fixed it up yet; it was something of a wreck. I'd bought it cheap from the Gardiners; it was part of the estate, but they'd never used it, and the plaster was cracked, a few windows broken, bats living in the chimney."

"Your mother saw it like that?" I asked, unable to hold in my smile.

"Well, I'd replaced the broken glass, gotten rid of most of the bats," she said, smiling back. "But there really was no way my mother could fool herself into thinking I'd come here for the social life."

"Why did you come here?"

"A combination of things," she said slowly. "I'd visited Capri on that trip after college. Instead of seeing glamour, the way my mother might have, I saw peace. It rained one day, and I felt a strange sense of belonging. I had this feeling inside. . . . I'd never felt I fit in anywhere before, but suddenly I was here, and I felt at home. And then the sun came out. . . ."

"And it was like this?" I asked, staring out at the amazing, unbelievable, indescribable sparkling blue.

"Yes," she said.

"And you always remembered it?"

"Yes," she said. "Both parts. The quiet rain and the dazzling blue. So when the time came, when I had to leave, I knew there was only one place to go."

"Capri," I said. "But Mom, this is just a **place**." I was asking her: **Did you really leave me and Lucy, and Dad, for a patch of earth?**

She nodded. We sipped our tea, and let the hugeness of our reality overtake us. The truth was the truth; we had spent the last ten years apart. I had always wanted her; our early bonding was radiant and total. During our separation I'd felt monsters clawing me inside. Was she now telling me she'd walked out on our life to come to this idyllic island?

"You mentioned 'showing you the way' before," she said. "That's what mothers are supposed to do. I don't really feel qualified to show you anything. I don't deserve to. I made choices you would never make."

"Can't you tell me about them?"

She stared out to sea, hot feelings seeming to pour right off her skin. "If I could tell you anything, it would be to follow your dream, whatever it is. Don't let anyone talk you out of it."

I stared at her. Did following her dream really mean coming to Capri, throwing me and Lucy and our dad away?

"Do you think it's impossible for a woman to do both?" I asked. "Follow her 'dream' and also stick by her family?"

My question hung in the air. As soon as I asked, I wished I could take it back. My eyes filled with tears, in anticipation of what she was about to say.

"It was," she said. "For me. Having you here, talking to Lucy . . . I hate so much of what I've done. But I want you to understand."

"The moon gate didn't work for you and Dad," I said, trying to make light. I didn't want to hear this.

"Pell," she said. I couldn't look at her, but I felt her kneeling in front of me. I heard her crying as well. She kissed my face, her lips on my tears. I should have flinched, but I leaned into her. She was my mother.

"There's a reason," she said. "That I did what I did."

"I want to know," I said. I felt myself shaking; I tried to hold it together, act cool and understanding. But right then I was her daughter, and she'd left me, and I was about to hear why.

"I was empty," she said. "Nothing inside. Going through the motions like a zombie, a sleepwalker. Miss Miller and your father took care of you. He was so good—he did everything. I was a skeleton mother."

"You were not," I said. "I know. I was with you. Our walks, our country, the map of Dorset . . . you, me, and Lucy. She pasted the stars on. . . ."

"You were too young to understand," she said. "Those were special times. But behind them, those days and the things we did, was nothing, Pell. I was nothing. I felt as if I was dragging you down—you and Lucy."

I felt chills. The look in her eyes was dark and frantic. What was she thinking? We'd had this day of closeness; it had started with her waking me up. But here we were, back to our reality.

"What are you saying?" I asked.

"Back then, just before I went to the hospital, I wanted to hurt myself."

"Hurt yourself?"

"Kill myself," she whispered.

No one had ever told me this, but suddenly I knew. I'd felt my mother's despair, her not wanting to be in the world. I forced myself to look at her, and I know I've never seen anything so terrible on another person's face. The torment was agonizing; it came from her bones. And I felt it in mine.

"Mom?" I said, reaching for her.

"I didn't kill myself," she said finally, "but I almost did. I almost . . . ," she said, then stopped.

"Is that why you left?"

She didn't answer. She stayed very pointedly silent. I could see her mind working, tumbling around something she wanted to say. Our hearts had once been so much in sync, I recognized the turmoil, the need to tell me fighting with some scruple about holding back. What couldn't she say? Instead of speaking, she took my hand. Together we stood.

We walked to the curved wall of the terrace. My mother and I held hands, facing out to the beautiful sea, so far below. A minute ago, I'd wanted to fling myself over. Right now the feeling had passed, and all I felt was exhaustion. We gazed out at the bay. The blue was deep and clear, the color of our eyes. I thought of what she'd said before, that she felt unable to show me the way.

That's what mothers do, I wanted to tell her. Whether conscious or not, their very existence is a map for their daughters. She didn't speak, but I felt her saying something back to me: the ocean is wide and deep, filled with beauty and menace. Life is a journey and a dream, exciting and treacherous. She was warning me and promising me, both at the same time.

"Okay," I said. "You can't tell me the whole story of why you left. But I need to know why you didn't come back. After you got well. Or even later—three years ago, after Dad died. Didn't you know we needed you? Why didn't you come back to us then?"

"Because I'd walled myself off," she said. "Once I

left, I gave up my rights as a mother. I couldn't come and go; it wouldn't have been fair to you and Lucy."

"We wouldn't have minded," I said. "We would have wanted you back for as long as you wanted to stay."

"I don't believe you," she said, holding my face in her hands, looking into my eyes.

"If you'd spent time with us, you'd have wanted to stay!" I said. "And never leave us again!"

"I knew that this was right for me, Pell," she said. "Being here, making a life for myself—it kept me alive. I had to literally shut the door on the past. If I looked back, even a little, if I called you on the phone, I'd be pulled home to you. And that could have been a disaster." The words were agonizing for her to say—I saw it in her eyes. They raked me inside like a branding iron. I caved in on myself, almost unable to stand the pain.

I wanted to scream. Anguish like a tidal wave. My mother returning to us would have been a disaster. Even after our father's death, when we'd been so alone, she'd chosen not to return to us. I stared at her. She'd used the word "almost," said it twice. Almost what? What had almost happened?

Or was it just an excuse?

My feelings were too much to take. I took a deep breath. My mother was waiting for me to ask more questions, but I had none—or, if I did, I was afraid to ask them. I told my mother I was taking a walk, and she just nodded and didn't try to change my mind.

I knew exactly where I had to go: the harbor, where I would feel like home, like Newport, where I would feel Travis with me, feel like myself again.

Ten

~

There were places on Capri no tourist ventured. Well, maybe a tourist who liked back alleys and what went on there. Midafternoon, Rafe drove the boat from his grandfather's dock to the Marina Grande. He saw the hydrofoils and ferries from Naples and Sorrento, yachts on their way to the south of France, small boats, low to the water, heading to the Grotta Azzurra. But he barely registered the activity.

His grandfather had been paying him to tend the dock and boat, mend the nets, paint the boathouse; he had cash in his pocket, and he told himself it was to settle his debt. Motoring into the channel, he pulled back on the throttle. Slowly he approached the pier where work and fishing boats docked.

Nicolas worked at the gas dock; he waved Rafe in, let him tie up on one of the finger piers. Wharf space was tight and expensive here; Rafe waved his thanks to the old man.

"What brings you to port?" Nicolas asked as Rafe stepped off the boat.

"Just an errand," Rafe said.

"Crazy summer day, just look at all these visitors," Nicolas said. But instead of looking around at the day-trippers and vacationers, he stared into Rafe's face. Rafe felt himself redden; he knew his grandfather's old friend was examining his pupils, his affect, watching him for signs of relapse.

"Thanks for letting me dock here," Rafe said. "I won't be long."

"You'd better not be," Nicolas said, arms folded across his chest. Rafe felt the old man's eyes on his back as he wound his way through the crowds, along the wharf. Shops and bars lined the shabby waterfront. The tide was out, and fishing boats were pulled right up on the shore. Guides hawking island tours called out and held up signs advertising trips to the grottoes and the Faraglioni. Rafe walked quickly along, ignoring everyone.

This used to be dangerous territory for him. Maybe it still was. Among the innocent shopkeepers and tour guides, there were people selling another kind of wares. Time was, he could find them no problem. He played a game with himself now: that guy with the black motorcycle jacket, the girl in the pink sundress. Were they holding?

Rafe lit a cigarette. He caught the eye of the guy in the leather jacket. He'd never seen him before; he was new here. But the way he looked at Rafe, a flick of his gaze, let Rafe know he had something to sell.

Walking on, thinking of his grandmother. In his mind he saw her smile, a knowing look. **Yeah, Grandma, I'm doing okay. I really am. This is just a game.**

She'd died two years ago. No game there. He'd been high, whacked out of his mind. But he saw certain things as clearly as if he'd been stone sober: the ambulance, her bird-thin body crumpled, the way she'd cried when they tried to lift her.

Asshole, he said to himself. **You fucking shit. You did that to her. You might as well have pushed her down.** Before and right after she'd died, he'd been one of the furtive ones down here at the wharf, or wherever he was: Trafalgar Square and Hyde Park in London; Washington Square Park and South Street Seaport in New York. Tourist areas were good: there was always someone selling whatever you needed. And Rafe had needed what they had.

"Hey, man," Arturo said, putting down his sign: thirteen euros for a tour around the island and a stop at the Blue Grotto. Arturo probably thought he was better off with Rafe's business.

"I came to pay you," Rafe said.

"Yeah?" Arturo asked, leading him off the beaten path, to an alley behind the funicular entrance. "That's good. Because then your credit is fine with me, and you can have whatever you want."

"I don't want anything," Rafe said. "Just clearing up my debt."

Arturo smiled and shrugged, as if he knew this was all just precursor to the real deal. Rafe reached into his pocket; his heart was pounding. He was going through the motions he'd gone through so many times before. Hand over the money, get something in return. Take it, feel better. His mouth was dry. By habit, he glanced around, looking for cops.

"I've let you slide on this," Arturo said. "I've been good to you."

"Thanks for giving me time," Rafe said.

"I didn't have a choice," Arturo said. "Nicolas and your grandfather have eagle eyes. You tell them about me?"

"No," Rafe said.

"Nicolas is always watching me. He and your grandfather told me they'd like it if I moved to Naples. Can you imagine that, those two old fucks? My family has been on Capri as long as Nicolas's people, centuries before the Gardiners came."

"I'm sorry they made it hard on you," Rafe said. His stomach clenched. Another way he'd messed things up, dragged his grandfather and Nicolas into his sordid problems. Maybe he should just fuck up once and for all.

"Anyone else owed me, I wouldn't have been so patient. But with your grandfather's influence, I had to hold back."

"Well, here's your money," Rafe said. "We're even now, so don't worry about it anymore."

Arturo counted out the euros. He glanced pointedly at a stone building, a maintenance shed owned by his family, where tools and fishing supplies were stored. Rafe had gone in there many times.

"No," Rafe said, before the question was even asked. "I'm done."

"No one's ever done," Arturo said.

Rafe didn't stick around to argue. He hurried down the narrow lane, stepping onto the waterfront just in time to see Pell Davis step out from under the awning of the funicular entrance. She blinked in the bright sunlight, getting her bearings. Rafe started toward her, but Arturo caught up to him.

"Here," Arturo said, handing him a small envelope. "This is for free. Old times' sake." He walked away, picked up his sign, before Rafe could shove the packet back at him. But not before Pell saw.

"Hey, Pell," he said.

"Hi, Rafe." She sounded cool, her gaze seemed unfriendly.

"What brings you to the marina?" he asked.

"I like harbors. How about you?" she asked, staring at the package in his hand. He wadded it up and threw it into a trash bin.

"I came to pay off someone I owed," he said. "That's over now, and I have the afternoon free. I know we said Monday, but do you want to take that boat ride to the Faraglioni? I'll show you the seahorses."

"No," she said. "Thanks anyway."

She started to walk away, down the waterfront. People jostled her, but she kept going. Rafe felt panicked that she had the wrong idea, ran after her.

"It's not what you think," he said.

"I don't think anything," she said.

"I owed him money from before," he said as she kept striding along. Her long dark hair swung as she walked, blocked him from seeing her face.

"You don't have to explain yourself to me," she said.

"But I want to."

They got caught in a throng of people jamming the dock for the next boat tour. Pell shouldered her way through, kept walking without looking at him. They passed a waterfront hotel, painted bright Pompeian red, and then she stopped.

"You should really get clear with yourself," she said.

"I am," he said.

"Are you sure? Because I saw him give you an envelope back there."

"Did you see me throw it away?" he asked.

"I did. But would you have if I hadn't been here?" she asked, staring hard into his eyes. The intensity made him feel uncomfortable, but he couldn't look away. Her eyes were bright blue, sharp with pain. Swamped with whatever she was dealing with, she felt concern for him too—he could tell. He'd felt it sitting beside her on the rock ledge, after his grandfather's party, and he sensed it now. Powerful emotions swept over him, reminding him of the way he'd felt in Malibu, talking to Monica.

"I would have tossed it no matter what," he said. "Honestly."

"Have you ever noticed how people say 'honestly' mainly when they're lying?" she asked. "You know, if you let your grandfather down, I just might have to hurt you."

"My grandfather?"

"Yeah," she said. "He adores you. It's so obvious, just spending an hour with him. You practically destroyed your life, but he's not giving up on you."

"He should have," Rafe said.

"Self-pity," she said. "Very attractive."

They walked along, then stood staring at the water. Dolphins leapt, following a fishing boat. Sun glistened on their black backs. He stared at her glossy hair, wished he could take her swimming, show her the beautiful world underwater, where it was quiet and peaceful and far from pain.

"What was in the package?" she asked.

"I don't know," he said. "Probably pills."

"What kind?"

"I used to take downs," he said. "I wanted oblivion. Just to sleep, all the time. I didn't want to feel."

"Because of your mother?" she asked.

The question shocked him. His mother had been dead so long, he rarely thought of her.

"I don't know," he said.

"Didn't you talk about it in rehab?"

"Of course," he said. "We talked about everything. But you know what? Plenty of people go through much worse shit than I did, and didn't start taking drugs. Look at you."

"Me?"

"Yeah," he said. "I know the whole story. How your mother bailed on you and your sister when you were little kids. How your father took care of you, and you were so close to him, and then he died and left you too."

"Who told you?" she asked.

"My grandparents," he said. "And my dad too, I guess. It's just known. Everyone on the island has a story. Lyra's is that she left her kids."

"People talk about it?"

He stared at her. A breeze off the harbor blew her hair into her eyes. She had dark, European beauty, but she seemed in some ways like a naive American. How could she understand the crumbling ruins of Capri, how they attracted broken people who'd stepped out of their other lives? His grandparents hadn't arrived here wrecked, but so many of the other foreigners had.

"Yeah," he said. "It makes her fit in here. The weather's been bright and sunny since you arrived, but wait for the first rainy day. The gloom and damp will pull you right down, remind you of every shitty thing you've done. There's no better place to brood, and I'm sure that's why Lyra likes it here."

The Chiesa di San Costanzo loomed behind them, the ancient whitewashed church reminding him of his grandmother's funeral, of prayers that had never been heard, of the suffering he had caused.

"She doesn't like me," he said. "You know why?"

"Because of Christina. She loved your grandmother," Pell said, sounding distant, catching Rafe's attention. What was that about?

"Yeah," he said. "Partly. But also because she knows I'm like her. A misfit who's screwed everything up."

"What's wrong with you?" she asked.

"Excuse me?"

"I can't believe you are Max's grandson, that you have even one drop of his blood."

"I was just trying to make a point, explaining why Lyra is so down on me. Everyone on Capri has their own story, their own reason for being here. It suits everyone for different reasons."

"You have a grandfather who loves you, believes in you. He's not looking backward at whatever you may or may not have done, thrown away, not appreciated. He's thinking of you right now, wanting you to stay healthy and well."

"I am," he said.

"How?" she asked. "By hanging out in the wrong places here on the dock, torturing yourself by getting envelopes from guys you should stay away from?"

"What do you know about wrong places on the dock?"

"I live in Newport," she said. She let it hang in the air. Although he didn't know that waterfront city, he was sure he could find an Arturo or two down by the harbor. He shrugged and gave her a slight smile, letting her know she'd made her point.

"What church is this?" she asked.

"San Costanzo," he said, thrown off guard. "Why?"

"I'm hot," she said as the sun beat down. "Can we go inside?"

They did, and it was dark and cool. Walking up the aisle, they sat in a pew near the altar. A cluster of candles burned brightly at the feet of the plaster saint. Rafe couldn't make himself look. He remembered coming in here the week before his grandmother had died. She'd fallen into a coma, and he'd lit a candle for her to get better. She hadn't.

Pell sat quietly beside him. He heard her breath, surprisingly fast, as if she'd just run a race. Glancing at her, to make sure she was okay, he saw her watching him. For a second, it made him think of Monica.

"Here's the difference," she said. "My father took care of me and Lucy. He didn't let up for a minute."

"But he died," Rafe said.

"Not before he made sure we were okay. We went through hell after she left. Real, true hell. My sister used to scratch her face at night, try to claw the skin off. She hurt so much inside, she had to make the outside match. And I pulled out hunks of hair, ripped them right out of my head."

"Why?"

"I don't know. I hated myself. I thought if she could leave me, I must be the worst person in the world. Ugly, and I don't mean in looks. I mean inside. I felt like a monster, a little ugly troll whose mother didn't love her."

"You're not ugly," Rafe whispered, and he wanted to take her hand. It was church, and he felt stiff, and he didn't know how she'd feel about it. His hand moved almost on its own, stopped just before he touched her.

"Neither are you," she said. "You were just a little boy when your mother died, and your dad didn't know what to do. He was working all the time, your grandfather said."

"Yeah," Rafe said. "And he's English. It's a cliché, but it's true—British people can be very stiff-upper-lip. My grandfather is unusual . . . but my father is classic. No confiding, no such thing as comfort. Just 'get on with it.'"

"You had all that emptiness inside," Pell said. "It started when your mother died, and it just grew and grew. That's why you wanted to sleep; to make that feeling go away."

"You never took drugs," Rafe said. "So how do you know?"

"Because I know the feeling," she said. "I lost my mother too."

"But she was still alive."

"Not exactly," she said. She fell silent, as if thinking something over. "Even when my father was still alive, we stopped talking about her—except with shrinks. My grandmother, once we moved to Newport, killed her in our minds. We didn't talk about her. We didn't look at pictures. After a while, it began to seem she was gone from the world. Not dead, not in a grave we could visit, not a saint we could pray to. Just someone who'd decided to move far away from us, in a life that had nothing to do with us. We knew she had chosen that. So we cut her out of our minds."

"Couldn't have been easy," he said.

"Easier than hoping," Pell said. "And she . . ." Again she paused, thinking hard. "Apparently she did the same thing. 'Walled herself off' from us, she said. That's what we all did. Kept each other out."

"But here you are," Rafe said.

"She's my mother," Pell said simply.

Rafe pictured his mother. Even though he'd been

just a kid when she passed away, her smile and eyes were as vibrant in his mind as ever.

Glancing at Pell, he tried to make sense of it. They'd both lost their mothers young; he'd taken one path to deal with it, she'd taken another. She'd seen him with Arturo's envelope, and she'd recognized what he really didn't want to admit: he'd been very tempted.

"Why are you here?" he asked.

"Here? You mean in church?"

"I mean on Capri. At your mother's house. Why did you come?"

"We need her," Pell said.

"Need her?"

"In spite of everything that's gone wrong, she's our mother. We want her back." The whisper echoed in the cavernous space.

"She's lucky," Rafe said.

"Who was San Costanzo?" Pell asked, as if she hadn't heard his words.

"The island's patron saint," he said. "He was on his way from Constantinople to Rome, got blown off course. Some kind of epic storm, sank all the other ships. But old Costanzo found a safe port here."

She looked up at him with wide blue eyes, recognition of a kindred spirit. He'd felt this way at rehab, meeting people who'd been through similar wars, who had their own language, whose hearts spoke to one another.

"Like my mother," she said. "And you."

"Yeah," he said, nodding. He took her hand, because he had to. She didn't pull away immediately. Her skin felt hot, as if she had a fever; Rafe himself was burning up. He and Pell stared at each other in the dark church, survivors of deadly storms, finding respite for the moment in the cool of the nave. She slid her hand from his after a few seconds, but not before he'd felt them together, really connected, not just their hands, but whatever it was that had kept their hearts beating through all the loss.

~

We could have gone into a café, or a gelateria, or even a bar. But a church? The darkness and the ghostly smell of incense and the glow of all those candles blazing on the altar made it all seem so much more intense. Being in San Costanzo gave the moment too much weight, something like an imprimatur. I'm thinking of Travis, of what he'd have thought if he had seen me there.

Rafe took me by surprise. All of it—not just when he held my hand in the church. That was a mistake, instantaneous, and I'm telling myself it was no more than what two friends might do. A quick clasp of the hand. Not a big deal. Right?

The first surprise was seeing him with the drug dealer, catching the wild look in his eyes when he was left holding that package—Rafe wanted to use; nothing he could say will ever convince me otherwise—and the passion I felt, caring so much about him and Max, my mother, the fragility of it all. My heart fell, just crashed, seeing him holding that envelope.

This is strange, but I'm thinking of my grandmother. Just before I left to come to Capri, she said, "You've always loved a lost cause." She was speaking of my mother. Is there truth in her words? My mother basically told me—no, **actually** told me—that she had chosen life without us. It had been a conscious decision. Never have I felt more abandoned, more wrecked. It's how I wound up in the church with Rafaele Gardiner.

After the hand clasp, it was as if we fell into a trance. Rafe and I sat there in the quiet church, not speaking or touching, just being still. I could feel my heart beating hard in my chest. I wanted to run away, make the feelings stop. I wanted to turn back the clock, not get off the funicular in front of him, not get drawn into the moment with him. I wanted there to be only Travis. I didn't want to have held another boy's hand, or be filled with these wild emotions.

But we sat there so long, my heart finally slowed down, and I felt overcome with sadness. My mother's words came into my mind; she'd knelt before me, held my face in her hands. My eyes filled with tears. She had been a good mother when I was little, but she hadn't wanted it. She had walked away from us, from motherhood. Rafe sat beside me, lost in his own world.

By the time we walked outside, onto the quay, I had lost track of everything: the sun in the sky, the time of day, the person I was before we'd gone into San Costanzo. The afternoon had somehow passed, and dusk was coming on. Capri's bright blue sky had dimmed. Violet haze coated the harbor as the sun went down.

"Want a ride home?" Rafe asked, gesturing at the yellow boat at the end of the dock.

I stood there, feeling dazed. He touched my shoulder. "Pell?" he said. "Are you okay?"

"I don't know. Are you?"

"I don't know either," he said.

I hadn't answered him about the ride home, but I fell into step with him. Our arms brushed, both comforting and jolting me.

We walked down the dock; Nicolas was there, putting gas in the tank of a big white yacht flying an American flag. When he saw me and Rafe, he gave us a solemn nod and a big smile. So big, in fact, I think he thought we were "together." I mean, as a couple. It doesn't take much to realize Max and his friends are worried about Rafe, and I'm nothing if not a good influence.

I climbed into the boat, we cast off, and went flying across the water. Salt spray cooled my face, and my hair blew straight back. I thought of Travis, an ocean away, fishing off the coast of Rhode Island. I said his name under my breath, just once. What had I done to us? I closed my eyes as the engine throbbed noisily, the boat bouncing across the waves as Rafe drove me home.

Eleven

Max stood in the lower walled garden as the sun began to go down. Staring at the bay, he watched for the boat to come around the headland. Nicolas had called earlier; he'd seen Rafe talking to Arturo. Max's heart felt heavy. Could the trouble be starting again? A second call from Nicolas reported that Rafe had bumped into Pell, and that they were heading home. Max concentrated his gaze on the bay, as if he could will them to make it back safely.

A school of silver baitfish broke the surface. Gulls wheeled and cried. Max barely noticed, his eyes focused as he waited. Here they came now. Rafe had the throttle open, and the yellow boat sped into view, white water shooting up behind.

There were sharp rocks just below the surface, hard to see in the dying light. Max told himself Rafe wasn't being reckless; he'd grown up summering here, and knew the water as well as Max himself. But if Rafe was back to drugs, hitting a shoal would put Pell in danger. And it would be the start of a treacherous trail.

Rafe pulled the boat up to the dock. Max saw Pell jump out, expertly catch and tie off the bow and stern lines. She started up the steps without waiting for Rafe, but he moved quickly and caught up with her. Max lost them in thick foliage as they climbed the steep stairs, but he was waiting for them when they got to the first landing.

"Hello," he said.

"Max!" Pell said, reaching up to kiss him.

"Hi, Grandpa," Rafe said.

"How lovely, to see my two favorite young people. Did you meet in town?"

"Didn't Nicolas tell you?" Rafe said, challenging and defensive. "I know he was watching me."

"He did tell me, as a matter of fact," Max said. He stared at his grandson, checking his pupils. They seemed normal-sized, not the pinpoints presented when opiates took him over.

"Rafe did the right thing," Pell said. "You don't have to worry, Max."

"You don't, Grandpa," Rafe said. He threw Pell a grateful look, but she didn't receive it with warmth. She inched away, not meeting Rafe's eyes, not even looking at him. Something powerful had gone on between them; Max couldn't tell whether it was good or bad, but he couldn't miss the electricity crackling all around.

"Pell, is your mother home?" Max asked.

"She was when I left a couple of hours ago."

"Do you know," Max began, "I rather feel like going out tonight? Let's find your mother, and go to Da Vincenzo for dinner."

"Maybe Pell's had enough of us," Rafe said.

"Never enough of Max," Pell said, giving the old man a big smile.

The three of them continued up the narrow, shady steps. As twilight fell, it became almost impossible for Max to see the stairs. His feet knew the way, they always had. Max's property included land on both sides of the steps, east and west, from the rocky shore up the steep hill to the very top elevation. Lyra's house and gardens occupied a large chunk about midway up, west of the stairs.

They reached Lyra's house a minute later. Max tried to get his breathing under control: it was racing not from exertion, but from the relief of knowing Rafe was okay, and the anticipation of seeing Lyra. He heard music coming from above, and her house glowed with warm light. The scent of honeysuckle surrounded them as they climbed the curved stairs to the terrace.

Max had been here infrequently at night since Christina's death. They used to have drinks and dine often with Lyra. She would play her favorite music; sometimes they'd watch a DVD after dinner. Back then Max had loved her only as a friend, neighbor, the young woman who considered his wife her mentor.

As he stepped onto her terrace, behind Pell and Rafe, he felt overcome with emotion. Their families were connected in deep, ineffable ways. He had seen her grief over losing Christina, and that had opened them up to talking more about her daughters.

Lyra and Max had comforted each other. Although she was hard on Rafe, he knew she had his, Max's, best interests at heart. And, especially, Max knew what this reunion with Pell meant to her, how both precious and terrifying it was to her. He could barely wait to see her now, witness the expression on her face as she began another evening with her daughter.

Voices carried through the vine-draped loggia, from inside the house. Max hesitated, not wanting to intrude if Lyra had company, but Pell led the way and he felt himself drawn along.

Lyra sat on her white sofa beside Gregorio Dante, their heads bent close together as they examined a large sheet of paper.

"Hi, Mom," Pell said.

"Pell!" Lyra said. "And Max . . . Rafe . . ."

"Buona sera," Gregorio said, standing to shake hands. "Ciao, Max."

"Ciao, Gregorio," Max said.

"Gregorio is building the moon gate for Renata and Amanda's garden," Lyra said to Max.

"Ah," Max said.

"Do Lucy's calculations help with the plans?" Pell asked.

"Perfettamente," Gregory said, tapping a photo of Lucy, obviously brought out by Lyra. "I wanted to see for myself this young genius who solved the problem so quickly. Lyra's daughters are both brilliant and exquisite. But why should I be surprised? They are hers, after all."

Max fought the urge to get sick. He gave Gregorio a long appraising gaze. The younger man could barely contain his desire for Lyra. Did Max show his feelings half as blatantly? He hoped not. Lyra seemed . . . what? She seemed to be flirting, smitten with the stonemason, smiling as she put her arm around Pell.

"They're wonderful all on their own," Lyra said. Pell stood there for a second, then eased away. Max didn't miss the way she reddened, looked down. Or the way Rafe leaned toward her, as if wanting to give Pell some strength, support.

"Her beauty is straight from you," Gregorio said stubbornly, and Max knew he had to leave.

"Have a lovely evening," Max said, smiling and giving a slight bow.

"But I thought you mentioned going out . . . ," Pell said. "We don't want you to dine alone, Max."

"Oh, of course not," Max said. "In my enthusiasm over greeting you after your boat ride from town, I forgot that I have a previous engagement."

"Max, are you sure?" Lyra asked. "Because we would love—"

"Quite positive," Max said. "Good night, all."

He left the room as quickly as possible. Turning, half expecting Rafe to be right behind him, he couldn't help smiling. His grandson had lingered behind, unwilling to leave Pell until he was pushed out the door. Which, considering the way Lyra felt, might well happen sooner rather than later.

Trudging up the remaining steps to the villa, he heard crickets in the brush, saw stars beginning to appear in the dark blue sky. The sight was so beautiful, but filled him with sadness. Certain things in life were eternal: the beauty of the stars, the way love made his heart feel. He glanced down the hill, through the trees, at Lyra's house. She was becoming attracted to a man much younger than he. How could he begrudge her that?

"Well, it's about time," John said, reclining on a settee on his terrace.

"What are you doing here?" Max asked.

"I came up here to offer a friendly ear. And this is the thanks I get?" John shook his head. "Bella let me in. We've been waiting for you. I assumed you would invite me to stay for dinner, and I in return would give you sage advice."

"About what?" Max asked.

"Anything you choose," John said.

"I suppose Nicolas sent you up."

"Well. It's possible that he did give me a quick call."

Max's friends were vigilant. When Rafe had stepped off the path in the past, disaster had occurred. Max briefly considered lecturing John on having faith in the young man, but restrained himself. He himself had expected the worst from the moment Nicolas phoned.

"I have seen my grandson, and he is fine," Max said.

"Excellent," John said, but his tone conveyed skepticism. "Where is he now?"

"At Lyra's, with Pell."

"Why aren't you over there with them?"

"Oh," Max said, walking toward the bar. He wanted his back to John, and busied himself pouring two glasses of Talisker. "Lyra has a guest."

"And?" John asked. "Do fill me in."

"Gregorio Dante. Bertoldi's son," Max said, handing him the scotch.

"A more unlikely pair could not exist. What is she doing with him?"

"He's working with her on Amanda and Renata's garden."

"Oh. Business. That's different. I hear the girls have a photographer coming," John said. "Some big magazine from the States is doing a spread on their house. So I suppose they're trying to get everything finished quickly. Still, upsetting to have that faux Adonis hanging around. Go rescue her!"

"Rescue her?"

"Yes," John said.

"She's strong. She doesn't need me."

John swirled the scotch in his glass, then took a long drink. He gazed at Max from his reclining position, giving the impression of a very large and old tortoise.

"Well," John said, "I suppose for some men, writing a play about love would be sufficient. I just never thought you were one of them, not when you're consumed with the real thing. However, introducing a specimen like Gregorio Dante will add quite a nice frisson of sex to the end of Act I."

"You're a bloody idiot," Max said.

"Excellent scotch," John said, draining the glass. "Do we have time for one more before Bella feeds us?" As if hovering just inside, Bella came out to say she'd noticed Max's arrival, and was preparing the meal.

"Thank you, Bella," Max said.

"We can play chess after dinner," John said, sounding content. "And discuss your plans for Act II. Perhaps the stonemason can have a wall fall on him!"

Rustling brush sounded from the stairs, and low voices drifted up the terrace wall. Max craned his neck to look over the side, saw Lyra, Pell, and Rafe standing in a semicircle, gazing upward.

"Why didn't you tell me you'd invited us to dinner?" Lyra asked.

"You looked busy," Max said. "I didn't want to interrupt."

"It was Gregorio, for God's sake!" Lyra said. "I was just giving him specifications for the moon gate. We were just finishing up."

"I hope you don't mind my mentioning Da Vincenzo, Max," Pell said. "It just sounded so fun. Besides, any chance to spend the evening with you!"

"Of course I don't mind," Max said. "It's just that I've—"

John scowled and mouthed **Shut up!**

"Please, Max?" Pell called.

Max looked down at the three faces. Rafe was silent, but Max saw him standing beside Pell, longing in his eyes. Lyra willing to go to dinner with his grandson was a first, a real breakthrough. Still . . . Max stared at her, wondering where any of it could ever go.

Sitting on the villa's terrace, the spot where he'd spent so many beautiful evenings with his wife, he felt the strangest sensation: a breeze through his hair, almost as if Christina were kissing the top of his head. He felt such yearning, a feeling that all was one, that these people he loved were all connected by invisible threads.

"Yes," he found himself saying. "Let's go to dinner."

Turning from the balcony's edge, he glanced at John. The three standing on the lawn below were unable to see over the villa's curved stone wall, and hadn't noticed that Max had a guest. John, surprising for him, had remained silent and avoided detection by the group. Max supposed there was nothing to do but invite his old friend along to Da Vincenzo.

"Care to join us?" Max asked quietly.

John shook his head and smiled as if Max was something of an imbecile.

"Take the lady to dinner, will you?" John asked. "I wouldn't want to intrude on the family scene. I believe I'll have another scotch right here, and make sure Bella's pasta doesn't go to waste."

"Good of you," Max said.

"Happy to oblige. We'll play chess and discuss Act II another time," John said. "Meanwhile, see what you can drum up in terms of inspiration. Dinner with the muse is always most valuable."

"Max, who's there with you?" Lyra called.

John drew his index finger, a dagger, across his own throat.

"No one," Max said, "I'm on the way."

~

Da Vincenzo was located in Capri town, off the main square. They drove down the crooked streets in Max's ancient Hillman. Lyra felt the summer breeze blow through the open windows and thought of how often she, Max, and Christina had driven in this old car to this, their favorite restaurant.

The kids talked in the back seat. Lyra glanced down at Max's hand on the gearshift. He'd once told her he'd had the car sent from England. It was sea green, small and compact, barely large enough for four. The salt air rusted it unmercifully, but Max cared for it and Nicolas kept it running. Lyra felt a rush of tenderness for the way Max loved things.

"What is it?" he asked, catching her looking at him.

"Nothing," she said. "I'm glad we're all together tonight."

"So am I," he said, the corners of his eyes crinkling in a deep smile.

They parked on a side street, fitting into an impossibly small spot. The rustic old house stood at the end of a dark and narrow alley, in a hidden park filled with lemon trees. Voices carried from the town square; doves roosted under the eaves of tall, crooked buildings.

Max held the door open. They all walked into the restaurant. Da Vincenzo was half used-book store, half trattoria, making it necessary to pass through stacks of books, over readers sitting on the floor, under a staircase leading to the second floor, where the poetry and drama sections could be found, as well as several cramped guest rooms where, legend had it, many now-famous young writers had once stayed.

All the way in back, through a heavy burgundy

velvet curtain, the trattoria was cozy and intimate, illuminated by scores of red candles. The menu featured local seafood, homemade pasta, and pizzas cooked in a wood-fired oven.

The dining room walls were lined with bookshelves, overflowing with old volumes that lone diners were invited to read while eating. Yellowed prints of great Italian writers hung below brass sconces, tarnished from the sea air; Lyra glanced up and saw Dante, Petrarch, and Boccaccio.

The place was favored by young intellectuals, and had been ever since Lyra had first come to Capri. She examined the menu and tried to picture Max here as a young man. She couldn't help turn her head, look at him again, as she had in the car. His leonine head was bent as he studied the menu, half-spectacles perched on the end of his sharp nose. Craggy and powerful, he was still a handsome man.

"This is charming and wonderful," Pell said, looking up from her menu. "I love it, Max."

"I thought you might," Max said. "There are fancier establishments in Capri, but none with quite so much warmth. And the food is superb."

"Grandpa's been coming here since he was our age," Rafe said, as if he'd heard the story a million times.

"Not quite, but close," Max said. "The original owner, Vincenzo Pertosa, was a friend to young writers and artists—not unlike Sylvia Beach at

Shakespeare and Company in Paris. When I came to Capri right after Cambridge, I rented a room from Vincenzo. Many nights he fed me for free while I wrote my first play."

"I didn't realize you'd written it here," Lyra said. "I thought London."

"That's where it was produced," Max said. "But I wrote it right here. Upstairs." He smiled up at the ceiling, as if in thanks and blessing.

"You were a starving writer," she said.

"Poor, yes," he said. "But not starving, thanks to Vincenzo. He housed and fed several of us that year. We were a colony of artists, giving one another support and making sure no one got discouraged. And eating well every night!"

Lyra resumed studying the menu. She thought of how different her post-college tour had been, how privileged she had been, how easily everything had been given to her. But how lonely, as well: there'd been no colony of like-minded young people. She had thought she was the only one in the world like herself.

The waiter came, and everyone ordered pizza. Max ordered a bottle of Taurasi, red wine from Campagna, for him and Lyra, while the kids drank mineral water. Lyra watched the way Max's eyes kept darting to Rafe, making sure he was okay, monitoring his interest in the wine. The next time Max glanced Lyra's way, she tried to give him a reassuring smile.

"Max, after dinner do you think we can go upstairs and see the room you stayed in?" Pell asked. "Is it still there?"

"I'm sure it is," he said. "The rooms are all named after characters from Italian literature. Mine was 'Beatrice.'"

"We have a minute before the pizza comes," Rafe said. "Want to run up and check it out?"

Pell nodded, and the kids excused themselves. Lyra lifted her glass, raised it to Max. The red wine sparkled in the candlelight.

"Here's to your inspiration!" she said.

Max seemed frozen, fingers wrapped around the stem of his glass, unable to move. He stared at her as if she had shocked him.

"This place," she explained, looking around. "Where you wrote your first play. It must have been very inspiring, right? That's what I meant. . . ."

"Oh," he said, clinking with her and starting to smile. "Of course."

"What did you think I meant?" she asked. A teasing glint entered her eye. "Did something go on here? Maybe before you met Christina? Don't worry, Max . . . your secret is safe with me. Did you fall in love with a young artist?"

He stared at her, warmth and great intelligence in his bright blue eyes, then looked away. She watched him gaze down at the bare wood table, rough-hewn and rustic, as if seeing something he couldn't quite bear to think about.

"Oh, Max," she said. "I didn't mean to tease you. I know that Christina was the love of your life. I just thought that maybe you'd loved someone before her, when you were young. It wouldn't be wrong if you did. I'm sorry for even mentioning it."

"Please, don't apologize, Lyra," he said. "I just . . . your words about inspiration made me think of someone."

"A young artist?" she asked, smiling.

He nodded. He met her eyes for a second, then looked down again. She watched him sip his wine thoughtfully, wondering why he was acting this way. Perhaps the restaurant was too full of memories, a reminder of days and people gone by. Wanting to comfort her dear friend, she reached for his hand.

"It's okay, Max," she said, leaning toward him. "Whoever she was, she was lucky you felt that way."

"Thank you, Lyra," he said.

Pell and Rafe returned. Lyra glanced up, saw Rafe pull back Pell's chair. He touched her arm as she sat down; Pell seemed unmistakably shaken. The sight chilled Lyra, and she gave Max's hand one last squeeze, keeping her eyes on Rafe. He registered her watching him and gave her a steady stare back.

"The room is empty," Rafe said, "so we got to go inside. Grandpa, we found your name written on the windowsill."

"We all did that," Max said. "Vincenzo insisted we leave our signatures, in case any of us had success."

"You sure did," Rafe said, sounding proud of his grandfather.

"There's a medallion on the door with a scene from **The Divine Comedy**—Beatrice standing in a garden," Pell said quietly.

"Fruit trees, flowering vines," Max said. "It foreshadowed you, Lyra."

"Thank you, Max," Lyra said, wondering about the intensity in his voice.

"Is it from the end of the work, where Beatrice and Dante unite in the Garden of Eden?" Pell asked, and Max nodded.

"Dante," Rafe said, gesturing up at the portrait. "Is Gregorio related to him?"

"To Dante Alighieri?" Lyra asked, and it struck her funny. "I doubt it, but I'll have to ask him."

"It makes you laugh?" Max said.

"Yeah," Lyra said. "Gregorio is a wonderful stonemason. But I don't confuse him with a poet able to write about a journey through hell to paradise."

"It takes a man like Max to do that," Pell said.

Lyra gazed over at her daughter, surprised that she'd make such a statement. It wasn't shy, reserved, polite, but it came from her heart, and Lyra was amazed at the way Max reacted. He bowed his head to Pell, touched his heart.

"Love can take you to paradise," Max said. "You might find tragedy and suffering along the way, in fact you probably always do. Not everyone knows that, or they might be too afraid to commence the journey."

"That's why Vincenzo gave you the room with Beatrice on the door," Pell said. "Because he knew you were worthy of her as your guide."

"She's right," Lyra said, thinking of Christina, of the selfless way Max had loved her. She thought of his devotion to her, his long and unwavering love, and felt bad for having asked him about the young artist; he suddenly seemed so thoughtful and sad. She glanced at Pell, overwhelmed with love for her and for Lucy.

"Thank you, both," Max said. "And Rafe too. You're far too kind, and I don't deserve a word of it."

"Yes, you do," Lyra said, squeezing his hand again. Just then the waitress brought the pizzas, and everyone looked so happy. Even Max; he'd forgiven her for mentioning the other woman, his old love. He gazed at her with such warmth and depth in his brilliant blue eyes.

Lyra felt stunned by her own feelings. Staring at Max, her own heart cracked open. He was so good; knowing he cared about her made her feel less terrible about herself. He accepted her for who she was, even for all the wrong she'd done, and she let herself imagine how it would have felt to be the young artist he'd once loved, to have him look at her in just this way.

~

In Newport, the day was sparkling bright. Lucy and Beck had walked Gracie down to Bannister's Wharf for an ice-cream cone, and to see the boats. They walked out on the pier to see **Sirocco,** and saw Lucy's grandmother serving luncheon under the blue canvas awning, holding court like a seagoing queen. Ducking so she wouldn't spot them, they went to the other dock, where all the fishing boats came in.

"Travis!" Gracie said. They'd brought her here before, and she knew where her uncle worked.

"That's right," Beck said. "Uncle Travis is out in Block Island Sound, catching fish."

"Ish, ish," Gracie said, her word for "fish," pointing at a cod-shaped weathervane on top of Keating Seafood.

"Very good," Lucy said, kissing Gracie's head.

"We'll have to teach her to say 'Auntie Pell,'" Beck said. "When she gets back from Italy."

"Auntie?" Lucy asked.

"Don't you think they'll get married? Pell and Travis?"

"They're only sixteen."

"Travis just turned seventeen."

"Still, they have senior year, then college. I think marriage is a long way off," Lucy said. She loved thinking about it, but lately she'd noticed stress on Travis's face after he talked to Pell. "If you're right, we'll be sisters-in-law."

"Totally," Beck said. "I'm all for it. They'll make it through college together. I can't imagine my brother with anyone else."

"I can't imagine my sister with anyone else," Lucy said.

"I don't know how Travis is doing it," Beck said. "He works so hard on the boat, and he doesn't sleep when he's home. He misses her so much. Have you noticed problems lately?"

"Kind of," Lucy said. "You have too?"

Beck nodded. "He seems really worried about something. Could she be falling out of love with him?"

"Never," Lucy said. But she wasn't sure. Something seemed wrong.

"When's Pell getting back?"

"As soon as she convinces our mother to come home," Lucy said. "Maybe she needs help."

"Good plan," Beck said, her eyes glittering in that "Eureka!" classic Beck way. "Let's get your grandmother to sail us over there aboard **Sirocco**!"

"Um, on second thought," Lucy said. Although she laughed and kept walking along the cobblestone wharf, she felt a pang inside. She ached for her sister. One of the side effects of losing touch with their mother so long ago was an unbreakable bond with Pell. No two sisters had ever been closer.

Pell called Lucy when she could, and Lucy called her. Phone conversations were one thing, but nothing even came close to seeing each other. No wonder Travis couldn't sleep either.

"Well, your grandmother's yacht isn't the only way to get there," Beck said.

"We could swim!" Lucy said.

"That isn't funny," Beck said, and Lucy knew she was thinking of the time Lucy had walked down to the beach in her sleep, strolled right into the rolling surf, nightgown and all.

"I know," Lucy said. "I'm sorry."

"Dude, don't apologize. Just, no swimming to Italy. How would you feel about a plane?"

"It's a thought," Lucy said.

"Works for many people," Beck said. "Air travel. It could get you there fast. Do you feel up to it?"

"Totally," Lucy said.

"You do seem a little better lately," Beck said, peering at Lucy's eyes. "The circles aren't quite so deep. You've been getting some sleep, right?"

"Yes," Lucy said, thinking of her mother's call, how it had soothed her more than warm milk and honey.

"Except around 2:01," Beck said.

"The bad time," Lucy said.

"It'll be less bad once you really have your mother in your life," Beck said.

"Really?" Lucy asked, staring straight into her best friend's bright hazel, green-gold eyes. She thought of Mrs. Shaw, Beck's mom, of how close they were.

Beck nodded, but with a tiny apology in her eyes, as if she didn't want to be too thoughtless in pointing out what Lucy didn't have.

"Yeah," Beck said, giving Lucy's hand a gentle shake. "Yeah, Luce. There's nothing like it. I want it for you."

Twelve

It's Wednesday now—five days since Da Vincenzo, and two days since I was supposed to go to see the seahorses with Rafe. I canceled. I've been gardening with my mother. Working hard, right by her side, not too much talking. I think we're both afraid of what we might say.

Well, it hit me over the head, sitting at dinner the other night. Max loves my mother. And I don't mean as her kindly old neighbor, watching over her in a benevolent, elderly way from the villa—I mean, he's **in love** with her. Sitting at a table in candlelight, watching the way he gazed at her, I saw it all. And the way he'd acted on our walk: he had seemed so full of longing. I'd seen it instantly, the way he'd spoken about my mother finding solace in the garden. But I'd doubted my perceptions then.

No longer. Da Vincenzo was one of the most romantic places I've ever been. The candles' warm glow surrounded us, held us together, kept us from having any secrets from one another. I saw everything at that dinner.

Max's love for my mother, my mother's doubts about herself, Rafe's . . . okay, this is where it gets upsetting. Rafe's feelings for me, are what I have to face. I do see them. What's more frightening, I'm having some of my own for him. He is a little older than I, but in many ways seems younger. Loss toughened me—not in a hard way, but in a realistic way. I know how life works, and I don't try to fight it. I try to accept what comes my way, go with the flow. Not Rafe.

He is really sensitive. When he lost his mother, he didn't have someone like my father to hold him, rock him, tell him it wasn't his fault. He didn't have a dad who'd sit on the edge of his bed when he had nightmares.

From the sound of things, David Gardiner isn't a bad guy—he's just a believer in the stiff-upper-lip, get-on-with-it-old-boy way of parenting. Rafe responded by needing to hide—to protect himself from the agony of his mother's death. Drugs and drinking provide a buffer. They're a really effective shield against the worst feelings a person can have.

I know all of the above without Rafe even telling me. This is the strange thing about me: I take in people's stories through my skin. Please don't freak out. It's just how I am. I see someone crying, and I feel the pain too. With just a little information, I figure out who the person is, what caused their grief; it seeps into me, into my heart. That's what's been going on with Rafe.

In the boat, on our way back from town the day we wound up in San Costanzo, we were silent pretty much the whole ride. When we got to the dock, I watched him scan the shore for starfish. He found one, silently threw it into the deep water. I asked one question.

"How old were you?"

I didn't have to say "when your mother died"—he just knew.

"Seven," he said.

Then we walked up the long stairs; I was transformed by what had happened during the afternoon, in the church, and could barely speak. But Rafe seemed to want to put it behind him, his show of vulnerability.

He began talking about New York, about school—he'd gone to St. David's, on the Upper East Side, with Ty Cooper, a boy who now attends Newport Academy—and I had to ask myself why he was telling me such mundane things. He must have wanted me to see him as "normal," with an untroubled past, a life I could relate to. He wanted to erase the image I had of him holding Arturo's envelope, of the wild look in his eyes. He'd wanted to use, and I saw, and he knew I saw.

And it touched me even more deeply, to think of

him wanting to manage my thoughts and feelings about him. As if he thought he wasn't good enough just the way he was, as if he had to pretend he was different.

If there's one thing I've learned, through the ten years of missing my mother, and especially after our last deep talk, it's that people are exactly the way they are. You can't change anyone, you can't alter the past. What is, is. And you have to go on from there. I'm grappling with an idea that I hate. I mean despise. And that's that my father was so good, so wonderful, my mother felt she couldn't live up to him.

With all her flaws, doubts, insecurities about motherhood, he'd filled in the blanks so easily. Maybe she really thought she could leave us with him, no repercussions. I wish I had pictures to show her, of my bald spot, Lucy's bleeding face, our fingernails bitten down to the quick. Maybe she'd realize there really is a place for a mother in every kid's life, no matter how inadequate she might feel.

When we got to the restaurant that night, I felt a little frantic inside. The skin on my hand prickled, sense memory from holding Rafe's hand in the church. I hadn't yet called Travis that day—I planned to later, after dinner—but he was foremost in my mind. I was in a relationship with someone I knew well and really loved. But I was having such intense feelings for Rafe. Just sitting next to him at the table made my heart beat in this very violent, thrashing, scary way.

Rafe is sexy. He's dangerous, because he hasn't yet realized he's not in control—of life, even of himself. He is tall and lean, with wavy dark hair that falls into his ice blue eyes. He lives in Max's boathouse, not up at the villa, and doesn't shower that often—his hair's kind of stringy, in a dissipated-poet kind of way. He smokes constantly; along with the way he drank and drugged, it's as if he's committing slow suicide. Something's going to kill him.

He's not the one for me. I know that. Travis is. Rafe is every mother's nightmare—I have only to look at my mother's disapproving face to know that. I'm psychologically in tune enough to question my own motives—am I attracted to Rafe just to get back at my mother? The answer to that is no. He pulls me in all on his own, without any help from her.

During dinner, when we went upstairs at Da Vincenzo to look for Max's old room, something happened. I can barely write it—not out of shame or guilt, I don't think, but out of not wanting to let it into the air, the world, take the steam out of it, take the power away. I think about it, and the top of my head nearly flies off.

We climbed the wooden stairs—narrow, crooked, dark. The second-floor hallway was lit only by one dim lamp on a table. There were doors on either side of the hall, close together because the rooms were so small.

Because it was so dark, we had to stand close to the medallions—ovals of wood, delicately and intricately painted with characters from books, a yellowing protective layer of varnish glinting in the low light, nailed to each door at eye level—to try to find Beatrice.

There she was, all the way at the end. I knew her instantly, by the romantic way the artist had depicted her, running through the garden, holding Dante's hand as if she'd never let it go. Trees bearing both fruits and flowers arched overhead, the garden in full bloom.

"How do you know it's Beatrice?" Rafe asked, flicking his lighter so we could see better.

"The garden," I said.

"Huh," he said.

"Did you read it in school?" I asked. **"The Divine Comedy?"**

"I might have," he said. "That's the thing about the way I went through school. Not remembering much . . ."

I nodded, and the lighter went out, and he turned away. I could tell that this was at odds with what had happened earlier, him talking about St. David's and school life. He stood there in the dark, looking at me.

"It's okay," I said.

"Not really," he said. "I've fucked up my life. And everyone else's."

"Start over," I said. "That's what you're doing right now, isn't it? You have a new life. You threw out the pills."

"You have no idea how badly I wanted to take them," he said, finally admitting the truth to me and, possibly, himself.

"But you didn't," I said.

He didn't reply, but knocked lightly on the door. No one answered; he turned the crystal knob, and we went in. The room was tiny, my idea of a monk's cell, but without the religion, other than the holiness of books and writing: single bed, small dresser, bookcase overflowing with old volumes, scarred desk, and straight-backed chair. I touched the chair, thinking that Max had once sat there.

Rafe looked through the room, a museum to his grandfather's early days. He did this funny thing—trailed his fingers over every surface. It was as if he were blind, had to see through touch. And maybe that's not entirely wrong—it's how we do so much in life, absorb the most important things through our skin. Or at least I do, as I mentioned earlier.

When he'd made a full circuit of the small room, he came back to stand beside me. We faced the window, which overlooked a narrow alleyway leading to the main square. Darkness leading into light:

trees in the town center were illuminated, hung with strands of tiny white lights.

Both Rafe and I happened to look down at the exact same moment, and there, in the aged wooden windowsill (and covered with the same protecting shellac as the door painting) was Max's signature. Of course I didn't recognize it, but Rafe did, and pulled me closer.

"Look," he said, pointing. "That's my grandfather!"

"Who are these?" I said, looking at other signatures.

"Must be other people who stayed in this room at different times," Rafe said. "Look at them all."

The window was open. A slight breeze blew in, and happy voices drifted in from the square. I heard the rustle of wind in the leaves and branches. The lights swayed, casting moving shadows in the room. I shivered, not because it was cold, but from something else.

Rafe saw. He turned to me. It seemed he was about to embrace me. He held his hands so close to my bare arms, I literally felt heat pouring off his palms. But he didn't touch me. He must have known he shouldn't—he could see in my eyes that I wouldn't welcome it. I wanted it, but I wouldn't let it happen.

A minute later, we left the room and went downstairs to rejoin my mother and Max. That's when I saw the look in Max's eyes, and instantly knew how he felt about my mother. Love was in the air. I'd carried with me vestiges of what had just almost happened upstairs. My blood was racing; I knew I had to call Travis.

Days passed before Travis and I actually spoke. He was out on the boat; the fishing had been so good, they'd stayed out longer than usual. By the time he called me back, I was so churned up. I felt as if the world was falling apart. My attraction to Rafe made me hate myself, and this is weird: it made me fear my mother. Her instability, the way she had left our family. Thrown away everything good and wonderful, and for what?

Paradoxically, that fear made me stick closer to my mother than ever. I went to work with her. Helped her prepare the flower beds for the moon garden. I kept an eye on her while Gregorio flirted with her unmercifully. I had the feeling he wished I'd leave them alone so he could really pour it on. As it was, he kept giving me smarmy compliments, then telling my mother he saw so much of her in me.

Getting through to Travis became my obsession. That plus staying away from Rafe. I never once went down to the water; from the terrace I looked only upward—at Monte Solaro and the clouds, at night the stars and the moon—instead of down toward the shore, the boathouse, and the tide line.

I'd left Travis several messages—both on his cell phone and with his family. Even though his mother told me what was going on, that the trawler was out past Block Island and not returning till the hold was full, I wondered why he wasn't calling—there's decent cell reception out there. I know, because I've gone out so many times on my grandmother's yacht. **Sirocco** has often cruised the New England waters with Lucy and me aboard, and we always called our friends from sea.

"Why didn't you pick up?" I asked Travis when he finally called me.

"I was ankle-deep in cod," he said. "Pollack too. My hands were slimy, and the fish kept coming."

"Oh," I said. "But couldn't you have called me back on one of your breaks?"

"Pell," he said, laughing, "I'm calling now. You seriously have no idea what it's like out there. We're either fishing, or gutting the fish, or icing the fish, or setting the nets, or trying to figure out why the trawl doors are stuck, or crashing for a two-hour nap. No such thing as real sleep out there. And another reason I didn't call was because there are always a bunch of guys hanging around, listening in."

"I'm sorry for being this way," I said, trying to laugh at myself. But the fact was, I'd been desperate to hear his voice, be reminded of who he was, and what we had, and how much I loved him.

"You can be any way you want," he said. "You're my Pell."

"I am?"

"Of course you are. Are you okay?"

"Oh, Travis. Better now, talking to you." I closed my eyes, relaxed into the sound of his voice, the connection between us. I could almost feel him holding me.

"How are things going with your mother?"

"Pretty well," I said.

"Have you laid it out for her?" he asked. "How you want her home with you and Lucy?"

"Not yet," I said. "How's Lucy?"

"She seems better. My mom said she's slept through most nights since that last call with you and your mother."

"I'm glad to hear that." I took a deep breath. "It would be so good to not have to worry about Lucy."

"She's your sister," Travis said, sounding sharp. "Of course you're going to worry about her."

"What's the matter?" I asked. Why was he attacking me?

"When are you bringing your mother home?" he asked. "Wasn't that the point of you going over there?"

"Yes," I said. "Of course it is."

Seething silence; I could hear the anger in everything he wasn't saying. I felt massively steamed up myself. Didn't he know how hard this was? I thought about my mother leaving us so consciously; I didn't want to put Lucy and me in a vulnerable position with her again. She'd known what she was doing, leaving us. Instead, and lamely, I found myself offering up excuses for her.

"It's a little trickier than I'd first thought," I said. "Getting her to come home. She has a real life here. She's working, has a gardening business. And her neighbor . . ."

"Max."

"Yes. Max—Travis, I'm pretty sure Max is in love with her."

"Really? I thought you said he was really old." Travis sounded warm again, as if he wanted the chance to make up as much as I did.

"He's seventy-something. I know this sounds strange, but to me he's not old at all. In some ways, he's the youngest, most hopeful person I know."

"Does your mother know how he feels?"

"I don't think she has a clue."

"There's no other guy in her life?"

I thought of Gregorio, the way he practically draped himself over her as they worked on the moon gate. It had almost made me wish Lucy had held back on the calculations; I wanted the project to just go away. I didn't like the way it reminded me of my father, of their honeymoon in Bermuda, of when my parents had been trying to be happy.

"There's one," I said, "but he's more interested in her than she is in him. I hope, anyway."

"You don't like him?"

"No. I like Max. But she . . ." I'd been about to say, **She always throws what's good away. My**

father, my sister and me, our family. Now, possibly, she'd follow her pattern and choose Gregorio over Max.

"Maybe things with Max will work out," he said.

I didn't answer right away. I was really in a state; nothing felt right to me. If things with my mother and Max did work out, it might mean she would never leave Capri; instead of giving the idea of returning home to me and Lucy a chance, she might lock into staying right here.

"Maybe," I said.

"What about his grandson?"

"What about him?" I asked.

"What's his name again?"

"Rafe Gardiner."

"Is he behaving himself?"

"Yes," I said. "He seems fine."

"He's not too—what did you say the other day—**troubled**?"

"No," I said.

I held my phone, closed my eyes, thinking of how terribly I'd wanted to talk to Travis the last few days. If I'd gotten him that first night, I might have spilled the whole story—the hand-holding, the almost-embrace. But time had passed, and I'd been avoiding Rafe.

We had planned to go to Il Faraglioni on Monday, but I'd left a message with Max that I was helping my mother garden and had to cancel with Rafe. That was true: I helped her plant Renata and

Amanda's herb garden, partly as a way of keeping an eye on Gregorio. Now the idea of telling Travis the truth about something that hadn't gone anywhere seemed needlessly hurtful.

"He grew up with Ty," I said instead.

"Tyler Cooper?" Travis asked.

"Yes," I said. Maybe I was using Rafe's technique of dropping the familiar name, Travis's football teammate, hoping to defuse his suspicions.

"Are you okay?" he asked, my strategy going right over his head, obviously not working.

"I miss you," I said.

"Pell, I can hardly take how much I miss you. Even on the boat, when I knew you'd called. I listened to your message in my bunk, and it helped me stand the way I was feeling."

"What way?"

"Just aching," he said. "It seems that you've been gone forever, and there's still so much summer left."

"Maybe I should come home early," I said.

"I should say no," he said. "I should encourage you to stay. You're there for a good reason. But, Pell, I want to see you so badly."

"I feel the same way about you," I said. "You have no idea."

"This is hard," he said.

"It is," I said.

"We'd better say goodbye now. Or I'll take back the part about you staying. I want you near, Pell."

"I want to be near you," I said. "I will be, before long."

When I hung up the phone, all seemed to be set right. But I made the mistake of walking over to the window of my room. Early-evening light turned the air golden. My gaze swept from Monte Solaro out to sea, then down to the rock-strewn shore.

There was Rafe. Instead of scouring the tide line as usual, he was just sitting at the end of the dock, staring up the hill. Not gazing toward the villa, but at my mother's house. At my window.

It felt as if he was looking into my eyes.

~

Travis glanced at his watch. It was noon, which meant it was six p.m. in Italy. He'd just hung up from Pell, and wished he hadn't been so noble. There were night flights from JFK to Rome; he should know, he'd put her on one. His mouth was dry; he felt tense, as if he could explode, and he had to fight the urge to jump into his car and drive to the Alitalia terminal, put down all his savings for a ticket. If she couldn't come home yet, he could go to her.

Walking into the kitchen, he wondered why he felt so uneasy. Pell had said good things, reassured him that she was still there, still wanted him. But there was a lost feeling in her voice—and it wasn't like her to be so desperate about needing him to call right back. Part of what made them special was how confident they were in each other. Travis knew he was behaving; he had the worst sense that the person Pell was doubting was herself. He wondered how much Rafe had to do with it.

Who had a name like "Rafe" anyway?

He stood by the refrigerator, looking for something to eat. His appetite was gone—partly from missing Pell, and also from the fact that he couldn't get the smell of fish off him. No matter how long he stood in the shower, he still reeked of cod. Even now, he lifted his wrist and smelled it.

Laughter behind him; he turned, and saw Lucy sitting at the table, legs drawn up as she bent over her notebook.

"What's so funny?" he asked.

"You," she said.

"Why, because I smell like a haddock?"

"Kind of," she said.

"Don't tell your sister," he said. "She might not want to come home to me."

"Ha," Lucy said. "That'll be the day."

"My mother said you talked to Pell the other day," he said.

"Every few days," Lucy said. "But yeah. She and my mother called."

"And you think her visit is going well?"

"Yes, except for the fact you're not there."

That made Travis grin. "Beck has good taste in best friends," he said.

"Thank you," Lucy said, bowing from the waist even as she sat scrunched at the table.

Beck entered the kitchen, carrying a stack of library books. Travis spied the titles, all having to do with Japanese and Chinese gardens.

"Okay, that's weird even for you, Beckster," he said. "Chinese gardens?"

"Lucy's mother needed specifications for a moon gate," Beck said. "We figured that the formula wasn't enough, and we should design the most spectacular moon gate ever seen."

"Moon gate?" Travis asked.

"Yeah," Lucy said. "When Pell called the other day, I gave her the quick answer. But did you know that moon gates are the most romantic structures ever built? They are perfectly round, reflecting the shape of the full moon. If two people walk through holding hands, they will have everlasting happiness."

"My kind of structure," Beck said. "Mathematical perfection, and scientifically guaranteed good fortune."

"You two are crazy," Travis said. "Brilliant, but nuts."

"Thank you," Beck and Lucy said, laughing as they returned to their books and drawings. Travis stared at the pages, thinking of Pell asking Lucy for the formula. Why hadn't she mentioned it to him?

It probably wasn't a big deal. But as he stood there in his family's small kitchen, he found himself thinking of Pell and Rafe, really hoping that she stayed as far away from the moon gate and Max's grandson as possible.

Thirteen

Over the next few weeks, Lyra was surprised to notice Pell sticking close to her. They went to the flower market together, walking along the tented rows, finding white flowers for the moon garden: artemisia, geraniums, impatiens, silver thyme, sage, white lavender, clematis, phlox, astilbe, and Echinacea "White Swan." After work they'd stop for coffee at the Gran Caffé degli Artisti, sitting under red umbrellas and passing late afternoons in the Piazzetta.

They checked on Lucy. Ever since the night Lyra had "tucked her in" over the phone, Lucy's sleep had improved. But insomnia seemed to have crossed the Atlantic, settled on Capri. At night neither Lyra nor Pell seemed able to sleep. Lyra would walk onto the terrace, find her daughter staring at the stars through the telescope.

"What are you doing?" Lyra had asked the night before.

"Plotting a course for home," Pell had answered.

"You want to leave?" Lyra had asked.

"There are people I love at home," Pell had replied. Lyra had felt her words like a slap across the face, then Pell continued, "But there's someone I love here too. And we're not done yet."

"No, we're not," Lyra had said, her heart splitting open and breaking, both at the same time. She'd wanted to deepen the moment, sit down on the settees and draw up their feet, talk through the night. She'd wanted to right the hurt she'd caused the other day, expand on what she had said, and heal the divide between them. But Pell stared at her for another long minute, then drifted down the loggia toward her room without another word, almost like a sleepwalker.

Today they strolled through the crumbling ruins of the Villa Jovis, along paths lined with oleanders and fig trees. The feeling that Pell was preoccupied stuck with Lyra. Her daughter seemed lost in thought as they meandered through antiquated remains of stone walls, vast rooms, baths, kitchens, temple, spread across terraces on the precipitous hillside.

Lyra watched Pell examine the floor's herringbone pattern, still intact after two thousand years. They stood near the cliff edge, looking into the blue water where some said Tiberius had thrown his enemies over.

"Tiberius's Leap," Pell said, watching a falcon glide past. "John Harriman talked about it that night we all had dinner at Max's."

"I remember," Lyra said. They stood well behind the row of people inching as close as possible to the edge. On this island of cliffs and drops, Lyra always kept a safe distance, remembering how close she once came. She saw Pell doing the same.

"Rafe said John was wrong. That Tiberius never did what they said—he never sacrificed people here."

"There are different views on that," Lyra said as they turned away. "I haven't seen you with Rafe lately, or heard you mention him."

"I've wanted to be with you," Pell said. But Lyra sensed it was more than that. Had Rafe offended her, scared her, done something to push her away? Lyra wouldn't be surprised and, in fact, hoped that it was true.

"He's done a lot of damage," Lyra said. "Has he upset you?"

"I don't know him well enough for him to upset me," Pell said, with chilly elegance that reminded Lyra of her mother. At the same time, she saw Pell trying to contain emotion that Edith Nicholson would never have, much less show.

"What's wrong?" Lyra asked. "You've seemed so distant. It started the day I tried to tell you about why I . . ." She'd been about to say "left."

"I don't know," Pell said, interrupting her. Bees

buzzed in jasmine cascading from a crumbling wall. "I came here for a reason. This is a huge thing for me, seeing you. But we're acting as if it's a vacation. Going to cafés, visiting tourist sites."

"Pell, what should we do? You've helped me with work—I'm so appreciative. You have a great eye, and you've picked out wonderful flowers for Renata and Amanda's garden. You got Lucy and her friend Beck to draw such beautiful plans for the moon gate. I'm blown away, and once the project is finished, I'm going to frame the drawings. Even Gregorio said—"

"Gregorio," Pell blurted out. "Who cares about him? Why are you even giving him the time of day?"

Lyra turned to her, shocked. They'd wandered away from the main ruins, standing near the old vaulted walls said to be the remnants of an ancient **Specularium**—observatory—overgrown with vines and wildflowers. Lyra had been saving this part for last, wanting to share with her daughter a memory of their own private observatory. Now she could only stare at her daughter, speechless.

Pell started to walk away, and Lyra grabbed her shoulder.

"What are you talking about?" she asked. "What about Gregorio?"

"The way you flirt with him. Those comments about your 'beautiful daughters' up at the house the other night. It makes me sick! To even think of you hanging out with a guy like him, when Max is around. And when you left someone like Dad!"

"Pell, I'm not 'hanging out' with him. I hired him to do a job. That's it. There's no comparison between him and your dad. I loved Taylor."

"No, you didn't," Pell said.

"You don't know," Lyra said. She felt hot and dizzy. Old feelings she'd been suppressing for years came close to the surface, and she forced them down again. If she got started on this, how would it end?

"What I know is that you were never happy. He tried so hard, and you threw it in his face. The Midwest wasn't good enough for you, our house wasn't big enough, Lucy and I were messy, boring, dumb little children, and Dad couldn't keep you. You said it yourself, you didn't like being a mother!"

"Pell, why are you doing this?" Lyra said. "None of those things is true. Not one. I was troubled, depressed, so confused. It had nothing to do with you and Lucy, except that I worried I couldn't take good enough care of you."

"Good enough," Pell said. "Do you know how little it would have taken for you to be that? All we needed was **you**. You at home with us. We needed you to love us, hug us. Color with us, like you always did. How hard was that?"

The words ripped out of Pell with such anger, as if she was unable to hold it inside, almost as if she was a child again, without the defenses of adulthood. Lyra stepped toward her, saw her shaking. She hesitated, not knowing whether Pell would push her away. But her maternal instincts took over, and she slowly put her arms around her daughter.

"Pell," she said.

"He was so good," Pell said.

"I know he was," Lyra said. "He loved you both more than anything. And he did everything for you. . . ."

"He did a lot," Pell said. "But so did you."

Did Pell really feel that way, or was this a revisionist memory? Lyra remembered some days when she couldn't get out of bed. Sleep would hold her down, just like a stone on a grave. Or if it let her go enough to slog out from under the covers, make a showing downstairs for the kids, she'd still be in her nightgown, hair messy and dirty, unable to smile or bring light into her eyes.

Taylor would work from morning till night at the law firm. Sometimes he'd come home during the day, to check on Lyra. Once, when Miss Miller had taken the girls to the park, he'd walked in on Lyra in her flannel nightshirt sitting on the couch, eating ice cream out of the container, watching **Days of Our Lives.** The look of confusion and disgust on his face came back to her now.

Then, later, their last winter together, Lyra had stopped sleeping altogether. The days were stitched together, sleepless nights, thoughts racing. She'd wander the house, standing by her children's beds, staring at them, wondering about their dreams.

"What did I do for you?" Lyra asked. "One good thing that helped you?"

"You loved us," Pell said.

"But your father . . ." Lyra began.

"No one hugged better than you," Pell said, nestling into Lyra's embrace now. "No one."

"Really?"

"Yes. And no one else made up a country with me. You were the only person I wanted to do that with."

"Dorset was ours," Lyra said. She pictured the map she and Pell had drawn, decorated with Lucy's foil stars. Pell seemed so raw, as if thrown back in time, emotions and flashes of the past sparking up. How long would it be before she remembered the river?

"Did you mean what you said last night?" Lyra asked. "About wanting to go home?"

"I don't know," Pell said. "I miss Lucy and Travis."

"Your boyfriend?"

Pell nodded. Lyra wasn't sure what she felt. She was glad Pell had someone else, so she wouldn't get taken in by Rafe. But she also wanted to warn her daughter against falling in love too completely, too soon. There were so many ways a young woman could block herself from reaching her full potential, keep from understanding the complexities of her own heart.

"There's so much I want to say to you," Lyra said. "Be careful."

Pell laughed softly.

"What's so funny?"

"You said that about Rafe. Now you're saying it about Travis. Do you want me to stay away from all men?"

"When I was your age, my mother was planning my wedding. It didn't matter that I hadn't yet told her about your father. She had generic, all-purpose ideas about me that involved nothing more than my being a debutante, then a bride."

"That won't happen to me or Lucy," Pell said. "Trust me."

"You say that now," Lyra said. "But love can take over very fast."

"With Dad?"

"Yes, but I was too young, and it was too soon. I needed to work things out first—to see what I could have become on my own. There are lines I think about: 'If you bring forth what is within you, what you bring forth will save you. If you do not bring forth what is within you, what you do not bring forth will destroy you.'"

"What didn't you bring forth?"

"I needed to find out who I was," Lyra said.

"And have you?" Pell asked, wheeling around, her eyes flashing.

"I think maybe I have."

"You couldn't have done that at home, with us?"

"This is very hard to say, Pell," Lyra began. "I was trying to escape my mother's plans for me, and I did that, partly, by marrying your father. I didn't give us a chance to find out if we were real, because I wasn't sure that I was real. I was a wreck, don't you remember?"

Pell didn't reply. Her blue eyes blazing, she took a step closer to Lyra. "Would you come back with me?"

Lyra had been waiting for the question to be asked again. Now it had, and she couldn't bear to answer.

Pell grabbed her wrist. "To Newport. Since you've done your soul-searching, would you come back and be a mother to me and Lucy?"

"I've made a life here," Lyra said, softly and slowly. "It includes you. You're here now, and I hope you'll come back to Capri over and over. You and Lucy, whenever you want."

Pell stared down the cliff, anguish in her eyes, as if Lyra had just rejected her all over again. Lyra wanted to hold her again, but Pell's posture warned her off.

"That's not the same as living with us," Pell said. "Is it? That nice warm glow you gave Lucy over the telephone. Do you think it's enough? And how about when I go to college? Am I supposed to give that up, to stay in Newport and take care of my sister? We need you, we always have. But you left us once, so how can I think it would ever be different?"

They stood on the high rocks of Tiberius's ruined observatory. Lyra's sentimental desire to tell Pell the sweet story of the engraving on the brass telescope dissolved.

"Do you really think I **just** walked away from you?" Lyra asked. She felt the truth surging up. "That it was that easy?"

"You did walk away. It's a fact. I don't have to think it."

"Pell," Lyra said, "I was sick. I told you, the winter before I left home, I tried to kill myself."

Pell stared, flushing red. "That's one thing Dad never talked about. But part of me always knew."

"The roads were icy," Lyra said. "I drove at night to the Detroit River. I brought the telescope so we could look at the stars. It's a miracle I didn't drive the car off the road, even before getting to the river. But I didn't. I parked right in the middle of the bridge, left the car running, set up the telescope. I wanted us to have one last look at the stars."

"Us?"

"I took you with me," Lyra said.

~

It was too hard to take, hearing it head-on. It shocks me to realize how life and memory work. A word here, a flash there, and suddenly the layer of grass is peeled back, a mound of earth is removed, and you're staring into the grave at the skull of what you loved. The bones had always been there; you just hadn't known where to look. Or perhaps you hadn't been brave enough.

I shivered that hot summer day; how spectacular the symbolism, standing on ancient ruins, an observatory no less. Because suddenly my memory spoke from exactly where I'd buried it. It showed me a little girl, arms around her trembling mother's neck, thinking they were about to look at the stars, feeling, instead, all attention drawn below, to the wicked frozen river. I couldn't actually remember this, but it was there, down in the depths. All I had to do was go in after it.

I backed away from my mother, then turned and pushed through a crowd of tourists walking up the path. I felt dizzy, surrounded by all the sightseers, and beauty, and history. My own history. Tearing through Tiberius's grounds, I had a stitch in my side, and I could hardly catch a breath. I stopped near the edge of the cliff, heard people talking, a cluster of American college-aged kids.

"Pushed them off, right here," one boy said, hands on his girlfriend's waist.

"Don't," she squealed, wrenching away.

"You think he just shoved them?" another boy asked. "They fucked up, he marched them to the edge and tossed them?"

"Man, I'd fight," the first boy said. "Someone tried to do that to me. Long way down."

"Very long way down," his girlfriend said, and now it was her turn to give him a pretend shove.

"Whoa," he said, turning to hug her.

I kept walking, my heart pounding. I thought of what Rafe had said at Max's that first dinner: that Tiberius had been misunderstood, vilified. He hadn't killed people here, thrown them to their deaths. "Tiberius's Leap" was just a marketing tool, invented to create a stir. Tiberius had come here to contemplate, that's all.

People aren't as bad as others want them to be. That is what I told myself. My mother had just come out and said she'd tried to kill herself. That had been a great fear of mine, one of the bad ones. I'd asked my father, Dr. Robertson, even Lucy if they'd thought she was suicidal. What a word: **suicidal.** It sounds clean and scientific. It's just a word. But hearing it from my mother, knowing she felt that pain.

Mom, what happened? How badly did it hurt for you to get to that point? The part I couldn't bear was what she'd said next: **I took you with me.** What did that mean? Was she bad? Was she one of the terrible mothers you read about? They kill themselves, kill their children.

Down in the depths: memory, memory. Should I go for it? Should I look deeper? I don't want to. I want to go back to what I don't know. But it's there, staring up at me, the skeleton of what happened that night.

I suddenly felt like a little girl, as if I'd lost years. I stumbled along, wanting my mother. I needed her to take care of me. I wanted her. Could she please tell me this new/old memory was wrong, that I had misunderstood, that these fragments of night and stars and the river were just a bad dream?

Please tell me I'm wrong, I thought as I turned to go back to the observatory. **Please just say you loved me then and you love me now and let's go home. You're a good person, a good person, no matter what you're a good person.** I walked back the way I'd come, and saw my mother there, waiting. She hadn't moved. She looked pale, and I knew.

I hadn't been wrong.

~

Lyra's heart was racing as she watched Pell approach. If she could have erased this moment, she would have: from the past, where it had started. But she had seen memory dawning on her daughter's face. Pell had started to put it together. Blue sky surrounded them; they stood in the ruined observatory, on the edge of Capri, floating above the azure sea.

"Are you okay?" Lyra asked.

"Mom, you're good," Pell said. Her voice was high, imploring; she sounded six years old.

Why had she said that? Lyra gazed at her, stricken, wanting to understand; she reached for Pell, but her daughter inched away.

"Tell me the rest," Pell said.

"Pell, are you sure?"

"You took me with you?" Pell asked. "To kill yourself?"

Lyra's eyes flooded with tears. "I couldn't leave you behind," she said. Pell let out a soft cry, covered her mouth.

They had been together on the bridge, Lyra holding Pell. They'd looked through the telescope, and Pell had named the stars. The river was frozen in parts, but there was a turbulent stretch under the bridge, rushing white water.

"You weren't going to kill us both," Pell said. It was a strong statement, as if she was sure of something Lyra never had been.

Even now, Lyra couldn't be certain. She wanted to affirm Pell, say of course she never would have. She had left the car running to keep it warm; she told herself she would have placed Pell inside, bundled her with a blanket, kept the window cracked open for fresh air, to save her from carbon monoxide. But Lyra had long been haunted by memories of those minutes at the bridge's rail, grasping her daughter and hearing the call of the rough water down below.

"Your father found us," she said. "I'd phoned him at the office, and something in my voice . . . I had mentioned the bridge to him once, as a place to end my life. He drove straight there, as if he knew where I was going."

"Or as if you **wanted** him to know," Pell said. "You wanted him to stop you."

Lyra stared at her. "Maybe . . . but it doesn't matter. He took us both home. I never even knew what happened to my car; I went straight to the hospital, and was there for months."

"And you came home, and we drew our map, and you left," Pell said.

"Yes," she said.

"I didn't want you to leave," Pell said, her voice low.

"Pell," Lyra said, reaching for her. "I left because . . . he wasn't sure—I wasn't sure—of what I might have done."

"But you didn't do it!" Pell said. "You stopped yourself!"

"Your father got there in time," Lyra said. "But if there was a next time—that's why I had to move away; he was afraid—I was afraid—that it could happen again."

"Why do you keep saying 'he'?" Pell asked.

"I was the one," Lyra said. "Who decided I had to leave. Because what if I tried again? And what if I couldn't keep myself from succeeding, from killing myself?"

"No, you wouldn't have," Pell said stubbornly.

"He was afraid," Lyra said, making herself be direct, look straight into Pell's cornflower blue eyes. "So I had to leave."

"'He'?" Pell asked. "You're saying it again! I mean, I'm sure Dad was worried about you, and wanted to make sure you were okay, but don't say it in relation to your leaving."

Lyra was sweating. She shook her head hard; why was she making this mistake? Her heart was racing as she saw Pell's expression change. The truth was right here on the cliff with them.

"You would have been fine," Pell said. "You learned an awful lesson. Besides, you didn't really want to kill yourself in the first place. Because you gave Dad whatever hint he needed to stop you—to get to the bridge and save you."

"I think he was most worried about you," Lyra said quietly. "That I could hurt you."

"No, you wouldn't have! He had to know that!"

"It's so complicated," Lyra said, seeing Pell's panic. "Being that depressed is like having the lights turned out. You can't see anything, trust your reactions. The despair is total. So even though the hospital helped me, I can't blame your father for not trusting that I'd never try it again."

"My father?"

"I told him that suicide was no longer an option.

That I was certain I'd never hurt you. Ever. But he wasn't so sure."

"Don't tell me this," Pell said, starting to pace. "It can't be true, it can't. I won't believe you."

"Okay, Pell," Lyra said. She would have stopped there. No more words had to be spoken. But knowledge is a boulder, and once it's dislodged, nothing can wedge it back into the mountainside, keep it from rolling down the slope, gaining speed. Staring into Pell's eyes, Lyra saw that she knew.

"He's the reason?" Pell asked, planting her feet and facing Lyra.

"We talked about it," Lyra said, wanting to start slow.

"Tell me!" Pell shrieked.

"I swore to him I was fine; my doctor did as well. But he couldn't take the chance. He loved you so much, and he was afraid of what I'd done, taking you to the river. What I might do again."

They stood alone in the old observatory, no one else around, water and sky gleaming as far as they could see, the blue crisscrossed by boat wakes and jet trails. "You're our mother, he knew we needed you! And he loved you too," Pell said. "So much, more than you can imagine."

"He did love me," Lyra said. "But he loved you more, don't you see? He couldn't take the chance."

"Dad," Pell said, turning away. And Lyra knew that Pell was speaking to her father. Addressing Taylor, asking him how he could have done it. Lyra wanted to hold their daughter, try to explain how it had been, how Taylor's feelings had changed, how Lyra had made him worry enough to want her to leave.

Lyra reached out, but Pell gave a violent twist and pulled away. She began to walk fast, then run. She tore down the path, out of sight. Lyra felt as if she'd just stabbed Pell, taken everything from her. She'd ruined the most important illusion of all: that her father was perfect, that he wouldn't have sent her mother away. Lyra sank down on the spot from where Tiberius had once gazed at the stars, and cried for what she'd just done to her daughter.

~

The river, the stars, the river, the stars.

My father in his hospital bed. **She never would have done it, she never would have done it.**

He was trying to tell me, as he was dying, the truth about my mother. Our whole family story contained in those few words. My mother had taken me to the river to see the stars that frozen night. I remembered now. Freezing cold, hands aching, the brass telescope as cold as if it were made of ice. My mother's breath on my ear as she'd pointed up at the stars.

"Capella, Pollux, Vega, never forget," she'd said.

"Which one is which?" I'd asked. I was shivering, but in her arms I didn't care.

"The three stars closest together," she'd said. "Even when they're not."

I'd laughed because what she'd said was a riddle. There were so many stars in the sky, and some looked so close, nearly touching one another. The Milky Way was a film of white sparks. The river tore beneath the high bridge, and even in the dark I could see chunks of white ice swirling in violent whirlpools, but I wasn't afraid. My mother was holding me.

Headlights came toward us, and my father got out of the car. He came so slowly, not saying a word, white breath puffing from his mouth. I remember my mother starting to cry. That scared me—not the river, not the ice, not the strangeness of being on a bridge on a winter night. Her tears at the sight of my father.

"I'm sorry, Taylor," she said.

"Give her to me," he said.

"I never would have . . ."

She never would have what? I wanted to know, but my father rushed at us then, yanked me out of her arms. He carried me roughly—no kisses, no hugs—to his car, buckled me into the back seat without a word, as if I'd done something wrong. I started to cry myself, upset with the way he was acting. Through hot, blurry tears, I saw him run back to my mother, grab her in both arms.

My father wrestled her into the car, and she

howled. Oh, God, that sound. **You're killing me, killing me, I'm dying.** In school we studied Inuit religion, native people who believe behind every human face is a wild animal. You might have a fox inside you, or a wolverine, or a mouse. That night my mother had a wolf inside her. Wild, unbridled, filled with terror and hunger. The sound was not human.

That's where the memory stops. I know he must have driven us home. I know for certain she went to McLean Hospital in Belmont, Massachusetts, and stayed for several months. My father never once discussed the bridge, or what almost happened there. He and Dr. Robertson helped me deal with my mother's leaving. But he never told me—or my doctor, as far as I know—that he believed my mother had intended to kill herself and me that icy cold night.

~

When I returned home from the strange and haunted ruins of Villa Jovis, from that devastated observatory, I tore off my sweaty shirt—I'd just run a mile in the heat—and put on a new one.

I grabbed my cell phone and my wallet, passport, and return airline ticket. I jammed them and a few clothes into my backpack. I didn't want to be there when my mother returned.

I dashed out the door and straight down the

steep, shady stairs toward the beach. The impulse felt primal.

Halfway down the stairs I stopped, sat on a step. My head was spinning, my throat raw from emotion. I was desperate to talk to someone. I dialed Lucy first. I wanted to tell her what had just happened, what I'd just learned. But the second she answered, I hung up. The sound of her voice was so dear, and she loved our father so much, I couldn't bear the idea of telling her the horrible truth.

I sat there on the cool stone step, shaded by pines and cypress trees, hiding in the shadows. I stared at my phone, wanting to call Travis, hear his voice, tell him I was coming home. But that didn't seem right either. I had a huge, cosmic rock in my chest, and to get it out, I needed blood family. I dialed my grandmother.

It was early in Newport, barely dawn. Her maid, Heloise, answered, and said my grandmother was still asleep.

"Wake her up, please," I said.

"Miss Pell, you know your grandmother doesn't like to be disturbed before—"

"Get her, Heloise. Right now."

Sometimes, when necessary, I can be not only persuasive, but quite imposing. It comes naturally, from spending the years immediately following my father's death with Edith Nicholson. Several minutes later, I heard her voice on the line.

"What is it, Pell?" she asked. "I'm very cross with you, waking me—"

"My father told my mother to leave?" I asked.

"What nonsense is this? Do you have any idea what time—"

"Tell me right now, Grandmother. Did my mother leave us because my father kicked her out?"

The sound of bedclothes rustling. I could almost see her slipping off her black satin eye mask, rearranging pillows, pushing back her summer-weight monogrammed coverlet.

"There was no 'kicking out,'" she said, as if I'd just used objectionable language. "He simply needed to find a solution based on your welfare. He was in a dreadful dilemma; she really left him no choice."

"Then it's true? It was his decision, not hers?"

"Lyra is my daughter," my grandmother said. "It pains me unutterably to see the absolute mess she has made of her life. From the day she married your father and moved to Michigan, I knew it was a terrible mistake."

That meant I was a mistake. "Grandmother . . . ," I began, staring out at the menacing silhouette of Mount Vesuvius, feeling volcanic.

"She was fragile. Emotionally and mentally. Your father told me what she did—he described every detail."

"She told him she wanted to kill me too?"

"No," she said, her tone somber. "Only herself. But she took you with her. Your father discovered her standing with you on the very edge of the tallest bridge, over an absolutely treacherous beat of river." She fell silent.

"So when she returned from the hospital, he was afraid she might try again. And he told her to leave?" I asked.

"It was a discussion between them. However, ultimately, yes. He did."

"But she must have been better. The hospital wouldn't have let her out if they'd thought she was a danger to herself or us."

"Your father couldn't take that chance."

I took that in. My father, whom I'd loved and trusted my whole life, had sent my mother away. He'd been **the grownups**. He'd been judge and jury, and neither she nor Lucy and I had had any recourse. Had he wrestled with the decision during the months she was in the hospital? Lucy and I had been so worried about her, missed her so much, we'd had fevers. He had comforted us. I pictured him sitting on the edge of my bed, reading **The Jungle Book** to us. His voice had been so calm. Was he, even then, thinking that he didn't want her home?

The grownups decided.

"How could he have let us think **she** wanted

to leave?" I asked my grandmother. "Why did he trick us?"

"He didn't, Pell," my grandmother said. "I don't know what your mother told you, but this was a shared decision. He merely suggested it, quite strongly, I'll grant you, as a solution. She was desperate; you're too young to understand how frightening it was to see her falling apart. He was terrified for you and Lucy."

"You let us think she had affairs."

"Darling, would you rather have known your mother nearly took your life?"

How could I even answer that? I felt scalding emotion starting in my toes; I really was a volcano. Hot fury overtook me; I pictured my grandmother in her perfect bed in her limestone mansion, and knew that she had helped my father hide every important truth from me and Lucy. He was dead, and I'd never get to confront him. I had enough rage for everyone.

"I was so alarmed for Lyra and you. So afraid for her health, and so ashamed of what the truth could do if it got out. I have never wanted to speak of this with you or anyone."

"Why not?" I asked. "Were you really afraid it would hurt us? Or just make you look bad to your friends?"

"Do not speak to me that way, Pell. I love you and Lucy. You can't doubt that, I won't have it!" my grandmother said in her most imperious and unshakable tone, and I didn't stop to listen. I knew that what she said and what was true were two different things.

"Our family is in pieces," I said.

"Darling, Lyra wasn't meant to be a mother," she said.

My mother wasn't meant to be a mother. Oh, wow. Those words would ring in my ears for a long time. They weren't unlike what she'd told me herself, that day at the moon gate. I just hadn't wanted to hear them.

I ended the call. My cell phone instantly rang—it was Lucy ringing me back, after missing my last call. I didn't answer it. I picked up my backpack, slung it over my shoulder, and ran down the rest of the stairs toward the rock beach.

Rafe stood by the boathouse, paintbrush in hand. He wore bathing trunks, no shirt, and he didn't see me right away; I watched him rinsing out the whitewash, cleaning the brush. When he was done, I stepped out from the shadows of pines growing on the hillside. My eyes were stinging, my mouth half open. I felt like a zombie, and all I knew was that I had to escape.

"Hey," he said. "Where've you been? I haven't seen you in a while."

"Il Faraglioni," I said. "Can you take me there?" I wanted to see the seahorses before I left.

"The stone arch? Sure," he said.

"And then to Sorrento?" I asked.

"Why, you taking off?" he asked, laughing.

"Yes," I said. I didn't smile.

His smile immediately disappeared. He nodded, finished rinsing his paintbrush. He pulled a shirt on.

"Let's go," he said.

Fourteen

Lyra ran as fast as she could, but Pell had made it home first. With a stitch in her side, running down the winding road, Lyra wished they'd taken the car to the Villa Jovis, so she could be home waiting for her daughter, so she could greet her and hug her and try to explain. As it was, she tore into the house, looking on the terrace, through the loggia, into Pell's room. Pell had been here—the T-shirt she'd been wearing earlier lay on the bed.

Sinking down, Lyra sat beside it. She held the shirt in her hands. It was soaking with sweat. Lyra spread it out on her knees, straightening it out: green cotton, with **Newport Academy** in white. Lyra traced the letters with one finger. She lifted the shirt, pressed it to her face.

She wished she could tell herself that everything would be okay. She wanted to reassure herself she'd done no harm, but she knew that wasn't the case. When she'd gone away ten years ago, she'd left her daughters to their father's love and protection.

They'd needed to idolize him, to make up for the fact their mother was gone. Today, in the ruins of a heavenly observatory, she'd ripped Taylor to shreds.

She'd finally told Pell the truth, but like all truths, it was far from black and white. This one, the story of what happened to their family, was filled with shadows, reflections, mirages, shades of gray. For a long time, Lyra had wanted to make Taylor the bad guy. He had told her he thought she should leave. Lyra had finally revealed that to Pell, but what she'd held back was the relief she'd felt at Taylor's suggestion.

McLean Hospital, winter, ten years ago.

To send Lyra there, Taylor had had to start by taking her to the local ER. She'd been admitted, kept seventy-two hours for a psych evaluation. She'd felt she'd stumbled into hell. The woman in the next bed had been brought in from the county prison. Serving a sentence for killing her boyfriend, she'd attempted suicide by swallowing bleach. Her sister, visiting, told Lyra the boyfriend had molested the woman's daughter; the daughter was now strung out on drugs.

After three days there, with a referral to McLean, a private hospital in Belmont, Massachusetts, Lyra had climbed into Taylor's car. He drove her to Detroit Metro Airport.

Just as if she'd been a child plotting to escape, slip out of the snare, he'd shepherded her through the airport, staying right by her side, waiting until her plane took off. He would have accompanied her all the way to McLean, but the girls needed him too much. Lyra remembered how pale he looked, how hollow his hazel eyes were as they said goodbye.

They'd embraced just outside airport security. She'd held him so tight, and she was so afraid. Not because of what she'd seen at the hospital, but because of what lay ahead for her and her family.

"I don't want to go," she'd said.

"Lyra, you have to get better," he'd said.

"I will. I promise. I'll work on it here, with you and the girls. I want to be with you."

"You wanted to **die,**" he'd said, tears brimming. "Three days ago, **that's** what you wanted."

"It was a mistake," she'd wept. "I didn't mean it."

"You were on the bridge," he'd said. "You were ready. And you had Pell with you."

"I never would have hurt her. Never!"

"Then what, Lyra? You'd have jumped off the bridge right in front of her?"

"No, Taylor!" But that had been Lyra's plan—as much as she'd had any idea at all. She loved Pell so much, had been unable to say goodbye at the house, before leaving for the bridge. Lucy was asleep, but Pell had still been awake. She had asked where Lyra was going, if she could come too, and Lyra had been unable to rip herself away. She'd let Pell into the car, and they'd driven off.

"You weren't in your right mind," Taylor had said, holding her, stroking her hair.

"I want to go home now," Lyra had said. "Make sure Pell is fine."

"She is fine," Taylor had assured her. "She'll be even better once you get well."

Lyra had sobbed at that, clutching Taylor in the middle of the airport. This was the same place she'd flown into their senior year of college, to be with him at his parents' funeral. She'd had so much strength for him then; how could she have gotten to this point?

They'd called her flight, and she had to leave. Taylor had stood there, right outside security. Her last sight of him before boarding the plane had been of him standing tall, watching her go. She knew he'd been guarding against her changing her mind, not getting on the flight.

The flight had been bumpy, through turbulent air from storms dumping snow below. The plane had circled Boston's Logan Airport for an hour, waiting to land. Lyra had sat in seat 1a, first row of first class, praying they'd have to turn back. She needed to see Pell; her mind raced with words to say, loving reassurances, to set things straight with her. But eventually the plane touched down, and a driver sent by the hospital met Lyra. She'd felt like a prisoner—seen off by her husband, greeted by hospital personnel, no chance to get lost or hurt herself.

A black town car drove her into the snowy Massachusetts countryside. She had grown up in New

England. The landscape felt like home. Except, instead of going to her mother's house, she was taken to a private psychiatric hospital.

Intake, medical exam, then an escort from one building to another. She'd be staying in Proctor. It looked stately from the outside; with red brick Jacobean Revival architecture, roof peaks, gables, decorative wrought-iron balconies, chimneys, white brick trim, it could almost have been a Newport mansion.

They took her to Proctor Two, a locked unit. No more Newport mansion. This was a hospital. There were some gracious old rooms with curved walls and ornate molding, a place to be elegantly insane, heavy mesh on the windows, no mirrors on the walls, checks every five minutes—even through the night, while Lyra lay in bed, a nurse would poke her head in, making sure Lyra hadn't killed herself.

Lyra was high risk. In spite of what she'd told Taylor, she still wanted to die. Her mind raced with ways to accomplish that: get to the roof, throw herself off. She felt it in her bones, a quivering, jelly-like shimmer, discomfort down to her marrow, a feeling that she had to end things, make the agony stop. Those first weeks, she felt she was being boiled alive. She knew she'd done something terrible, taking Pell to the bridge.

The doctors were the best in the world. At the beginning she'd tell them how much she loved her children, then in the next breath sob that she wished her life was over. Over time she began to see that she actually felt worse now than before going to the bridge; half of her anguish came from what she'd done to Pell.

They wrote letters to each other. The high point of every day was mail call, when Lyra would pick up letters from Pell and Lucy. Taylor too. He never stopped writing to her, telling her he loved her, giving her encouragement for the shock therapy, telling her to work hard with her doctors and get better.

Twice a day, morning and night, the nurses would take Lyra and all the other crazy women on Proctor Two walking outside. The nurse was the only one with a lighter; patients were not allowed to have sharps or fire, so many of the patients would take the opportunity to have her light their cigarettes, and they'd walk around the "campus" in a big cloud of smoke.

The paths led all around the lovely, snow-covered grounds, through groves of maple, oak, and elm. On walks after dark, Lyra would look up through the bare branches at the constellations, missing Pell and Lucy more than ever. She'd stare at the stars, wondering if they were gazing out their window at the same sight.

The nurse was a little like a dog walker you see in cities, leading a pack of dogs to the nearest park. They were under constant watch and supervision. It began to sink in, one morning when the snow was starting to melt, run in rivulets down the winding drive, that Lyra had brought herself to this moment in life—being led through the lovely grounds on her way back to a locked ward, unable to make decisions for herself. That was the instant her real work began.

She'd gone at it with a vengeance. Art therapy: collages, drawings, clay sculptures. Two themes emerged: gardens and stars. She exalted in her creativity, happily amazed by how much she had inside. She explored her discoveries with Dr. Wilson, her psychiatrist. She told him that her father had once said, "Day and night were created for Lyra; sunlight because she loves gardens, and darkness so she can see the stars."

Her father told her she'd been named for a star: Alpha Lyrae, also known as Vega, of the constellation Lyra, the fifth-brightest star in the sky, the second-brightest in the northern celestial hemisphere, after Arcturus. She'd adored her father; a yachtsman, he'd navigated by the stars, given her a brass sextant and telescope for her first Christmas. She didn't know what had happened to the sextant, but she'd never part with the telescope.

Her earliest happy memories were of looking at the stars with her father. They'd walk around her family's estate, just as Lyra would do later with Pell and Lucy in the backyard, and he would point out all the heavenly bodies.

"There's Capella, in the constellation Auriga, the

eleventh-brightest star in the sky," he'd say. "And there's Pollux, an orange star, in the constellation Gemini."

Those were Lyra's nights; but because she also loved the day, she and her father would go strolling through the gardens. As a young boy, his nanny would take him to Roger Williams Park in Providence. She was Irish, and her father had been a gardener; she'd taught him to identify every tree, each plant. Lyra's father did that for her, testing her as they walked the gravel path through their formal gardens.

She'd told Dr. Wilson about wanting to be an astronomer and a gardener, and how her mother had laughed. "What you'll be, darling, is a wife."

She'd confided in him a secret not even Taylor knew. Like her father before her, she'd named her children after the stars: Pell was Cappella, and Lucy was Pollux. Her Pell, her Lulu, Lux, Lucy. Taylor had thought they were just nice names; he hadn't realized they were talismans holding Lyra together.

When she was ten, her father gave her a window box. It had been their secret. He'd shown her how to fill it with potting soil, let her plant seeds. The box couldn't go on any window in the main house; they'd set it out back, in the window of the garage. Lyra had tended it all that summer. The petunias she'd planted had bloomed, coral pink and white, more beautiful to Lyra than any of the English gardens on her family's grounds.

She'd gone to boarding school that fall. Her parents got divorced that winter, and the next summer, Lyra didn't touch the window box. Her father wasn't there to help her. He married a younger woman, and they spent summers in East Hampton. They eventually had two children, and Lyra hardly ever saw him after that. Her mother was on the party circuit, mostly in Newport, but sometimes going to Europe. She never took Lyra with her.

Dr. Wilson had helped Lyra see how all her dreams had been killed: her interest in astronomy and gardening put down by her mother, and with her father gone, no one to encourage her or help her. She told him about her graduation trip through Europe, how she'd visited Capri and felt she'd come home: the gentle sadness, the dangerous landscape, the deep sea and blue mists, had matched the way she felt inside. Sometimes she felt it calling to her.

She'd cried at that, the idea of a foreign island she'd visited only once feeling more like home than her beautiful house, her husband who loved her, her two children. The sense of isolation, the dream of life in a place where no one knew her, felt more comforting than the thought of returning to her comfortable home.

Dr. Wilson had been the one to show Lyra the lines from Thomas, about "bringing forth what is within you." She'd been so full of love and brightness and interest, but it had all been stopped, and that had nearly destroyed her.

"It's why I wanted to kill myself," she'd said, finally realizing. And that day, for the first time, she'd admitted the most dreadful thing she'd ever felt: maybe, deep down, she had wanted to take Pell off the bridge with her. Because life had felt so impossible and cruel, how could she escape and leave Pell behind? That reality had scared her more than anything she'd ever encountered in life.

By the time she left McLean, it was springtime. She asked to meet Taylor alone first, without the girls. He'd picked her up at the airport. She remembered the look on his face: so happy to see her. She'd melted at the sight of him, and they'd held each other.

They'd driven partway home, parked on a side street. She'd told him everything she could—about her past, and her parents, and her thwarted dreams, and how it had all led her to the bridge last winter. He'd listened, avid but cautious, watching her face so carefully.

"Are you sure you're ready to come home?" he asked.

"I want to say yes," she said.

"But you can't?"

"I was ready to leave the hospital," she said slowly. "I know there's nothing more they can do for me. I have to do it for myself."

"But you're better," he'd said. "Right? You're not

depressed anymore, you won't try to hurt yourself again?"

"Or Pell," she'd said.

"You're admitting it? You were going to take her with you?"

"I don't know," she'd said.

"But you're safe now. You won't ever feel that way again."

"I can't promise," she'd said. "I want to tell you it will never happen again. That it was a one-time slip, that I'll never want to hurt us again."

"If you can't promise that, why did they let you out?"

"Because they have faith in me."

"Lyra, you have to have it in yourself."

"Do you?" she'd asked.

She'd stared at him, watching the doubt in his eyes. The hospital had given her another chance at life—maybe her first real chance. She was thirty-two years old, and she'd never lived.

"How can I take care of our girls," she'd said, there in the car with Taylor, "when I've never learned to take care of myself?"

"You don't want to be with us?"

She squeezed her eyes tight. The words wouldn't come. She didn't know what she wanted. When Taylor spoke again, his voice was hard.

"I can't take the risk," he said.

"Of what?"

"Having it happen again. If you're not sure

you're ready, you can't be with the kids. I love you, Lyra. But I can't put Pell and Lucy in that kind of jeopardy."

"I know," she said, tears welling.

"You can go away for a while," he said. "And come back when you're really ready. When you know it's right, when you're sure you can be safe."

Sitting on Pell's bed now, her face buried in the green T-shirt, she thought of how the years had passed. She'd left Michigan a week after returning home—drawn the map with Pell, kissed her sleeping children, and flown away. She'd come to Capri, to make a home on these craggy white rocks, to find a way into her own heart. She'd always told herself she would return to her family.

She had kept waiting for that moment when she was sure she could be safe; later, she'd started building walls to keep them out. Love was too hard. She'd been unable to let herself try again, even with her kids. Now, ten years later, holding Pell's shirt, she shook.

Taylor had seen how it was going. The kids kept asking about her. He'd decided it couldn't go on, and he'd asked her for a divorce. By the time she signed the papers, it was almost a relief. No more expectations. No more hope.

Lyra had missed her kids' childhoods; she'd given up the chance to nurse Taylor through the end of his life. She'd been waiting to feel good, steady, right, told herself that as soon as she figured it all out, as soon as she could be guaranteed she was on an even keel for the rest of her life, she'd return. She'd been on hold, waiting for safety that didn't exist. Love was extreme, it was a precipice, the night sky, the deep blue sea.

Somehow Lyra hadn't figured that out, and now it was too late.

~

A sea breeze cooled the Villa Andria's terrace, and hummingbirds darted into the bougainvillea. Shade dappled the marble table. Max bent over his notebook, writing a scene in his play. Love came easily to his characters, as it had to him. But, as in real life, theater demanded obstacles, heartbreak. Could anyone really be happy? Against all odds, Max believed it was not only possible but necessary. Find love or be doomed. He'd staked his life and his body of work on it.

The doorbell rang, and a moment later Bella directed Lyra onto the terrace. She stood there, out of breath, hair disheveled. Max saw her panic and fear, felt instantly worried himself. He stood up, looked her in the eyes.

"What's wrong?" he asked.

"Pell," she said. "She's gone."

"Maybe she's out exploring the island," Max said.

"No," Lyra said. "She's taken her knapsack, her ticket home. Max, I've done something awful."

"What?" he asked.

"I told her about her father."

Max nodded, took a deep breath. He pulled back a chair from the table, eased Lyra into it. He remembered talks, when Christina was still present, about the marriage Lyra had left.

"Pell is intelligent," he said. "And she's old enough to hear the truth."

"She idolized him," Lyra said. "She's hung on to the fact that he's wonderful and I'm bad. **I'm** the one who left."

Max stared at her across the table. He reached over, tenderly brushed the hair out of her eyes. "Lyra, are you really so dense?" he asked.

She drew back, gazing at him.

"Pell came here to see you. She loves you."

"I don't deserve it," Lyra said. "I've been out of her life since she was six."

"Dear girl," Max said. "Christina used to say you were punishing yourself. You felt you'd let your daughters down, and you wouldn't let yourself feel their love. She said the reason you were such a brilliant gardener was because you poured so much love into the earth. She said you had so much to give, because you were holding it inside for your children."

"Christina was too kind to me," Lyra said. "And so are you."

"Someone has to be," Max said. "Because you certainly are not kind to yourself."

Lyra stared at him, as if trying to decide whether

to believe him or not. For the moment, the jury was out. She rose, pacing the terrace. "None of this matters now," she said. "Until I find Pell. Max, I'm worried that she's heading for Rome, to fly home. She's done with me."

"Have you tried to call her?" Max asked.

"Her cell phone is turned off," Lyra said. "It went straight to voicemail."

Max closed his notebook, pushed back his chair. He went to the house phone, dialed the boathouse. Rafe had been restless lately, and Max had been concerned. But he knew no one had a better heart than his grandson; there wasn't a soul who knew the island more, and once Max told him that Pell was upset and had wandered off, Rafe would be happy to help find her.

But the telephone down below just rang and rang. Max heard the bell echoing up the hillside. The distant sound drew him to the edge of the terrace. He scanned the rock ledges, all along the shoreline. Perhaps Rafe was dutifully patrolling the tide line, saving starfish and other stranded creatures.

And then Max saw: the boat was gone. He replaced the receiver in the cradle, frowning as he stared at the dock. Would Pell have gone to Rafe, asked him to take her to the mainland? He wanted to reassure Lyra, tell her he knew she was wrong about Pell leaving without even saying goodbye to her mother. His heart told him the Pell he had already come to know and love would never do that.

But hurt children could do unexpected and damaging things. He thought of Rafe, all the anguish he'd caused himself and their family. He pictured Christina lying in the grass, where she'd fallen, after Rafe had left her alone. Unintended, horrible consequences of a young man's pain and mistakes. When he turned to meet Lyra's eyes, he wanted to tell her with certainty that all would be well. But she saw the doubt on his face, and she crumpled.

Max went to her. Lyra wept, and he rocked her with all the love he had, knowing he would do anything for her, set the world straight, help her begin again.

Fifteen

Rafe steered the boat around the mountainous island, Pell sitting in the bow. She wasn't talking. Something about the way she held herself made her seem breakable, so he drove slowly, and it took a long time to reach the rock islands. They passed the fleet of small tourist boats heading for the grottoes. He saw Arturo, who saluted and grinned. Rafe didn't even acknowledge him.

Salt spray blew into their faces; Pell didn't duck or flinch, just stared straight ahead. Rafe wondered if she even felt the water. A pod of dolphins swam alongside, and she showed no sign of noticing. Rafe drove the boat past sheer cliffs and hidden coves. He would have liked to show her each one, all his favorite spots.

But she sat so still, leaning forward, as if her desire was to get away from the island, to leave Capri behind. Something must have happened with her mother. Or had she had a fight with her boyfriend, over the phone from the States? She'd been so nice to Rafe, he wanted to ask her what was wrong, give her the chance to open up. He wanted it to be the way it had been with Monica. Her posture didn't invite that, though. She faced the water ahead, as if he wasn't even there.

Pointing southeast, they finally approached the mysterious, wind- and sea-sculpted shapes of Il Faraglioni. Iconic images of Capri, these enormous rock islands just off the southern coast had always fired Rafe's imagination. As he motored closer, Pell finally turned toward him.

"There are seahorses here?" she asked.

"Yes," he said. "I'll show you."

He drove the boat through a natural arch in one of the rocks, a bridge formed by thousands of years of erosion. Looking down into the shoals, he saw water dappled turquoise, jade, and azure. Sunlight penetrated the top layer, and tiny gold shapes danced just below the surface.

"Pell," he said, cutting the engine, motioning her toward the stern. Small waves slapped the boat.

"What is it?" she asked.

"Right there," he said, pointing into the water.

The boat rocked in the wake from a passing tour boat. Pell teetered, and Rafe grabbed her, held her steady. She leaned into his body. His feelings had been so tamped down, first by grief, then by drugs. But he'd been coming back to life this summer, and Pell was a huge part of it.

"I don't see," she said. The boat was even now,

no longer rocking, but she didn't pull away. She clung to him, smooth tan arms and lean waist, and he wanted to kiss her. She stared into the clear, shimmering blue pool, and he wanted to taste her lips, lick the salt spray from her, and he was about to. Their eyes met for a second. She wanted him to. Or no, she didn't.

"Are you okay?" he asked.

"Not really," she said.

"What's the matter?"

"Everything," she said, choking up. He smoothed her dark hair back, feeling so tender toward her. That day in the church she'd let him hold her hand, and now his arms were around her, their faces nearly touching.

"Rafe," she said softly, backing away. She crossed her arms across her chest. He'd stepped over some invisible line. She'd been upset, but now she was agitated.

"I didn't mean . . . ," he began.

"I know," she said.

What had changed? Was this because she had a boyfriend? She never talked about him, and she seemed so upset; had they fought? Rafe had spent so much of the last years getting high and trying to get clean, then getting fucked up again, chasing oblivion, he didn't know how to trust himself.

He'd been with lots of girls. In New York, in London, even here on Capri. Parties on yachts, at the marina, in the grottoes. But this was so different. It reminded him of Monica, a way he'd started to feel back in rehab, never had the chance to find out. Now his feelings for Pell were exploding.

He reached for her again, but not coming on strong. Just easy, hand on her shoulder. He touched her hair. It felt like silk, the smoothest sensation against his skin. The boat rocked, and she leaned into him again. He tried to say her name, but his voice wouldn't work.

Sun beat down, baking their skin. What if they just went swimming? He would show her the underwater caves. They could climb up onto the rocks, and he would kiss her, they would make out, he would caress her, make her forget her boyfriend. Was this what falling in love felt like? Was this what would have happened if he and Monica had had a chance?

After another minute, Pell eased out of his arms, knelt in the boat, and leaned her head against the gunwale. At first he thought maybe she was seasick. But he saw her shoulders shaking, and realized she was crying.

Rafe knelt beside her. He didn't touch her, just was with her. The moment was so quiet. Boat engines hummed far away, but they were alone in this small cove, the tallest pine- and cedar-crowned spire of white rock rising beside them. Sunlight bounced off the cliff, splashing into the glinting turquoise sea.

Rafe reached his hand into the clear pool. Pell

didn't raise her head, so he bumped her lightly with his elbow. Even then she wouldn't lift her eyes; she didn't want him to see her crying, or she was too gripped by whatever thoughts had driven her to leave her mother's house. So he touched her again.

"Pell," he said. "Hey."

No response.

"Look," he said. "Seahorses."

At that she raised her eyes. When he'd stuck his hand into the water, the seahorses—delicate, fragile—had swarmed around it to investigate. He extended his index finger, and the largest seahorse, three inches long, wrapped his tail around so Rafe could pull it from the water.

He handed the squirming seahorse to Pell. She held it cupped in one hand, and she began to smile.

"See them all?" he asked, gesturing toward the cerulean water. "They came to see you."

"Oh, Rafe."

"They're for you," he said. "All the seahorses."

The old him would have gagged at what he was saying. Would have laughed at what a jerk he was being. How corny, how stupid. Where had his words come from? What about Pell made him this way? He felt the way he'd seen his grandfather act toward his grandmother. He wanted to shield Pell from all hurt and wrong. He gazed at her as the boat moved beneath them.

He reached over, wiped tears from her eyes. Leaning close, his lips brushed her cheek. Then he took her hand, guided it into the water. She resisted a little, not wanting to let the seahorse go. But she did, and even as it swam away, scores more bumped her hand, wrapped their fine tails around her slender fingers.

"How did you find these?" she asked.

"My parents brought me here when I was little," he said.

"You must have loved it. Other kids see seahorses at aquariums, you had them in your backyard."

"Yeah," he said. "I'm pretty lucky."

"You became the **lanciatore della stella**. The star-thrower. The boy who saves starfish and other living creatures."

"That's me," he said.

"Seahorses and starfish," she said, almost to herself.

"Why do you love them so much?" he asked.

"They used to remind me of my father."

"Used to?" he asked.

But she didn't reply, and he saw her smile dissolve as she gazed into the sunlit sea at hundreds of tiny seahorses.

~

Lucy Davis knew something was totally, utterly, indisputably not right. Pell had called, then hung up without leaving a message. Very unlike her. Pell was the über–Older Sister, the one who always left the encouraging word, who inquired about Lucy's welfare, well-being, and sleeping, who was always on Lucy's case.

Sending Pell out of the country, away from Lucy's side, had taken yeoman work. Seriously, Lucy and Beck had had to double-team her, convincing her that the trip would benefit Lucy in the long run, considering Pell was planning to bring their mother back, and not that Lucy was getting her hopes up or anything, but who didn't want their mother to return after years away?

Lucy had found some peace. Just hearing her mother's voice that day, talking her into sleep; it didn't mean everything was going to be perfect. But it told Lucy that she was loved. That's all she'd ever wanted.

Not only had Pell not left a message, when Lucy returned the call, Pell's phone was off. **Off.** That never happened. What if Lucy stubbed her toe and couldn't get through? What if Lucy had a nightmare and Pell wasn't available? What if their grandmother tried to force Lucy to attend some horrible black-tie-for-the-younger-set thing at the Breakers and Pell wasn't there to absorb Lucy's venting? What if Lucy stopped sleeping again? Or sleepwalked into the ocean like that time before?

Sitting at Beck's kitchen table, lost in the latest round of drawings in their attempt to design a mathematically perfect moon gate, Lucy stared at her best friend.

"Still not answering?" Beck asked, leaning over the paper, drawing yet another circle with her compass.

"Nope," Lucy said.

"Are you ready to take the next step?"

"Call my mother?"

"Yeah."

Lucy nodded. She had to admit, she loved this part. Any chance to talk with her mother. She had secret thoughts she kept from Pell. Both girls treasured their father, but Lucy believed their mother's real problems had started with him. Taylor Davis had been such a wonderful man, such a perfect dad, their mother must have felt like dog poo in comparison. Literally. He was like the golden sun, and she must have felt like a big pile of poop. **Look at me! I abandoned my children!**

Even when she'd still lived at home—and although Lucy was only a toddler at the time, she remembered clearly—their mother had been kind of a downer.

Dressed in her nightgown, never really washing her hair that well, watching soaps and eating cup-o-soups while Miss Miller, starched and prissy as ever, marched Lucy and Pell off to the park, and to nursery school, and to playtime at their friends'; and while their father, in his beautiful suits, went to the law office where he was a partner, and made lots of money, and gained the respect of the community, and still managed to come home on time and have dinner with the kids because his wife was in bed sobbing—well, who wouldn't have the slightest, wee bit of a hard time showing her face around the country club?

"Okay, fine," Lucy said, punching in the number for her mother's house as Beck looked on. "Dialing now . . . ringing . . . more ringing . . . oops, no one home. They must be out together having mother-daughter fun, that's it, they're . . . oh!"

"Hello?" her mother said.

"Mom?" Lucy asked.

"Lucy!"

Lucy beamed. Her mother sounded so thrilled to hear her voice, she almost wanted to hang up and call right back just to feel the jolt again.

"How are you?" Lucy asked.

"I'm fine," her mother said. "But I can't find Pell. Have you heard from her?"

"It's strange you'd ask," Lucy said. "Because she did call a while ago, but she hung up before I answered. Is everything okay?"

"I'm afraid I upset her," her mother said. "I didn't mean to, but I said the wrong thing, and . . ."

"Pell isn't like that," Lucy said. "Whatever you said, she forgives. She taught me that when we were little." Could Lucy say this, go out on such a limb? "Because of you. Because we loved you so much, no matter what you did or said, no matter what, she told me to forgive everything."

"Oh, Lucy," her mother said.

"If she didn't love you more than anything," Lucy went on, "she wouldn't have kept the map all this time."

"The map?" her mother asked.

"Of Dorset!" Lucy said. "Don't you remember? The country you and Pell made up. You drew it with crayons, and I stuck stars in the sky. Tiny foil stars. They were there so long, the glue dried up and some of them fell off. Pell re-glued them."

Her mother was silent so long, Lucy thought maybe the connection had been broken.

"Mom?" she asked.

"Pell kept that map?" her mother asked.

"Of course," Lucy said. "She'd never throw it away."

More silence, and suddenly Lucy felt more worried than before. Her heart raced, and she gave Beck a look of dread. Travis came in from fishing, kicked off his rubber boots. Lucy smelled fish guts, but that's not what made her feel sick: it was the idea that something bad had happened to her sister.

"Is everything okay?" Lucy asked. "Are you all right? Is Pell?"

At the sound of Pell's name, Travis stopped what he was doing and stared across the kitchen, straight into Lucy's eyes.

"I'm not sure," her mother said. "Honestly, I don't know."

They spoke another minute, and then hung up.

Lucy felt afraid, because she hadn't heard from her sister, because it was so unlike Pell to let her worry, and because it was clear that for some reason Pell had let their mother think she'd destroyed the map of Dorset. Lucy had felt left out by Pell's trip, as much as she'd wanted her to take it, and as badly as she'd hoped she'd bring their mother home.

"I'm going," she said, looking from Beck to Travis.

"Where?" Beck asked.

"Capri," Lucy said. "Pell needs me."

"I'll go with you," Travis said.

"Yes!" Beck said.

"Oh, shit," Travis said, starting to rummage through his drawers. "Do I know where my passport is?"

"Mom has it," Beck said. "She kept it after you and the team got back from skiing."

Lucy and Beck exchanged a look. They weren't supposed to know that Pell had gone too. She and Travis had been new back then—last winter, start of second semester. As a reward for their outstanding football season, some alum paid for the team to take a trip to Toronto. Pell and two of her friends—Logan Moore and Cordelia St. Onge—had met them at their hotel.

"Only one problem," Travis said. "How much are plane tickets to Rome?"

Lucy reached into her backpack, pulled out her wallet. Her hands were shaking as she dug the credit card out of its compartment. She stared at it, at her name in raised black print.

"For emergencies," she said. "That's what the trust officer said it was for. And this is an emergency."

"You'd probably better check with him, be sure," Travis said.

"It's my sister," Lucy said. "And I can be very persuasive. I just . . . I've never made flight reservations before. Our father always did it, or Pell. Travis, do you know how?"

"I can figure it out fast," Travis said.

Sixteen

Do you know about family myths? Your family has one—we all do. They are shorthand versions of your story, usually accenting noble angles. Here are a few examples: "My grandfather was a hero in World War II and never talked about it." "My mother built her business from the ground up but never forgot her roots." Our family myth, Lucy's and mine, was, "Our dad was both father and mother to us; he picked up the pieces after our mother abandoned us."

Seeing the seahorses was a mistake. It was a magical sight, gazing into that azure pool with Rafe, watching the tiny golden creatures swim around our hands. But the reason I'd loved them was because of my dad. His nicknames for us: Seahorse and Starfish, me and Lucy.

I told Rafe I wanted to leave Il Faraglioni. The rock formations were mystical and poetic, as if the great rock islands had been shaped with an artist's hand, but I couldn't even appreciate their terrible and magnificent beauty; our family myth had been shattered, and all I could think about was getting home. My mother hadn't "abandoned" us; my father had told her to leave.

"Let's go back to the dock," Rafe said. I knew that he could see I was agitated, and I suppose he might have been concerned. He'd put his arm around me, and I'd let him. I felt terrible about that, and wanted to get to Travis.

"I have to get to Sorrento," I said. "I understand if you can't take me. Just drop me off at the marina, and I'll get the ferry."

"Of course I'll take you," he said. "If you really want to go."

I did and I didn't. One regret was that I hadn't said goodbye to Max.

Blinding sunlight struck the water, bounced off the rocks. I was surrounded by so much beauty, and I just wanted to hide. I found myself wishing it would rain; during the weeks I'd been on Capri, other than morning mists and the occasional late-afternoon storms, I'd seen nothing but blue sky and sun. You'd think I'd be grateful, but suddenly I wanted clouds and gray, the sound of rain.

Rafe set off toward the mainland. It wasn't far. I had my backpack, plane ticket, passport. There would be a bus to the airport. I clutched the backpack to my chest. I had a picture of my father in an inside pocket. If I looked at it now, would I even recognize him?

My dad. Now I knew. He was one of the "grownups," the ones who'd decided it would be better for my mother to go. I suppose that, deep down, I'd suspected that all along. In all our years of therapy, there were certain specifics we never discussed. Our mother had been depressed, unable to care for us, and the focus had always been on us—not the whys of our mother's leaving, but the hows of us surviving, getting along without her.

Each year brought its own struggle: first we'd had to stop mutilating ourselves with wild, primal grief. We'd literally needed to heal the scratches self-inflicted on our arms and faces, the raw patches of scalp from torn-out hair. Next we'd needed help concentrating in school. Ways to pay attention to basic lessons, reading and arithmetic, without having our thoughts instantly, constantly go to her. Our father and doctors had worked with us through all that, giving encouragement, helping us.

I was six when she left; twelve when my father got sick, thirteen when he died. Maybe if we'd had more time, if he were still here when I was more grown up, like now, the truth could have come out.

All of a sudden I noticed the boat slowing down. Turning, I caught Rafe's eye.

"Hey," I said.

"I can't," he said.

"What are you talking about?"

"I can't take you to the mainland," he said.

"Why?"

"It's the wrong thing to do."

"Give a friend a ride?" I asked.

He shook his head. "Not that. I'm talking about you. You should stay and talk it out with your mother."

"Rafe?" I asked. "Are you serious? You don't know what's going on."

"Exactly," he said. "And I don't want to see you make a mistake like this before you tell me."

"I don't want to tell you, I don't want to talk about it, I just need to get to the airport!"

"Then someone else will have to take you," he said.

The boat bobbed on small waves for a moment, and then he turned the wheel and we began heading back toward Anacapri. My heart was racing, and I felt hijacked. Still gripping my backpack, I watched the island of Capri slide by as we took the long boat ride home.

When we approached our little cove, Rafe steered the boat into an unfamiliar inlet, a quarter mile or so from the dock. Rocks were everywhere, sticking out of the water on all sides as he piloted through a narrow channel. The shore was all rock, with a dark slit opening in the sheer cliff ahead. I held my breath as he drove us slowly through the aperture.

We were in an almost-cave; I say "almost" because the rocks rose and curved around us, but instead of being closed at the top, there was a wide chimney reaching up to blue sky. Light streamed in, turning the water bright, dazzling, emerald green. This had to be one of the grottoes.

"What is this?" I asked, my voice echoing through the chamber.

He didn't answer right away, motoring slowly over to the grotto wall. Just when I thought we were going to hit it, I heard a slight crunching sound and felt the boat slide onto a ledge. Looking over the side, I saw we were beached on a black sandy bottom. Rafe jumped out, walked through shallow water to the bow, and made the bowline fast to an iron ring bolted to the rock wall. Now we were all tied up, but where?

"You might want to take off your shoes," Rafe said.

"What is this?"

"A grotto on my grandfather's property."

"What's wrong with the dock?" I asked.

"Look," he said. "My grandfather keeps pretty close watch on me. He and your mom are close, and if you two are fighting, or whatever this is, odds are she'll talk to him about it. He's seen the boat is gone; if he spots it at the dock, you won't have time to figure things out before your mom's all over you."

"So, you're going to help me figure things out?" I asked.

He nodded. "Yep," he said.

I kicked off my flip-flops, and stepped over the side of the boat into cool salt water. The waves lapped our ankles as we walked along the grotto's rock, out the opening, into bright daylight. I glanced up, saw thin cirrus clouds, long, swooping ribbons: mare's tails.

Rafe and I walked around the rocky point, just at the very base of the steep hill. We kept to the shadows, and I knew he was trying to stay out of sight of the houses up above. The whitewashed boathouse lay ahead, set on concrete piers to allow the tide to flow beneath. Just beyond were the stone steps up to my mother's house and the villa.

Unlocking the door, Rafe let me in. I felt surrounded by the sea: the sound of waves was everywhere, coming through the windows, through the floorboards. The place was sparely furnished: a single bed, a desk, two wooden chairs. Outside, the cry of mournful seabirds.

My skin tingled. Not just from the surging sea, the breeze, and feeling wrecked about my dad, but something else: Rafe stood so close to me. He stared, his blue eyes so wide-open.

"What am I doing here?" I asked.

"You can talk to me," he said. "It was noisy in the boat, but it's quiet here. Tell me how I can help you."

"No one can help," I said. "It has to do with me and my father. He's the one I need to talk to, but he died three years ago."

"I get that," he said. "Same with my grandmother. She's the only one I want to talk to about what happened, but I can't. In a way, it's worse, because it's my fault she died."

He was right: at least I couldn't blame myself for my father's brain tumor. I'm almost seventeen, pretty young in some ways, but older than my time in others. My father's death, and all that had gone before, had made me grow up fast.

"It's going to be okay," he said.

And he kissed me.

~

Travis was known for getting things done. At Newport Academy, after just one season, he'd been elected captain of the football team for the coming year. Workouts started in mid-August; he'd been in touch with all his teammates, making sure they were good to go.

Even on the trawler, his first summer as a commercial fisherman, the captain gave him a lot of responsibility. When the insurance company had refused to reconsider raising the rates, Captain Zeke had thrown his cell phone across the wheelhouse. Travis had been the one to call the agent back, calmly go over the policy, talk her into getting more quotes—and she had, and Zeke wound up with lower rates than before.

Zeke had no problem with giving Travis a long weekend off—Thursday through Tuesday—to reward him for great fishing, and taking care of business. It seemed incredible to Travis, the idea of flying to Italy for such a short time, but that's how much he needed to go. Lucy had called her mother back, and still there was no sign of Pell. The main problem was airfare.

"Just do it," Beck advised, when he got home from work that day. "Who cares what it costs? There's no price tag on love."

"You're fourteen," Travis said. "You might be a genius, but you don't get it. I'm saving up for school."

"You're worried about Pell, and you're putting tuition before her? You're **right,** I don't get it."

His sister made him think. Travis excused himself, went into his room. He looked through the Newport Academy directory, looked up Ty's number in New York. He lived on Park Avenue; it sounded rich. The maid answered, gave Travis a different number to call, 516 area code.

"Hey, man," Travis said when Ty picked up.

"How's it going?" Ty asked.

"Great. Where are you, anyway?"

"Southampton," Ty said. "At our summer place. What's going on? You calling an early practice?"

"Not exactly," Travis said. "I wanted to ask you about someone."

"Who?"

"Rafe Gardiner."

Long silence. Travis had time to think about the

difference between him and his school- and teammates. Most people who attended Newport Academy had money. They came from families who could afford fancy Manhattan apartments, big houses in the Hamptons; they didn't have to rely on grants, loans, and the largesse of their girlfriend's grandmother to get through school. Mrs. Nicholson endowed his and Beck's scholarships, and it burned him thinking she saw his family as a charity case. It gave her a chance to look down on him.

"Rafaele," Ty said after a minute. "He lives, or lived, a floor below us. We went to St. David's, but, man—that was a long time ago. And that incident, that only happened once. Who the fuck told you, anyway?"

"Told me?" Travis asked.

"What, some asshole who wants my position on the team told you about Central Park? The charges were dropped, Trav. . . ."

"Hey," Travis said, his heart starting to thump. "What are you talking about?"

"You're team captain," Ty said. "I assumed you were getting all hard-ass about past infractions of the honor code. Is that why you're asking about him?"

"No," Travis said. "I don't care what you did in Central Park—it won't affect you being on the team. But I'd really appreciate it if you told me, if it has anything to do with Rafe—Rafaele—Gardiner."

"Okay," Ty said, taking a deep breath. "I'm trusting you, man. I don't want to fuck up my senior year with getting kicked off the team for something that went down two years ago."

"You won't. Tell me, okay?"

"We were smoking a joint in the park. Cops came along, we got busted. I got out of it, no problem—good lawyer, first arrest. But Rafe had coke on him. And oxycodone, enough so they said he was dealing."

"He's a drug dealer?"

"No, not like that. He's just fucked up, can't stay out of trouble. He got out of jail time by enrolling in a rehab. Too bad he didn't go straight there—I heard he went to Italy and some weird shit went down, and his grandmother wound up dying."

Travis froze. "He killed her?"

"I don't know the details, but yeah. It was an accident, but still. My parents know his dad, and he's pretty much washed his hands of old Rafe. Why are you asking all this?"

"You mentioned Italy," Travis said. "Capri, right?"

"Yeah," Ty said. "How do you know?"

"Pell's there," Travis said. "Her mother lives next door to his grandfather, and he's around this summer."

"Keep her away from him," Ty said. "She's a sweet girl."

"Would he hurt her?"

"He hurts everyone," Ty said. "I kind of feel bad for him. He was best friends with my brother when they were little, but then his mother died, and he just lost it. He became the kid no one wanted to play with. Long story, but he kind of went bad. His dad's a big deal in a British bank, never around. Rafe just basically ran wild. He always had a girlfriend, usually some nice girl who goes for the bad-boy thing. Pell wouldn't, but some of them got into coke with him."

"You're right, Pell wouldn't," Travis said.

"Still, keep her away from him," Ty said.

"Thanks, Ty," Travis said.

"You sure this won't affect me on the team?"

"It won't," Travis said. "See you in August."

He hung up and dialed Pell. What was he going to say to her? He felt like a dad about to deliver a lecture, or someone in a horror movie yelling "Get out of the house, the madman's about to strike!" Straight to voicemail. He'd already left so many messages, he didn't even bother. Sitting on the side of his bed, he stared at the wall and knew what he had to do.

~

Lucy's grandmother hadn't liked the plan, but Lucy wasn't really asking her permission. At fourteen, she was obviously a minor, and there were many decisions she could not make on her own. To access her money, for example, or to leave the country, she needed the permission of her guardian. That person was not Edith Nicholson. It was Stephen Campbell, one of her father's best friends. Lucy had explained the situation to Stephen, and he had put in a call to her trustee—William Crawford of United Stonington Trust.

William was cool. He'd been a friend of Lucy's dad, too, and he'd known her mother back in their prep school and college days. He'd listened to Lucy and Stephen, agreed to approve the trip. Normally it wouldn't have taken such a powwow to plan a visit to Lucy's sister and mother, but there was one complication that had to be addressed.

Stephen had picked Lucy up at her grandmother's estate; they drove straight to Beck's house, and Stephen waited in the car while Lucy ran to the door.

"Is he here?" Lucy asked when Beck answered.

"Yes," Beck said. "He's in his room, filled with angst."

The two girls hurried through the small house; Lucy checked her watch—there wasn't much time to lose. When they got to Travis's door, Beck knocked hard.

"I'm busy!" he called.

Beck and Lucy exchanged glances, and Beck rapped again.

"Open up now! It's urgent!"

"Come in."

Beck threw open the door, and Lucy saw Travis

sitting at his computer, scrolling through some travel website. He had pulled up discount flights to Rome, and she saw he'd been making notes on a pad.

"Hi, Lucy," he said. "You on your way?"

"You should know," she said. Travis had reserved the flight for her; he'd wanted to get a seat for himself, too, but it was full price, beyond his budget.

"Well, I'll try to catch up with you," he said. "If I can find—"

"No," Lucy said. "You're coming with me now."

"I want to, you have no idea. And I would—Beck, you were right, what else is money for? But I don't have enough; even if I use all my savings from fishing so far, I can't afford the full-price fare. I have to—"

"It's all taken care of," Lucy said.

"What do you mean?"

"Remember what I told you, about emergencies? I explained it to my trust officer, and he agreed—you are needed, Travis."

"Lucy, you're the second-most-capable fourteen-year-old I know," Travis said, with a glance at Beck. "You don't need a chaperone."

"No," she said. "But Pell needs you."

Travis took that in; he couldn't argue with her, didn't even seem to want to try.

"I'll pay as much as I can, owe you the rest," he said.

"It's a done deal—you don't owe me anything.

Just hurry," Lucy said. "Stephen's giving us a ride to the airport. He's waiting outside now. Pack your stuff, and let's go!"

"Take a shower, dude," Beck said. "You don't want to arrive in Capri smelling like codfish. I'll pack for you."

Travis ran into the bathroom, and they heard the shower running. It was just noon, and the flight left New York at eight that night. Lucy and Beck grinned at each other, taking the opportunity to turn Lucy's watch and Beck's clock radio six hours ahead, sync them to Italy time.

Seventeen

By twilight, high clouds covered the sky, obscuring Monte Solaro in mist. Pell hadn't returned home all day. Lyra and Max had looked all over the island, then he had dropped her off at home to wait. She'd walked through the garden, thinking maybe Pell had gone somewhere quiet to think. But she knew, and so did Max, that Pell was with Rafe, that they had gone somewhere in the boat.

Lyra sat on the terrace, watching weather move in. Dampness surrounded her, and clouds were settling, vast and gray. A sharp breeze picked up, blowing through the trees. How quickly the azure water lost its blue, drained of brightness. No lights sparkled across the bay; haze enfolded the mainland.

The dock was barely visible down below. Lyra kept her eyes on it, waiting for the yellow boat to return. Max had called Nicolas and John, Stefan, and all his other friends, asked them to watch out for Rafe and Pell. Nicolas had accosted Arturo, threatened him with the loss of his boat slip if he didn't tell him where Rafe was. Arturo defensively said he'd seen him heading toward Il Faraglioni hours ago, and Nicolas had taken a boat over to look. Max was still searching Capri, going to the places his grandson had been known to go.

Lyra sat on the settee, arms wrapped around drawn-up knees. Ten years of being alone, not having the day-to-day guardianship of her children, and right now she was so scared she couldn't breathe.

The damp grew so thick, moisture dripped from the leaves. Lyra thought of Pell, dressed for a sunny day, wondered if she was getting chilled. The brass telescope stood on its tripod, anchored to the stone parapet. Lyra unfolded herself to move it inside. She turned on some lights in the living room, used a cloth to wipe it off. Her stomach flipped; she was taking care of a "thing" again, when what she really wanted was to be holding her daughter.

She thought back to the week before Pell arrived. She'd busied herself, cleaning and polishing, making the house as perfect as possible. She'd planted window boxes for the guest room, polished the silver tea set. Max had laughed at her—he didn't think she knew, but she'd realized immediately what he was thinking. Who cared about the house, about objects? It was people who mattered.

Her daughters.

She drifted toward a large painting, three feet

square, hanging on the wall. Abstract, soft pastel, it showed three rounded green shapes—one large, two small. The green was a shade of mint, rain-washed, the shapes smudged around the edges. They might have been hills.

Christina had painted it for Lyra the year before she died. She'd been losing ground, forgetting words, everyone's name, even Max's. But during that time, her art had deepened. It was as if without clear thoughts and language, nothing blocked the true spirit welling up from inside.

"What a beautiful landscape," Lyra had said when Christina presented her with the painting. And it really was: three defined hillocks in the foreground—the larger flanked by two smaller ones—overlooking a vast sea of blue. "The ocean, and three hills."

"No, **girls**," Christina had said, correcting her.

Lyra had smiled; her friend often mixed up words. But Christina pointed, starting with the shape in the middle. "Lyra," she'd said. "And her daughters."

Immediately Lyra saw. "Pell," she'd said, touching one hill, "and Lucy," the other.

"Yes," Christina had nodded. "Lyra and her children."

Lyra gazed at the painting now. It captured the way one flowed into another, whether hills or people. Separate, independent, yet necessary to the landscape, to the larger composition.

The phone rang, and Lyra ran for it.

"Hello?" she said.

"Mom, it's Lucy."

"Hi, Lucy," she said. "Have you heard from Pell?"

"Not a word, and that's so weird. It's not like her. Mom, I'm on my way."

Had Lyra misheard her?

"On your way?" she asked.

"Yes. I know it's last-minute and all, but you don't have to worry about getting things ready or anything. I'll sleep on the floor. It's okay. The main thing is, I want to be there for Pell. And you too."

"Lucy," Lyra said. She stared at the painting. "You shouldn't have to come all this way just to check on your sister. I'm supposed to be taking care of her. I want to see you—I've had it in mind to call and ask you to come. Why didn't I do that? And why have things gone so wrong with Pell?"

"How could it be easy?" Lucy asked. "We love you so much. All this time and distance between us is what's hard."

"You're only fourteen, and you know that?"

"Of course I know it. Pell's my older sister." The words were simple, direct, enough said. The girls' sense of each other was so intense, one sister knew when the other needed her.

"When do you land?" Lyra asked. "I'll make arrangements to have you met at the airport."

"Thank you, Mom," Lucy said, and gave her the flight details. Lyra wrote them down. "I'm bringing someone with me," Lucy continued. "Travis Shaw. Pell's boyfriend."

"Lucy, I'm not sure," Lyra began.

"Mom," Lucy said. "You don't know how it is. This is the way we do things. Travis is part of our lives."

"Okay," Lyra said. "He's welcome, of course. And I can't wait to see you."

They said goodbye.

Lyra heard footsteps on the terrace. She turned, saw two people through the tall windows: Pell and Rafe. It had started to rain, and they were dripping wet. Lyra had ten seconds to feel relief before worry took over. Pell looked miserable, and walked straight through the living room, past Lyra, toward her bedroom.

Rafe stood just outside the door, in the rain.

"Where were you?" Lyra asked. "Where did you take her?"

"To Il Faraglioni," he said.

"I swear to God, Rafe," Lyra said. "If she's not okay . . ."

The young man stared at her. His eyes seemed clear, alert, but darkness hung on him like his wet clothes.

"Go check on her," he said. "She's pretty upset."

"I can see that," Lyra said. "What happened?"

"I made a mistake," he said. "I'm sorry."

And he walked off the terrace, back into the steady rain.

Another boy's arms around me.

His lips on mine.

And I'd leaned into him, wanting everything to go away, losing myself in his kiss for ten, thirty, sixty seconds.

I couldn't tell myself it was just a quick peck, that he tried something and I instantly turned away. Because that's not what happened.

The boathouse, so spare and clean, the changing weather sweeping through the two small windows, that first gust of wind, and the breath of rain. I'd wanted mist, damp, cool rain, and here it came.

Rafe's arms strong and lean, and the danger so sexy, the knowledge that he'd stepped off the path and made it back alive. Kissing me, hot and wet, pulling me down on the narrow bed, and I'd let him.

Thinking everything in my life had been a lie, the word **everything** starting and ending with my dad. Because that's what he'd been to me, nothing less. Running home from school, there'd been one person I wanted to see: him. Having a bad dream, there'd been only one who could give me comfort: him. His goodness had erased all the dread and badness of my mother's leaving.

So what am I saying? My mother's bombshell, the disillusioning news that my father had been one factor in why/how she'd left us, had thrown me into crazy disarray. The Pell I'd always been disappeared in that moment. Steady, helpful, loving, caring, responsible me—gone.

Don't think I haven't known how people saw me. After my mother left, once we got through the first horrendous year, Dr. Robertson's help enabled me to find my center, realize what was important, know that Lucy needed me, that I had to be the best older sister possible. At the age of seven, I pulled myself together. I remember it so clearly—I saw the alternatives: be good, be there like my dad, or be a wreck, be gone like my mom. I elected to be like him.

All through my life, and I do mean all through, up until today, I've been hyper-responsible. Walk my sister to school, help her with her homework, make sure she gets to bed on time. When our dad was sick, I acted as a nurse. I filled a basin with warm water, used a washcloth to wash his face, helped him shave. Once he stopped being able to work, he was home all the time. His illness took him down over the course of a year; sometimes he'd go to the hospital—when he got pneumonia, then a staph infection, two surgeries to relieve pressure on his brain.

I insisted on knowing the details. His doctors had instructions to tell me the truth; my dad trusted me and my strength **that** much. So at the end, when he came home after surgery to remove infected parts of his skull—"debriding the bone," it was called—and a nurse would come to our house to clean out the wound—I would stand right there, holding his hand, while she swept the crater in his head with hydrogen peroxide on a Q-tip. I was thirteen; other kids were at after-school sports, at the library, with their friends. I was with my dad.

"You're the strongest girl I've ever known," he said.

"Thanks, Dad," I said. "It's easy, I love you."

We'd beam at each other, even as he was turning into a skeleton, losing so much weight he barely weighed more than I. We were there for each other—I couldn't forget what he'd done for me and Lucy. Other dads might have brought someone else in to care for the kids—like a nanny, or a governess, or a girlfriend. Not him. He let us know how much we mattered to him.

He neither pushed us nor forbade us to talk about or call our mother. But the feeling became, it was easier without her. When we did talk to her on the phone, we were all left feeling so empty. She should be here, she shouldn't be here, we didn't know. That might have been the time my father could have told us the whole truth. He could have let himself be a little more of the bad guy, to save her from being completely, one hundred percent wrong.

Now, in my room at my mother's house, I heard the rain pouring down outside, pattering on the roof and leaves. My mother's voice at my closed door. "Pell," she said. "Please, let's talk. Will you come out?"

But I wouldn't. I went into the bathroom, tried to scrub Rafe's kiss off my lips. The feeling of his hands off my arms and shoulders. What I couldn't erase was the excitement I'd felt. I did it all myself—kissed him, turned myself inside out lying on that bed in the boathouse, wanted him with everything I had. My mother's voice kept going outside the locked door, saying Lucy and Travis were on the way.

I already knew. I'd listened to my voicemail.

"Pell, Lucy's worried about you. We're flying to Italy tonight. I can't wait to see you," he said.

Travis, my boy.

Threw him away, didn't I?

Responsible me. The girl I used to be, let's go back to her for a minute. Even after my father died, and we moved to Newport, and started school there . . . even then, I was steady and reliable. I didn't see the point in breaking rules. Life handed me certain opportunities, and I accepted them, respected the boundaries along the way.

There were few exceptions to that. I'll give you an example of one, and show you how ignoring the boundary, the rules, made me feel bad. Guilty, if you will—not in a religious sense, but in a moral, ordered one. Stepping outside the lines seemed, at that time, an unnecessary risk. I could have been expelled, and where would that have left Lucy?

Here's what happened. Last winter:

Travis and I had been getting closer, had started going out just before Christmas. Our relationship had bloomed slowly. He'd arrived at school just that fall, fresh from Ohio, where he'd had a long-time girlfriend. They'd broken up. I wasn't the reason, but I wanted him to be sure. I'd felt the wild, amazing attraction to him—not just physically, but emotionally, in my heart and every other part of myself. And when he'd reached for me, I'd slowed it all down. Not to drive us more crazy than we already were, but to give him time to get over Ally.

Christmas came—that's when I first realized I wanted to travel here, to Italy, to connect with my mother, stay with her, bring her back. Being with Travis, seeing the closeness he had with his mom and sisters, realizing their family had been broken and had come back together—that's what started me thinking. I'd even considered Capri for Christmas, but realized two things: it wouldn't give me enough time to really get to know her, and also it would take me away from Travis, just when we were getting started.

Walks on the winter beach, coffee in a candlelit café on the wharf, kisses in the far stacks of our boarding school library in grand, gilded, haunted Blackstone Hall. Travis and I fell in love. Then, right after the holidays, a trustee of Newport Academy decided to reward the football team for a winning season. He funded a trip to Toronto during February break.

Impossible! Travis going away for five days. He didn't want to leave, but the team had just voted him captain for senior year. I couldn't bear to part with him because I was head over heels. A whole lifetime of doing the right thing suddenly felt like the biggest obstacle ever. All I could think about was stowing away in his duffel bag.

My friends came to the rescue. Logan Moore had a car—a Range Rover, to be precise. Her mother is Ridley Moore, the film star, and I'm pretty sure the phrase "spoiled Hollywood brat" was invented for Logan—I say that with adoration and sympathy, because she is a sponge for love. Cordelia St. Onge, of the Boston St. Onges, her father the head of neurosurgery at Bay State General, came along.

We told school that we were heading to Logan's mom's film set. Ditto the St. Onges. We told Logan's mom that we were going to South Beach. She gave us George Clooney's number, said he was shooting a movie there with Robert Pattinson, said they'd be happy to take us out for mojitos. The fact we are nowhere near twenty-one didn't faze her. The only people who knew where we were really headed were Lucy and Beck, and they cheered us all the way.

The drive to Toronto took all day, into the night. The team was staying at the King Edward Hotel, downtown. Lovely and old, it was graceful and centrally located for the boys to visit the alum's office—he owned businesses, a minor-league hockey team, and was trying to start an American football program for Canadian youth.

Logan, Cord, and I checked in to the King Edward. We had to take care not to be seen by the coach or chaperones, one of whom was Stephen Campbell, our math teacher and Lucy's guardian.

After dinner, when the team returned to the hotel, I was hiding in the lobby. Well, I was in plain sight, but shielding my face with the **Globe and Mail**. The guys didn't notice me; the coach and teachers headed into the bar. I saw Travis, Ty, and Chris hesitate outside the bar's entrance; maybe they thought they'd head in, have a soda or something. That's when I made my move. I lowered the newspaper.

Travis and I have antennae for each other. He must have felt the tingle I was giving off, because he turned and saw me. Didn't even say a word to his friends, just walked straight over.

"What are you doing here?" he asked.

"Don't you know?" I asked.

He must have been shocked by my behavior. I was a little stunned myself: me, perfect girl, rule follower, the one who'd kept him at arm's length all through the fall, so he could get over Ally, had driven to Canada to be with him.

Travis took my hand. Instead of taking the elevator, easier to be seen there, we climbed the stairs. He was sharing a room with Chris, so that was out. I led him instead to my floor, and we let ourselves into my room.

The maid had been by—turndown service. The heavy silk curtains drawn tight over the windows, radio playing low, one lamp casting a warm glow, queen bed neatly turned down, chocolates on the pillows. We stuck the Do Not Disturb sign on the doorknob.

We lay down together.

Kissed, so slowly but with everything we had. Alone in a hotel room. He tasted so good, the boy I had been falling in love with all year. All my good behavior, my holding myself back, afraid to give myself, so fearful of being hurt or left or of letting someone down, it all dissolved. We were together, Travis and I.

Our hands unbuttoned our shirts, slid off our jeans. I'd never felt like this, my skin against a boy's skin. The air was cool, our bodies were hot. We scrambled under the covers, and we kissed more deeply, he was hard and I was soft, the down quilt held our heat beneath it and we warmed up fast. We said each other's names over and over, because we wanted to be sure we knew what was going on.

Travis, Travis.

See, we loved each other. Our bodies were proving it, showing it. This was a new way. Words didn't say what we had to tell each other, we had to find a new language. His eyes never left mine.

We fell asleep, held each other all night long. My legs were wrapped in his, his arms were around me, our mouths kept finding each other. Soon gray light spilled through the narrow space between the curtains. Day had come.

"I don't want to go downstairs," he said. "I want us to stay together all day."

"Okay," I said.

We didn't laugh; it wasn't a joke. What else in life mattered but this? I came alive that night-into-day. I swear, I did. I'd been a good little grownup for so long, always doing my best, anticipating what was expected of me, for the difficult situation otherwise known as life, but not then—then, with Travis, I lived without thinking. I just let my heart pull me along. The tide had me, and I couldn't fight it.

Of course we got in trouble.

Logan got drunk. No George Clooney/Robert Pattinson mojitos, but she got some guy to buy drinks for her and Cord, and Stephen Campbell caught them both the next morning, hungover out of their minds, Logan so sick she threw up right in the lobby.

Questions were asked, my name was spilled, the front desk consulted, and soon the phone in my room began to ring.

I answered—vestiges of my vigilance, worried that maybe Lucy needed me—and heard the solemn voice of my dad's old friend, and our math teacher, Stephen. Only at that moment he was Mr. Campbell.

I tried to protect Travis—not let on that he was with me. But he took the phone, wouldn't let me be in trouble alone. When we returned to school the next week, Ted Shannon, our headmaster, gave us a stern talking-to. He said that strictly speaking we hadn't broken any school rules—if we had, we'd be expelled.

But Stephen said we'd used poor judgment. Travis was about to be football captain; I was a shining star, daughter of his dear friend Taylor. He mentioned Lucy, how much she looked up to me.

He put us on unofficial probation—which basically meant that we were off the hook, as long as we didn't get in trouble for the rest of junior year. We didn't.

Because that's Travis and me—in spite of the passion we have for each other, the desire to be together, we are ultimately who we are, Travis Shaw and Pell Davis: good kids. We can't help ourselves.

I would have sworn that was true, until earlier tonight.

Kissing Rafe, as if there were no Travis. That's all it had been, a kiss—but a long one, a minute. And the way I'd felt. Animalistic. All need. Plus, in there somehow, a crashing thrill of being bad. Like, take this, universe.

My father, my role model, has let me down.

So I did something awful in return: I betrayed the boy I love.

Travis, Travis Shaw.

Travis, I whisper now, knowing he is on the way here. **I'm sorry. . . .**

Eighteen

Rafe thought of the very first time he'd seen Pell stepping off the boat; the feeling had started then. Her long dark hair, wide blue eyes that took everything in, a gaze that made you feel you wanted to know her, and be known by her. He'd been so hungry for a friend, for company, for someone to love. The empty place left by Monica had felt unfillable. But then Pell had come along.

Getting to know her, then today: on the boat, seeing her so tense and upset, knowing something was eating her up. He'd shown Pell the seahorses and in that instant—when she first saw them—she'd lit up with such happiness, he'd thought, **Okay, yes, I can make her smile, we actually have something.**

Now, standing on the steps in the rain, he looked up at Lyra's house. There were lights on. Which one was Pell's? Did it matter? He wanted a chance to redo the ending—they'd been having such a good, quiet time. He'd felt good about bringing her back to the boathouse, so she could pull herself together and go home.

He'd gotten up the courage to kiss her. Led her over to his bed, and eased her down, and he'd thought they were good, that everything was going to be great. He'd felt her wanting him—he knew about girls, arching backs and pressing and murmuring. And to have that kind of sexual heat with Pell, along with her singular depth and intelligence and kindness, he'd been ecstatic. And then she'd pulled herself back, yanking her arms away.

So hard. Jumped off the bed, pacing, saying, "What have I done?"

"Nothing, Pell, I just wanted to kiss you, I thought I could help."

"Travis," she'd said. "Oh, my God, Travis."

Travis, her boyfriend.

What had Rafe done wrong? He felt frantic himself, not understanding. He'd thought something special was starting between them. Had he misread her signals so badly, or had he just been blind, yearning to replicate what he'd wished for with Monica? He wanted to talk to Pell now, try to explain. Lyra wouldn't let him back into the house, he was sure of that. And Pell herself seemed unable to get away from him fast enough. Rain poured into his eyes, and his clothes were soaked through.

He might as well go get the boat out of the grotto, tie it more securely to the dock, in case the storm got worse. Or he could drive it to the marina. It was midsummer, the height of the action on Capri. Boats in from the States, Spain, the south of France. Docks full, bars packed. Young people looking for each other. Rafe's familiar old cravings kicked in, worse than ever.

He wanted to get Pell's eyes out of his mind. It wasn't their beauty that was killing him now; it was the despair and disgust he'd seen in them after he'd kissed her. She felt sick for betraying Travis. And Rafe suddenly admitted how lost he felt without Monica.

The problem with loving drugs was that it kept you from loving everything else. Life became a series of forgettable pleasures. Then, after they wore off, you hated yourself and whoever you were with.

At rehab there was a rule against getting involved with other clients. His last rehab, in Malibu, the rule was strongly enforced; get caught in a compromising situation, and you were out.

You were supposed to concentrate on your own recovery. "Keep the focus on yourself" was one of the slogans. You had to learn to recognize the whole spectrum of feelings. The average person might think that was no big deal, but addicts lumped them all together, got high whenever anything got too intense, good or bad. There was actually a wheel—a big pie chart on the wall—every wedge a different feeling: happy, sad, nervous, doubtful, excited, tired, hungry, lonely, angry.

"HALT can be a trigger," the counselor was saying. "And make you want to use. So don't let yourself get too hungry, angry, lonely, or tired. We have to learn to take care of ourselves in a whole new way."

Rafe had heard it all before. The acronyms, the quaint sayings, the hopeful cheerleading. He felt worn out—why wasn't that on the chart? What good did any of this do? Across the classroom was a girl with a pixie haircut and huge green eyes, skinny in a pink T-shirt, black jeans, with a huge linen scarf-shawl thing wrapped around her neck. When the counselor started in on the feelings wheel, she'd glanced at Rafe. He'd happened to be looking over, and they started laughing.

Her name was Monica, and she came from Santa Monica, just a few miles south of the rehab's Malibu location.

"Your parents named you for your town?" he asked.

"Even worse," she said. "Santa Monica Boulevard. I was conceived in a parked car outside a pizza place in West Hollywood."

"But how does that make you feel?" he asked, and they laughed. They walked through the rehab grounds smoking cigarettes.

"Is this your first time in rehab?" she asked.

"No," he said. "Third. Yours?"

"Also third."

"Maybe three's the charm."

They walked and smoked, aware of the staff watching. No fraternizing with the opposite sex.

Groups were okay, one-on-one was frowned upon. Rafe didn't ask her her drug of choice. Another rule, one he didn't mind keeping. Once you started talking about what you took, you wanted to take it. And hearing what someone else once used, realizing you never tried it, could plant a seed in your mind for when you got out.

"Where are you from?" she asked.

"New York."

"Where'd you go before?"

"Wernersville, Pennsylvania. Antigua. Now here."

"Nothing but the best," she said.

"How about you?" he asked.

"I always come back here," she said, smiling. "Feels like home."

They'd gotten to know each other over the stay. Walks around the campus, supervised hikes into the Malibu scrubland, Friday night movie excursions. They talked about their families; her parents were divorced, her mom a screenwriter now married to a director, her dad an actor who'd stopped working to shoot heroin.

Rafe told her about his mother. Monica listened as if she cared. When he told her about his first Christmas after his mother had died, how he'd asked the elevator man in his apartment building to take him to the roof, so he could leave her present up there, closer to heaven, she'd cried.

His father had stopped visiting. The first two times in rehab, he'd shown up on family day, and for family counseling. But this time was different. Rafe's father was finished with him—not just because he kept relapsing, every rehab stay costing him thousands of dollars, not to mention legal bills for the Central Park arrest—but because of what had happened on Capri.

Because of what Rafe had done to his grandmother. His grandmother, who'd never been anything but wonderful to him, all he'd had to do was stay with her for an hour. An hour. Sitting on the lawn, Pacific Ocean gleaming blue on the horizon, Rafe told all that to Monica.

"That's why you have to stay clean now," she said, staring at him with enormous green eyes.

"It's why I don't think I can," he said. "She took care of me when I was little and would visit her, and all she needed was one hour—keep her safe, from falling and hurting herself, and I couldn't even do that. I keep seeing her face looking at me. And I just want to block it out."

"Don't you know you can't?" Monica asked. "For as long as you live? All you can do is find a way to live with it."

"I can't," he said.

"What was her name?"

"Christina Gardiner."

Looking up, Monica stared at the sky. "Christina," she said. "Please help Rafe. Be with him, and help him."

Rafe had a lump in his throat. It was as if Monica knew his grandmother, realized she was the kind of woman who **would** help him if she could, would watch over him. Who would forgive him.

At the movies a month before he left rehab, he'd sat next to Monica, watching **The Lost Pawn.** There, in the dark, he'd felt her elbow touch his on the armrest. Then she'd taken his hand. They'd clasped hands all through the film; he'd barely seen what was happening on the screen.

"Did you like it?" she asked afterward, standing on the sidewalk under the marquee.

"I loved it," he said, wanting to kiss her in the warm California night air, aware of the counselor watching them.

"I meant the film," she said, smiling.

"Oh," he said. "Yeah, it was good."

They smiled, walked to the van. Something stirred in Rafe that night. He wanted something—or someone. Lying in his bed back at rehab, he thought of Monica. He wondered what life would be, having a woman to love, wanting to get up in the morning because you didn't have to feel so alone. She didn't hate him for what he'd done—she understood addiction, knew she'd almost lost her own soul along the way.

People were allowed to contact each other once they were discharged. Rules were strict inside the rehab gates, but it was a free world outside. Rafe had every intention of getting her address and phone number, contacting her when they were both released.

The suggestion was "no major changes during the first year," including relationships. But something between them had already developed over the months together; wouldn't it be an even more major change if they left each other's lives? He had planned to wait a month or so, to make sure he could stay clean. Then he would call her.

Rafe never got the chance. One day he went downstairs, and she was gone. No one could tell him why—confidentiality. He heard that her insurance had run out, that her mother wasn't willing to pick up the difference this time around. Rafe knew the despair and frustration of three-time-rehab parents; his father had told him this was the last chance. But he wished she'd left him her number.

When he was released, he called information first thing. Her stepfather's number was unlisted; her mother's office wouldn't even take his call. He'd kept waiting for Monica to search him out, but how would she find him on Capri? Had he even told her that's where his grandparents' house was?

Now, staring up at Lyra's house through the rain, the lights shimmered and blurred. He blinked, hoping Pell was okay. The sound of her saying "Travis" haunted him—not just because she felt so bad, but because it woke Rafe up to his own heart. He should have been saying "Monica" with as much regret, grief. She was in him, as much as he'd tried to think it didn't matter.

"Rafe?"

Hearing his grandfather's voice, he turned.

"Hi, Grandpa," Rafe said.

"What are you doing, standing here? You're soaking wet. Come up to the house with me."

"How'd you know I was here?" Rafe asked.

"Lyra called to tell me you'd seen Pell home. I assumed you were down at the boathouse. I don't want you staying there tonight."

Rafe felt frozen in place. He'd lived in the boathouse these last four weeks. Going to the villa made him feel raw, too close to his grandmother and what he'd done.

"Come, Rafe," his grandfather said, reaching for Rafe's hand.

Rafe flinched—he felt undeserving of tenderness, of his grandfather's love, and the touch of the old man's hand threw him back to childhood, when he'd still been good, before he'd caused so much destruction.

The slope was wet, the stone stairs carved into the rock slippery, and in that instant Rafe let out a huge yell as his feet went out from under him. His grandfather clutched at him, trying to hold on, and all Rafe could think of was stopping the fall, keeping his grandfather from crashing down the rocks, and he went backward into darkness.

~

Lyra heard a shout; the voice echoed off the hillside, dissolving so fast, she wondered if she'd imagined it. She stepped outside to investigate.

A steady drizzle was coming down. She shielded her eyes with one hand, peering into the dark. Rustling sounds came from the stairs, then a groan. Moving cautiously, Lyra inched her way around the cypress grove to see who was there, what was going on. Through the mist she saw Max with one foot on the stairs, one over the side, planted in the wild scrub.

"Max, what is it?" she called.

"Lyra, thank God!" he called back, and she saw his shoulders straining as he bent over trying to haul something heavy out.

Running over, she saw that it was Rafe. By a quirk or miracle, Max's grandson had fallen not into the abyss, but onto a narrow strip of crumbling soil, old branches, and brambles clinging to the rocks. Blood poured from Rafe's temple, trickling away in the rain; his eyes were shut. Her heart seized; for a moment she flashed back to Christina's fall.

"Is he . . . ," she began.

"He's breathing," Max said. "Please, help him."

Lyra climbed down beside Max. They were balanced on the steps, looking into a sharp ravine that fell a hundred feet down to the cove. Rafe had gone over backward, must have struck his head on the step, landed on a foot-wide strip of hillside between the stairs and precipice. Fallen branches, shallow pine and cedar roots, and cascades of dead leaves and debris had woven together to form a cradle, a web between the stairs and plunging rock face.

Max held Rafe in his arms, one foot digging into the precarious weave of earth and roots, and Lyra realized that if Max's weight broke through the fragile basket of knit-together ground, or if Rafe woke up and rolled the wrong way, the two men would go over.

"What should I do?" she asked.

"Can you brace me," Max asked, "while I try to pull him onto the stairs?"

"Okay," she said.

"Stay on solid ground," he said. "One foot on the stairs, that's right—the other on the rock."

"I've got it," she said.

Stepping forward, Lyra grabbed for his arm. She felt Max's weight straining toward the edge, reaching around Rafe's inert body, easing him toward the steps. Hearing Max's labored breathing, she prayed that he wouldn't have a heart attack.

She stared down at Rafe's pale face, the blood dripping from the cut in his head; he was clearly unaware of any of it. Two years ago she'd found Christina where she'd fallen, just a hundred yards away. This young man had already been responsible for one disaster, now there was another in the making.

Lyra glanced at Max's face, saw the strain, and hope, and desperation. No matter what Rafe had done, Max loved him with everything he had. Lyra thought of Pell upstairs, shut in her room. All day Lyra had been worried; no matter that Pell had run off on her own, Lyra had wanted to blame Rafe for taking her away.

"He's slipping," Max said. His voice broke; she heard so much love. The rain was coming down harder, and Rafe's weight plus the way Max was wedging his foot into the root system made the cradle of branches and earth start to give way with a terrible tearing sound.

"Hold on," Lyra said, bending down, grabbing Rafe by the collar.

"Get back," Max said. "Lyra, make sure you're on the steps."

Lyra couldn't let go. She closed her eyes, hearing Max's voice: "I have you, Rafe, I have you, my boy." In that moment she knew he was prepared to go over the edge with his grandson. There was no way Max would let Rafe die alone.

And in that moment, Lyra felt flooded with love of her own. Pell; she had come to this island, she loved Lyra enough to forgive her for all that she had and hadn't done; Lucy was on her way. And for Max, her dearest friend, who taught her with everything he had to believe in goodness, to open her heart a little more, a little more, each day. He was crouched in the pouring rain, holding on to the boy who'd thrown his own life away over and over, who'd caused Max's beloved Christina to die, ready to give everything for him.

Christina was with them. Lyra heard her voice, right there on the craggy stairs, in rain driving so hard it seemed to want to wash the earth, the trees, Max and Rafe, every living thing off the rocks.

"Rafaele," Lyra heard Christina say. "Rafaele . . ."

Max turned his head; he'd heard it too.

And Rafe woke up. His eyes flew open; he jolted, but Max held him steady. Lyra offered Rafe her hand, pulled him toward her as Max stepped carefully backward, onto the steps. Very slowly Rafe got to his knees, crawled to safety.

Lyra and Max supported him. He walked between them, one arm around each of their necks. They made their way gently, both not wanting to jar Rafe and perhaps not wanting to discuss what had just happened.

"You saved me," Rafe said to Lyra and Max when they got to the car parked outside the villa, to take him to the hospital.

"Thank God you woke up when you did," Max said, helping his grandson into the front seat.

"It was Christina," Lyra said.

They both looked at her, confused. "You heard her, didn't you?" Lyra asked.

"I heard you," Rafe said, reaching for her hand. "You said my name, and I woke up."

"That wasn't me," Lyra said.

"Really?" Max asked, and she saw him smile.

"Really," Lyra said.

"My grandmother," Rafe said, bowing his head.

Lyra crouched by the open door. He looked up again, and she gazed into his blue eyes, this young man Christina had loved so much. "You are so loved," she said. "Do you know that?"

"I don't deserve it," he said, his voice low and hoarse.

"I don't either," she said. "But I seem to be surrounded by it. You helped Pell come back home today. Thank you."

He nodded. "She wasn't ready to leave," he said.

"I'd better get him to the hospital," Max said, and Lyra felt his hand on the back of her head. She stood up, face-to-face with him. Her heart was pounding—she'd been so afraid of losing him back there on the hillside. She reached up, touched his cheek.

"I'm coming with you," she said. "I'll call Pell from there, let her know what's going on."

"You don't have to come," he said.

"Yes," Lyra said. "I do." She looked into his blue eyes, felt something shift in her heart. She'd heard Christina's voice back there, no matter what Rafe and Max thought. And she knew her old friend had been giving them all her blessing. Perhaps Lyra had actually spoken Rafaele's name, inspired by Christina herself. But this was all Lyra, straight from her own heart.

"I'm with you," Lyra said. "We're going together."

Nineteen

The flight took eight hours. Every minute felt tense, as if the plane would never land. Lucy's grandmother had tried to make her fly first-class, but she'd traded in her ticket to sit with Travis in coach. They ate sandwiches Travis's mother had made them, watched the movie, slept. Well, Lucy had. Travis was used to having a little sister lean against him on long trips. To him, Lucy was as much his little sister as Pell's, and she slept most of the way with her head on his shoulder.

They arrived in Italy, Travis's first time in Europe. He knew it sounded lame, but he barely noticed anything: not the architecture, the cars, the landscape, the cathedrals. He could only think about getting to Pell.

The storms that had buffeted their landing had passed, and the day sparkled bright and sunny. At the bustling dock in Sorrento, they were met by an old fisherman, Nicolas. Travis felt instantly at home—he was just like Joaquim, a Portuguese fishing captain he knew from Newport. Tan, lined face, great friendly smile with a gold front tooth.

"Lucy Davis?" he asked.

"Yes," she said. "That's me."

"And Travis Shaw?"

"Yes," he said.

The grin became larger. "Come aboard, I am your **traghetto**. Your water taxi."

"I got my mother's message," Lucy said. "Thank you for coming to get us. She said something happened, she'd see us later . . . but I thought my sister might have come."

Nicolas's smile dimmed. "There was an accident," he said. "Max's grandson was injured, went to **ospedale.** They are there with him."

"Oh, no," Lucy said. "Is he badly hurt?"

"Yes, but he will recover."

They climbed aboard, set off across the deep blue water. Travis barely noticed the boat's fishing rigs, barrels, nets. Approaching Capri, he hardly saw the green, mountainous beauty. His mind was racing.

He hadn't spoken to Pell since before he'd decided to come. He'd checked his messages since landing, and she hadn't returned any of his calls. At least they knew where she was. But was Travis going to walk into an Italian hospital and find out she was in love with someone else?

Nicolas drove them to the marina on Capri. The wharf area bustled; shops and restaurants backed up to a steep, soaring mountainside. Travis took it in, and in spite of the dramatic landscape, felt a connection to Newport: two worlds here, the fishing boats and the yachts. When Nicolas pulled up to the dock, Travis jumped out, caught and cleated the lines.

"You are a good boatman," the old man said.

"Thank you," Travis said.

"You work?" Nicolas asked.

"On a fishing boat," Travis said.

"Excellent," Nicolas said. "Work is good. Especially on the water."

Travis nodded. They were alike, Travis and this old man, and looking around the glamorous port, Travis felt the same division he sometimes felt in Newport—between his family and the rich people, between the Shaws and the Nicholsons and Davises. What if Pell had changed, had decided she wanted to be with people more like her?

He lifted their bags, and Nicolas led them down the dock, across the wharf, and under a large arch to the funicular office. Nicolas got them tickets; Travis tried to pay him back with the euros he'd converted at the airport, but the old man refused. Standing in the crowd, Travis wanted to leave everyone behind, just sprint to wherever Pell was.

Five minutes later, the funicular arrived, and they climbed aboard a red car, between a train and cable car, attached to a track running up the steep mountain behind the marina. Out the window were wide views of the bay they'd just crossed. Travis didn't care. He stared out but didn't see, couldn't smile. He sat beside Lucy; she couldn't comfort him because she didn't know what was going on either.

"Don't think what you're thinking," Lucy said.

"How do you know what I'm thinking?" he asked.

"Because I'm jet-lagged out of my mind, and my thoughts are going crazy. I figure yours are too."

"A little," he said, forcing a small smile, so she wouldn't worry.

They crossed the Piazza Umberto, saw the sign for **Ospedale.** Travis glanced at Lucy to make sure she was okay with Nicolas. She nodded, and he started to run. He tore through the crowd, still carrying his and Lucy's bags. Weaving and dodging as if he were flying down the football field, he'd never run this fast before.

He found the hospital building, didn't slow down. Through the front doors, straight to the front desk, where he was all ready to start butchering the name Rafaele Gardiner, to try to find the room. But he didn't have to.

"Travis."

Her voice. Pell. He turned, and she was there, waiting.

Eyes so blue, filled with pain. She was going to tell him right now, it was over, she'd come to her senses. He was just a scholarship kid, a teacher's son; she could do so much better. He walked over to her, afraid to speak. She reached out, her hands shaking.

"Pell," he said.

"I knew you were coming," she said. "Nicolas said he'd bring you to the hospital."

"I called," he said. "But you didn't answer."

"I know," she said. "I got your messages."

"Why didn't you call me back?" he asked, trying to keep his voice steady, stay strong.

"Because I couldn't take hearing your voice until you were here, until you were really here. Oh, Travis," she said, falling into his arms and starting to cry.

~

Lucy was in heaven.

Italy was the most beautiful place she'd ever seen, the buildings ancient and graceful, the accents pure music. She had enjoyed the funicular ride, had her guidebook open and was following along, even as Travis's panic grew by the mile.

In spite of her momentary jet-lag-induced qualm, she'd wanted to tell him not to worry, he hadn't known Pell as long as she had. Pell stayed true; she didn't stray or wander, just remained steadily on the path. That had been so Lucy's entire life, and she doubted one trip to Italy could change something so deep at the core.

Lucy had missed her sister so much, and once Nicolas's boat pulled in to the dock on Capri, she smelled the wild herbs and saw the crowds of people passing along the waterfront, and knew she was about to be reunited with Pell. She wouldn't even let herself think about the other amazing thing that was about to happen. It seemed too impossible and wonderful to believe.

She and Nicolas walked slowly across the cobblestones, watching Travis tear into the hospital, and through the window they saw him and Pell embracing. They were still in love, of course they were.

"Amore," Lucy said, trying out her Italian on Nicolas.

He beamed, then stopped still, right there in the square surrounded by charming ancient cafés, umbrellas, church tower, and stone arches. At first she thought maybe she'd botched the pronunciation so badly, or possibly it was considered laughable to say "love," or . . . And then the wonderful, impossible thing she hadn't let herself think about happened.

"Mom!" Lucy said.

The hospital door opened, and she came forward. Tall, with flowing dark hair with a white streak in front, looking exactly like Pell but a bit older, Lucy's mother stood there. They stared at each other for the longest minute ever measured on earth.

The seconds ticked and took Lucy all the way back to her birth, to her mother's arms in the hospital, to their very first meeting. And they swept her through her first four years, the happiness of their beloved time. The dreaded 2:01 a.m. had started losing its power during that phone call when her mother had talked her to sleep. Love wasn't a time of day or night.

"Lucy," her mother said, opening her arms.

And Lucy ran; no, she flew. All the way across the remaining space between them, Nicolas smiling and all the people watching, and Lucy didn't care. It was a dream, a waking dream. She threw herself into her mother's arms, and the two of them were back together, they were back together, it already felt as if they had never been apart.

~

Rafe's condition had stabilized during the night. Max stepped away from his grandson's bedside long enough to go downstairs to the hospital lobby, gaze through the window to witness the reunion: Pell and her young man, Lyra and Lucy. Seeing Lyra with both her daughters did something to his heart so powerful he had to lean against the door.

"Are you all right, sir?" a woman asked, entering the hospital with a bouquet of flowers.

"Yes, thank you. Quite," he said, smiling at her. He resumed watching the gathering.

Max's chest felt so full, as if it might burst open. His heart was healthy, but proving inadequate to contain so much emotion—joy and sorrow. Lyra had been by his side, with Rafe, ever since bringing him into the emergency room last night. She'd held

Max's hand, but not in their old, familiar, friendly-neighbors way. In a way that told him they were each other's family. He wanted to tell her that she was even more: she had somehow, along the way, become his life.

Max stood just inside the hospital door, watching. He saw Pell and Lucy hug, then Pell introduce the young man to Lyra; Max hung back for the moment, not wanting to intrude. He knew what this meant to her—the moment she'd most needed and feared for ten years: reuniting with her daughters. What if they'd rejected her? Deep down, that had always been in Lyra's mind. But watching the two girls circle their mother, Max knew she needn't have worried.

Across the cobblestone square, Nicolas stood like a sentry. Arms folded, watching the same scene from a different angle. Max watched as John Harriman approached Nicolas, received the report from him. John, old gossip that he was, watched Lyra, her daughters, and the young man with avid interest. But even the sight of John touched Max; what good friends he had. Max had called Nicolas, told him about Rafe's fall, asked him to pick up Lucy and Travis in Sorrento.

Nicolas had told John, and they had both come directly to the hospital. They'd stayed in the waiting room with Max and Lyra for a few hours last night. Rafe's head wound was deep, he had a concussion, and had suffered a seizure. After midnight, concern arose about brain swelling. A surgeon had been consulted.

Although surgery had been avoided, Rafe was to stay another night under observation. Max had called David in New York, told him the situation. The dark end to the day, the deep sorrow, was his son's reaction.

"He's using drugs again," David said.

"No," Max said. "It was raining, he slipped on the stairs."

"Dad, you can't believe him."

Once when Rafe had started using drugs again, David had confronted him and Rafe had denied it. David told Max the rehab counselor had said, "How can you tell an addict is lying? His lips are moving."

"I was there, David," Max said. "I saw what happened. It was dark, he was standing on that steep section of the hill by Lyra's house. The truth is, he fell trying to protect me—to block me from going down."

"Dad, you saw what he wanted you to. You're believing what he says, not what he does. Ask yourself, what was he doing there? Who stands on those stairs in the rain, at night?"

"Rafe had just walked Lyra's daughter home. I think he was concerned about her."

"He's concerned about one person—himself."

"You haven't seen him recently," Max said. "I've tried to tell you, things have changed. He's staying away from trouble, he's a good worker, he's been a caring friend to Pell. I'm very impressed with him, the changes he's making. If you came and saw him, you would be too."

Silence as David took that in. Max could almost hear his skepticism, his grave disappointment.

"Dad," David said, "you're too good to him. Mother is dead because Rafe thought it was a better idea to take some pills and get high than stay with her for—what? How long were you gone that afternoon? Thirty minutes? An hour? How can you forgive him for that?"

"Because I love him," Max said. "He made a terrible mistake, and he has to live with it. And because your mother would want me to."

"I have to go now, Dad," David said.

"David, do you have a message for me to give Rafe?"

"Goodbye, Dad."

Max held that inside now, his son's goodbye. David was a good person, brilliant in his way. Max and Christina had sent him to Eton, then Cambridge. He had tried his best with Rafe after Violetta's death, but Max had watched with dismay as he'd spent most of his energy rising high in the Bank of Kensington instead of tending to his grief-stricken boy.

"Max!"

Lyra had spotted him through the window, was calling him onto the square. He smiled, pushing his own private disappointment in David down, and stepped outside into bright sunshine. Lyra linked her arm through his.

"Max, I'd like you to meet my daughter Lucy," Lyra said. "And Pell's boyfriend, Travis Shaw."

"How do you do?" Max said. He shook Travis's hand, but Lucy spontaneously stood on tiptoes and kissed his cheek. "Thank you," he said.

"Pell's told me so much about you," Lucy said.

Pell nodded, but didn't speak. Max gazed at her; in so short a time, he'd come to love her. She was Lyra's daughter, but wonderful in her own right. She'd shown up at the hospital last night, right after Lyra called. Max had watched her checking her voicemail, staring into space, wide-eyed with some kind of private torment. She was present for her mother, Max, and Rafe—but her heart and mind were elsewhere. Now he realized where: with Travis.

Max saw the way they leaned into each other. There was silent, unspoken support flowing from one to the other. Pell's eyes looked stricken, as if she was carrying a secret weight. He knew that it had something to do with why Rafe had been on the steps last night.

"Did you have a good trip over?" Max asked Travis. "Nicolas met you?"

"Yes, sir," Travis said. "Thank you."

"I would have gone to get you myself," Max said.

"But your grandson's been injured," Travis said. "How is he?"

"Improving," Max said. "You're kind to ask." He watched as Pell looked down at her feet, and Travis put his arm around her.

"I hope he's better soon," Travis said.

"Thank you," Max said, knowing that all would be well between him and Pell. Travis's great heart shone out.

Max felt Lyra take his hand. Whether for support or from sheer joy, he didn't know. Glancing down at her, he saw a completely different woman. Her eyes sparkled, and she beamed up at him. "My daughters are here!" she said.

"Nothing could be more wonderful," Max said.

John took that moment to pull Nicolas across the tree-lined plaza to get a closer look at the Davis family reunion. Lyra happily introduced him to Lucy and Travis, and Nicolas made a kind remark about Travis being a fisherman. There was plenty to interest John, but Max couldn't help note his old friend seemed most fascinated by Lyra's and Max's clasped hands. John's eyes glinted with delight. Max really couldn't begrudge him. Except for Rafe's condition—and David—Max felt fairly delighted himself.

Twenty

~

Travis and I were together again. But things had changed.

I had left Newport as one person, but now I was another. Life adds up. It also subtracts. Love is cumulative. Doubt is corrosive. Nothing is set in stone. Illusions in a family, in life, can cause terrible damage. I'd set my father on a pedestal. Seeing him knocked off nearly caused me to destroy everything.

How can I explain how hard it was, waiting for Travis to arrive? I'd heard his messages, the growing concern in his voice. In my room at my mother's, I lay on my bed, hand on my stomach, wondering how I could have kissed Rafe, nearly thrown myself into something I'd never come back from. Travis was my only one. Rafe had been a stand-in. And what a way to treat a person—Rafe, I mean. As if he didn't matter on his own.

When my mother called from the hospital, I

nearly fell apart. Because I cared about Rafe—my feelings for him, although confused, were real. By the time I got to the hospital, he'd taken a turn for the worse. He'd had a seizure, lost consciousness. There was swelling in his brain; a doctor came to talk to Max about surgery to relieve the pressure.

My mother paced the floor. While Max consulted with the surgeon and then, I gather, called Rafe's father in New York, my mother was inconsolable. She and I hadn't really talked since my return home from the boathouse. We hadn't cleared the air, and I was still angry with my father, and shocked and horrified at the idea that she had really thought about killing us that night at the bridge. But I was also taken by the fact she wasn't apologizing to me, trying to explain, to smooth things over. All of her attention was on Max and Rafe.

"I thought he was okay," she said. "I really did, I was sure of it. . . ."

"The doctors are with him," I said. I'd been with my father through many surgeries. I'd seen him have seizures. I felt I knew about head trauma.

"He could have died, there on the hill," my mother said. "But he didn't. He made it here. . . ."

"And he'll get through this," I said. I felt cold and, as I've mentioned, a little superior in my hospital and bedside experience.

"Max won't be able to take it," my mother said, suddenly falling apart, starting to cry. "If he loses Rafe. Please don't let it happen, please, please. . . ."

My mother was praying. I stood up from the chair where I'd been sitting. I watched her bow her head, sob into her hands.

"Mom," I said.

"Pell," she said, almost as if seeing me for the first time. "Is it me? Do I bring such terrible things to people I love?"

"No," I said.

She grabbed my hand. "What I did to you . . . putting you in such danger. I am so sorry. Please, Pell—don't be mad at your dad. It was all my fault."

Fault. What a useless word. It hit me—we were together, my mother and I. She was praying for Rafe, a boy she'd previously—even hours earlier—seemed completely unable to stand. And she'd just said "people I love." My mother.

All these years without her, I'd pictured her on the glamorous island of Capri, surrounded by rich, famous, shallow, beautiful people. I hadn't expected to find her in a warm, cozy house, perched on a rocky overlook full of gardens, surrounded by some of the most wonderful people I'd ever met. I hadn't anticipated Max, and the way he felt about her, and the way my mother obviously felt about him, and how depths and heights of love could heal every heart.

"Mom," I said, hugging her.

We stood there a long time. Max came back, and my mother took his hand. They went to sit quietly in a corner of the waiting room. I watched her try to soothe him. The nurse came out to say they could see Rafe. I watched through the door, saw my mother lay her hand on Rafe's forehead.

It's strange. Seeing her that way, so warm and caring toward Max in his moment of crisis, toward Rafe as he lay injured in bed, I felt my father with us. As if he'd come back to be with me, stand by my side, bear witness to my mother's transformation. I felt him forgiving all she had done, all she'd been unable to do. I felt his spirit, but I wished I could see his face. I closed my eyes, brought him close in my mind.

"She's good," I said to him. And I meant it two ways. She's doing well—she's healed herself from the pain that drove her away from us, and she's a good person, someone I can feel proud of, someone who cares.

My father had only wanted the best for me and Lucy. I knew that. He would never have driven my mother away, and he couldn't really explain to us the truth of why he'd needed to protect us from her. It would have planted a dreadful, immutable fact in my mind: my mother had considered killing me.

Instead, my father let us keep our love for her. He'd never told us she might have hurt me, might have intended the worst there was. Because of him, we'd been able to hold her close, Lucy and I, in a golden glow of what once had been and what we'd never stopped hoping could be again.

And here we were. All three of us together.

While my mother took Lucy home, to let her settle in and get over her jet lag, and while Max stayed at the hospital with Rafe, I walked with Travis. We sent his bag in my mother's car. He and I climbed the Phoenician Steps—all eight-hundred-something of them. My legs ached, but the physical exertion was nothing compared to the difficulty of facing what I'd done.

"I should bring the team over here," he said. "A few times running up and down, we'd be in shape and ready for the season."

"Travis . . . ," I said.

But he just kept walking up, as if he didn't want to slow down, stop, listen to me, hear me confess. He sensed it, I could tell. I must have looked like a wreck—I'd been up all night, and even though I'd showered after the boat ride and making out with Rafe, I felt disgrace and betrayal clinging to me.

When we finally got to the top, I grabbed Travis's hand.

"I have to talk to you," I said.

"This is amazing," he said, not hearing me.

He chose that moment to look around, and for the first time seemed to see the spectacular view. Rain had washed the air so clean, there wasn't a trace of humidity to dull the sparkling blue. The cerulean bay gleamed, hardly a line between water and sky. We saw the white wakes of brightly colored fishing boats; my gaze was pulled southeast, in the direction of Il Faraglioni.

"You have to listen to me," I said, shaking him.

He tried to keep ignoring me, just staring out to sea at Ischia, then right toward the mainland, over the water to the dark shape of Mount Vesuvius.

"I did something," I said.

Finally he looked at me. "I know," he said.

"How?" I asked.

"Because I know you, Pell," he said.

We sat down on a grassy slope, shaded by olive trees. Sunlight dappled through the silver leaves, and tiny lizards skittered across flat rocks. There was space between us; we didn't touch, just stared out to sea. I wanted to explain everything, but suddenly I couldn't speak. He knows me, he said. I thought he did. But I also thought I knew myself.

"I want to tell you what happened," I said.

"You don't have to."

"Yes, I do." And I started talking. My mother, my father, the revelation about what had happened on the bridge, my father telling my mother he didn't want her to live with us if she couldn't keep us safe. My running out, deciding to leave. Rafe, the boat ride, the seahorses.

"He showed you seahorses?" Travis asked. For

some reason, that detail seemed to hurt him more than any so far. He'd heard, all along, about my father's nicknames for me and Lucy.

"Yes."

"Go on," he said, steeling himself.

I told him how Rafe had refused to take me to Sorrento, wanted me to have it out with my mother. How I'd been crazed, thinking of my father, of what he'd kept from us, of how everything I'd believed about him, and about our little family, was suddenly flipped. My wonderful father, so flawed he'd actually driven my mother away.

"I wasn't ready to go up to my mother's house," I told Travis. "I couldn't bring myself to face her. So I went to the boathouse."

"What's that?"

"It's where Rafe sleeps."

Travis looked away again, staring at the bay, at the boats, as if he wished he were on one of them, fishing far away from me. My heart was beating in my throat. I took Travis's hand. He had to look at me for this part; I tugged, so he'd turn his head, and he did, and I was staring into his eyes.

"I kissed him," I said.

He looked momentarily stung, then blank. And then he walked away. He stopped looking at me, and he started back down the steps, as if toward the marina, to find Nicolas, to get him to take him as far from me as he could get.

~

Travis felt stung, as if wasps had gotten him. But instead of his skin burning, it was his insides. Little venomous insects had flown down his throat, jabbing him with poison. Could he die from this? The picture of Pell kissing another guy.

He felt sick, burning up. The image was there in his mind, it wouldn't go away. Had Rafe put one hand on her head, the other on her waist? Had he touched her face? Had the kiss been slow? Had it been intense? How long had it lasted?

Pell had told Travis she loved him. He remembered the first time. It was even before Toronto, before things got so physically serious. Going back to last winter, the start of Christmas vacation, right after the wreath-throwing. His family had just gotten back together. Carrie had returned, bringing Gracie.

The baby in the house had distracted everyone from the fact Carrie had disappeared for a year, all the reasons for her taking off. Gracie was so cute and sweet, funny and curious. The whole family congregated around her, staring at every move she made. Travis started feeling as if they were watching a magic show so they wouldn't have to talk.

He and Pell walked the school grounds, just as they had a few weeks earlier, looking for Beck at the height of the drama. Winter, and snow was a foot deep. The paths were shoveled but icy, and a bitter ocean wind blew between the buildings.

"How are you?" Pell asked, after they'd walked in silence awhile.

"I don't know," he said. "It's all weird."

"Which part?"

"Things are messed up," he said. "Carrie's home, and that's great. But she had a kid. No one even knew."

"Your family had a lot going on," Pell said.

Travis nodded, his chin buried in a muffler. She was right. Trauma had hit the Shaws. Family secrets; sounded like the title of a chick flick, but they were real. His mom had been with another guy before marrying his dad. Carrie had come from that relationship, and when the truth came out eighteen years later, it nearly destroyed everyone.

Travis's dad had died in a terrible accident, Carrie had run away, and it had taken a year for her to return home, for them all to start to come back together. Travis had been going out with Ally, a girl from back home in Ohio, when he'd first moved to Newport. Pell had seen him through everything, even the breakup.

"Why did it have to happen?" Travis asked Pell, walking through the snow. "Why'd my dad have to die? Everyone's sitting home, smiling at Gracie, and he's gone—he'll never know his granddaughter."

"I don't know why such terrible things happen," Pell said, taking his hand.

"If my mom had told the truth back when they were young," Travis began, and Pell stopped him.

"I'm sure she did the best she could," Pell said. "She must have decided it would hurt him less to not tell him the truth."

"It hurt him more," Travis said.

"I know," Pell said. They walked a few more minutes, then stopped. She looked at Travis in that deep way, her blue eyes knowing so much, as if she'd lived her whole life already. Her eyes were filled with sadness, and that's when she said it. "I love you, Travis."

"I love you too, Pell," he said.

They held each other, their bodies pressing together as the cold wind blew around them. Then she tilted her head back and looked up at him. He'd seen a sharpness in her blue eyes—a promise. He'd had the feeling she wanted to say more. But they hadn't been going out long—they were so new. Maybe she'd felt it was too soon to say that much.

Now, walking down the crooked, rugged stone steps on Capri, Travis burned with the news about Pell kissing Rafe. He hated what she'd done, more than almost anything he could think of. It had hurt him worse than anything since his dad's death. But suddenly he stopped, one foot in the air, before it hit the next step. And he knew: exactly what Pell had been thinking that snowy day.

He turned around and started running up the steep flight, two stairs at a time, hoping she would still be there. She had to be. He had to look her straight in the eyes and see if he was right.

~

Travis came back.

I hadn't moved.

In fact, I'd used my mother as a model. That day at Tiberius's Leap, when she'd told me the first part of the story about taking me to the bridge, I'd been unable to hear the whole thing, and gone running off. Once I'd processed her words, I returned, and she was right where I'd left her.

As Travis came flying up the craggy Phoenician Steps, I saw the relief in his face when he spotted me standing there. I know I felt immense comfort, realizing that he hadn't commandeered Nicolas to take him back to the mainland.

"Pell," he said.

"Oh, Travis," I said, reaching out. But he stopped short, didn't take my hand.

"I have to ask you something," he said.

I nodded, steeling myself. He wanted to know about the kiss—the details of how it had happened, why I'd let myself get into that situation. "Travis, I'm just so sorry," I began. But he shook his head hard, stopping me.

"Back at school," he said.

"Newport?" I asked. What was he saying?

"Last winter. On that walk."

That walk. There could be only one. "When we said we loved each other?" I asked.

"Yes. You looked at me."

I nodded. I'd been unable to look away from him, and I felt that way again, and my eyes were riveted to his.

"You wanted to say something else," he said.

Had I? I thought back, couldn't remember. "I don't know," I said now.

"I think you wanted to say you'd never lie to me," he said. "Like my mother did to my dad. Even if it hurts, the truth is better."

My eyes filled with tears. Travis was right. I had been thinking that exact thing, on that cold walk through Newport Academy. His family had been ripped apart when his dad found out the truth, that Carrie wasn't his daughter. Mrs. Shaw is one of the best people I know—kind, smart, caring. But she'd tried too hard to protect her husband, instead of trusting his strength, and his goodness, and his capacity to forgive.

"Is that why you told me today?" he asked. "About you and Rafe?"

"Yes," I said. "Because I can't keep a secret from you."

"Thank you for telling me."

"Travis, I'm so sorry."

"Yeah," he said. "I am too."

I froze. Was he breaking up with me?

"Can you ever . . . ," I started to say, but it took a minute to get the words out, "forgive me?"

"Pell," he said, sounding weary.

I was terrible; he couldn't get past it. I started to blather. "Back in Newport, when you were still with Ally . . . once you started having feelings for me, you broke up with her. You could never be with two people at the same time. And I . . ."

"You were 'with him'?" Travis asked.

"No—I mean, we didn't do anything. More than kissing . . . but isn't that enough? I let something happen, and you never would have. You don't deserve it. But if I can just explain, tell you . . ."

"Pell," he said. "You can tell me it was all because of the news about your father, and the seahorses, and all that. But I've been worried about Rafe Gardiner since you first told me about him."

"Why?" I asked, shocked.

"You really want to know?" he asked.

I nodded, and now it was my turn to gaze out over the sea. Birds sang in the trees, raucous song, and I felt my heart pounding. Travis took my hand, held it hard.

"Your mother didn't like him," Travis said. "He had, has, some kind of dark secret. You said he was 'troubled.' Pell, since I've known you, you've been the best person on this earth. Nothing has ever shaken you. Your dad's death, your grandmother's whatever, your mother living so far away, having to look after Lucy as if you're her mom, helping me through my family craziness."

"But I love you," I whispered. "If you think I'm attracted to someone just because he has a dark secret . . ."

"Pell," he said. "You're the one with the dark secret."

"What?" I asked.

Now he was tender. He stroked my face. I felt his lips on my skin. He held my hand even tighter.

"You've tried to carry it all for so long," he said. "Put it down."

"What?" I asked. "Put what down?"

"The heavy rock, the dark secret. Your mother left you and Lucy. Whyever she did it, whyever it happened, for whatever good or terrible reason, whether your father was the most wonderful dad in the world and made everything as good as he could, you've been without your mother since you were six years old."

He was right, and tears welled up again. I stared at him, the boy I'd loved since the day I first saw him.

"Rafe is like you," he said. "I don't know how or why—I don't even know him. But he's suffered a lot. And you saw, and it made you feel at home. Because that's you, Pell. You've been through so much."

"Travis," I said, falling into his arms.

"You told me the truth," he said, kissing my lips.

"As long as you're not in love with him, what happened doesn't matter."

"I'm not," I said.

"That's good," he said.

I gazed into his blue eyes. I believe that when you meet the one for you, you just know. That happened for me and Travis a year ago, when he first moved to Newport. I remember the first second I saw him, across the campus. Our eyes met; we became friends after that, and then better friends.

He had to figure out things with Ally. Then he did, and they broke up, and we got together. We were **still** together. Life was hard; it had been so painful for both of us. But we had each other.

I thought of last winter, back at school. Snow everywhere, all over campus. His family had recently reunited after their own period of working their way back together. Our school has a ceremony once each year, where we commemorate the history of Newport Academy, honoring its founder and one of the students who died long ago.

A week before I told him I loved him, we were all gathered on the school's snow-covered lawn. Travis watched as his sisters and niece, Lucy, and I threw a wreath into the sea. Then we all went to stand with his mother. The sea wind blew, and we were all chilled. We huddled in a circle, to keep warm. Travis's father had died, his older sister had had a baby, his mother was sorting out the damage her secret had done.

I was struck by how, out of great sadness and turmoil, the Shaw family could arrive at this amazing moment. Getting to know Travis had inspired me to think more clearly about my own history—about my parents, and the fact of my mother living so far away—and had strengthened a growing desire of mine to find her and bring her home. That day, freezing cold, seeing three generations of Shaws, I realized how every**thing** in a family affects every**one** in a family. . . .

Ghosts in the nursery. That's the phrase used by the psychoanalyst Selma Fraiberg to explain the way parents bring their own issues of childhood—their own pains, fears, wishes—with them as they start to raise their own children. That idea resonated with me, and was one of the reasons I wanted to become a psychologist. For me, it was more the ghosts in second grade.

That's how old I'd been when my mother left.

Sitting with Travis now, gazing into his blue eyes, I felt my second-grade ghosts flying away. I could almost see them, white as mist, rising into the clear air, through the branches of the olive trees, disappearing somewhere above.

"I love you, Pell," Travis said.

"I love you, Travis," I said. "You came all this way."

He smiled. His eyes looked relaxed now, getting tired, jet lag catching up with him. The blue sky and water surrounded Capri, and it felt like it belonged to us, all of that beauty and wildness, all of the mystery.

"It wasn't so far," he said. Then he put his arms around me, eased me onto the soft green grass, and we fell asleep in the sun.

Twenty-One

The next morning, Rafe lay in bed, hooked up to IVs. He had the world's worst headache, and when he opened his eyes, he saw double. Peering at the door, he saw the nurse—two of her, actually—coming toward him. She held up the syringe, and he shook his head.

"Really?" she asked. "It will help the pain."

"That's okay," he said. "I'll skip it."

What had come over him? Legal painkillers were being offered hourly. Back in rehab, starting with the first one, he'd met people who'd been sober a few years, who'd gone out, started using again, during hospital stays. They counseled skipping the narcotic cocktail when possible, going with Tylenol instead. Their faces and stories came back to Rafe now.

He'd spent two nights in the hospital. Last night, when his headache had gotten really bad, he'd picked up his cell phone and called a number he had stored, but rarely used since his stay in Malibu. His sponsor answered—Kevin McCauley.

"Hello?" Kevin said.

"Hey, man," Rafe said.

"Is this who I think it is? I was pretty sure you'd fallen off the planet."

"Almost did," Rafe said. He went through the short version of what had happened. Hitting his head, standing up and being able to walk on his own, then getting to the hospital and having everything crash. Losing consciousness, having a seizure, slowly getting back to some kind of normal.

"Sounds as if you're lucky to be alive," Kevin said.

"Yeah, I think so," Rafe said.

"You said you were at your grandfather's?"

"That's where it happened, yes."

"Ironic, right?" Kevin asked. "That you should take such a bad fall right there. Was it near the spot?"

"A hundred yards," Rafe said, knowing Kevin meant the place Rafe's grandmother had died.

Twice a week, the rehab residents would go to outside twelve-step meetings. He'd met Kevin at a Sunday morning AA meeting, chosen him to be his sponsor because Kevin had managed to stay clean and sober for eleven years, didn't sound as if he had all the answers, and worked as a gardener for the movie stars of Malibu. Because Kevin knew the garden, loved the earth, he reminded Rafe of his grandmother.

"There are no coincidences," Kevin said, using a phrase Rafe had heard a hundred times in rehab and meetings. It had always set his teeth on edge—one of the pithy things people in recovery said to sound spiritual, or to connect dots never meant to be connected. But just then, Rafe knew Kevin was right.

"Lyra came to help me," Rafe said.

"The neighbor you think hates you? Your grandmother's friend?"

"Yeah," Rafe said. "I was out cold. Hanging on the edge, and I heard a voice. It brought me back, woke me up. It was Lyra, calling my name. But this is weird. She says she didn't. She says she heard it too, and it was my grandmother."

"That sounds right," Kevin said.

"But how?" Rafe said.

"Why wouldn't she be looking out for you?" Kevin asked.

"Because she's dead," Rafe said. "And it was my fault."

"Look," Kevin said. "I don't know about these things. But it seems to me maybe she was trying to tell you to stop thinking that way."

He looked around the hospital room, seeing two of everything. His grandmother had come here after her fall. Rafe thought of how sharp and alive she'd been when he was young, how like a little girl she became as she aged. Losing all that she knew, regressing, forgetting names. He'd come to see her here, in bed with a broken hip. Sobbing like a child, she'd called him "David," his father's name.

"I wish I could," Rafe said. "They keep coming around with shots, and those syringes are looking pretty good. My head's killing me, and I'd really like to stop thinking about my grandmother."

"Here's the rule," Kevin said. "If it's medically necessary, take the shot. Sounds as if you're doing better. So you should ask yourself—is it worth it? You've put together how much time now?"

"A year and thirty-five days," Rafe said. "Clean and sober."

"Great, Rafe. So why screw that up? Take ibuprofen, and know 'this too shall pass.' Do the next right thing."

"Okay, thanks. That's what I called you for," Rafe said. "Oh. And something else. You know that girl Monica?"

"From the rehab? I remember her."

"Do you ever see her around?" Rafe asked. "She lives out there. Santa Monica, I think; I thought maybe you'd bump into her at meetings. You don't have her number, do you?"

"No," Kevin said. "You know, I have my four meetings a week, all up here. Santa Monica's got some good ones. I hope she's going."

"Me too," Rafe said, thinking of her, praying she could make it this time.

"They have meetings in Italy too," Kevin said. "I'm sure you can find some right on Capri. Recovery is like a campfire. You want to stay together, close to the warmth. Once you start wandering away, you can get lost in the woods."

"Thanks, Kevin," Rafe said as he hung up. He knew his headache was less intense than yesterday, that he could get through it without Vicodin. A couple of hits, and he'd be heading down to see Arturo, as far from the campfire as he could get. But he wished Kevin had had Monica's number, and he wished his thoughts would stop swirling up to torment him.

Rafe drifted in and out. The hospital was its own netherworld. He felt restless and imprisoned, alternating with too exhausted to move. He knew Pell had spent most of the first night waiting with his grandfather and Lyra. At least he was mainly unconscious then. When she stopped in to visit, an hour after his call to Kevin, he felt embarrassed to see her.

"Are you awake?" she whispered, coming to stand by his bed.

"Yeah," he said.

"Does it hurt?" she asked.

"A lot," he said. "If you're talking about my pride." He tried to smile.

"How can you say that?" she asked. "You've been one of the best parts about being here. I'm the one who was a jerk."

"I guess I was mixed up about your situation," Rafe said.

"I put you in a bad position," Pell said. "Seeing my mother after all this time has been intense. Having you here made it so much better. My feelings have been all over the place, and somehow they landed on you."

"Well, I wanted them to," Rafe said.

She smiled. "You were so good to me, taking me to see the seahorses. And even more, not letting me leave without seeing my mother."

"'Do the next right thing,'" Rafe said.

"Exactly," Pell said. "Are you okay?"

"Getting there," he said.

"That's good," she said. "Because the starfish can't do without you." She and Rafe both smiled, remembering their first talk, that walk along the tide line. He thought of how high and dry he'd felt himself at times, out of the reach of the ocean, of the life-sustaining sea.

"So, your boyfriend's here?" Rafe asked.

"Yes," Pell said. "Travis. He's waiting for me downstairs. I just wanted to stop by and see how you're doing. Make sure you're okay."

"He's a lucky guy," Rafe said.

"Somewhere out there is a lucky girl," Pell said, kissing his forehead. "Get better fast, and go find her."

"I'll try," Rafe said.

"Get back to the beach soon. The starfish need you."

And it was funny, but Pell's words made his headache go away. Just like that—no Vicodin, not much more Tylenol. He felt absolved from his own stupidity, thinking he could substitute one girl to care about for another.

He thought of Monica, remembered that day on the lawn when she'd prayed to his grandmother, to look over him. More than anything, he wanted to find her, tell her what had happened that night on the stairs. He felt goosebumps, thinking his grandmother had called his name.

Rafe stayed in the hospital one more night. The doctors did more tests, to make sure there was no bleeding in the brain. The X rays looked fine, and they let him out that afternoon. His grandfather drove him home, slow and easy, winding up the serpentine road from the hospital to the villa.

"How does it feel to be home?" his grandfather asked as they pulled in to the driveway.

"Good," Rafe said, but he felt sad. This wasn't really his home. Neither was the boathouse, nor New York. He was nineteen, untethered. Most of the last five years, he'd been too busy bouncing in and out of rehabs.

"You don't sound as if you feel good," his grandfather said, glancing over.

Rafe looked around at the parklike grounds.

Craggy rocks, terraces of green lawn and brilliant flowers, the white villa silhouetted against blue sky. This place represented his grandfather's life. A lot of people didn't realize that his grandfather was a self-made man. He'd earned a lot of money early, from two hit plays that were turned into films. But he'd grown up in Nottingham, the son of a factory worker.

"What made you start writing plays?" Rafe asked.

"I was curious about other people's lives," his grandfather said.

"Really?"

"Yes. I'd look at row houses and imagine the stories going on inside. A light behind a curtain. Two people leaving a bar. Your grandmother painted beautiful pictures of gardens, flowered terraces, exteriors. That was her domain. Mine was the interior, what went on under the family's roof."

"Does writing help you figure things out?" Rafe asked.

"Sometimes," his grandfather said. "But not always. Lately I've found life to be completely unfathomable. The mysteries are too great for a humble playwright like me."

"Come on, Grandpa," Rafe said, laughing as they parked the car. "You're the wisest person I know. What's so unfathomable?"

"The fact," his grandfather said, not opening the

door, just turning to face Rafe, "that such wrong assumptions can be made about people you think you know well."

That was a loaded statement. Was he speaking of Rafe's father? Probably. Rafe knew his grandfather had called to tell him about Rafe's fall. Rafe hadn't heard a word from him, and didn't expect to. His grandfather, on the other hand, never stopped hoping that Rafe and his father could have a rapprochement, hug it out, and go play a nice round of golf.

"Don't worry," Rafe said. "I've messed up so badly, I can't even blame him. It'll take a long time before he trusts me, if ever. I can't really expect to have a relationship with him till then."

"You're speaking of your father?" his grandfather asked. He smiled. "Yes. He surprised me. But I was actually thinking of Lyra."

Rafe opened his mouth to reply, but didn't get the chance. Speaking of Lyra, here she came now. Her daughters too, and that tall guy with Pell had to be Travis. Everyone was carrying something: Lyra a big canvas bag and a bouquet of flowers; Pell a huge ceramic pasta bowl; a young girl, obviously her little sister, with a straw basket overflowing with tomatoes and basil; and Travis with a string of fish.

"What's going on?" Rafe asked.

"Nicolas took Travis out fishing," his grandfather said. "They had good luck. Lyra says it's your grandmother, still watching over you."

"Me? I didn't go fishing. . . ."

"No, but it's your homecoming," Max said.

"For me?" Rafe asked. "But I didn't do anything."

"Rafe, you don't have to 'do something.' We love you. Everyone is just so glad to have you home. Bella has kindly consented to letting Lyra, Pell, and Lucy use the kitchen to cook for you. Lyra insisted."

Rafe gazed through the windshield at Lyra Davis. Something had transformed her. Instead of the angry woman who he'd assumed hated him, she appeared wreathed with love. Surrounded by her two daughters, a miracle in itself. Rafe wondered how they'd done it, come back together after so much pain. He glanced at his grandfather, saw him beaming. **We love you,** his grandfather had said.

Love had come to the villa, Rafe realized as he opened the car door. He saw Lyra stand beside his grandfather, watching him take the basket from Lucy. Kisses all around. Rafe felt tired. He knew this was in some ways for him, but he felt it was really a celebration for everyone else. His grandfather and Lyra had something new going on; Lyra was reunited with her daughters.

"Grandpa," Rafe said, "I'm a little tired. You mind if I go down to the boathouse and rest for a little bit?"

"Rest, of course," his grandfather said. "But not

the boathouse. Please, Rafe, I'd like you to stay up here until I'm sure you're steady."

"My stuff's down there," he said.

"I'll get it for you," the tall kid said. "I'd be happy to run down."

"You must be Travis," Rafe said.

They stared at each other a few seconds, then shook hands. Out of the corner of his eye, Rafe saw Pell smiling.

"And you're Rafe," Travis said. "Glad you're okay."

"Thanks," Rafe said. Then he turned back to his grandfather. "Anyway, thanks for thinking up the party idea, but if it's okay with you, I'll just—"

"Rafe."

A voice Rafe hadn't heard in months, not since he'd flown to New York from California, after getting out of his full year in Malibu rehab. Gazing at the villa's terrace, Rafe saw the dark silhouette, sunlight glinting behind him. Years flew away. Rafe might have been ten again, just home from fishing with his grandfather, seeing the man he looked up to more than any other.

"Hi, Dad," Rafe said.

~

While Rafe and David sat on the terrace, Travis built a fire on the grill, using dried olive branches; Pell and Lucy cooked pasta, dressing it with olive oil, ripe tomatoes, and fresh pecorino; Max stood at the sink, cleaning the fish; and Lyra picked sprigs of rosemary and thyme. At one point, passing by, she leaned into him. Just for a moment—no words were exchanged. But he felt the quick pressure of her body, almost as if she was touching base.

He watched her stand between her daughters, admiring their cooking. He stared at the backs of their heads, three dark-haired women, so similar in their grace of movement. They spoke in low voices, happy and excited. Max felt a wave of doubt and sorrow—they were all so young. How could he be feeling this way, was he a complete old fool? But when Lyra turned, their eyes met, and she smiled.

Max was in that strange, blessed phase of writing a play when the characters have taken over and seem to be creating themselves. His new work had started as a love story between two sets of characters, but as he wrote it, he'd started to realize that he'd made his landscape too small. Life, as it had presented itself to him this summer, was proving to be too enormous and generous to be expressed through four characters, in three acts.

To the list of characters representing himself and Lyra, Pell and Rafe, he had added Lucy and Travis, Bella and Alonzo, even John and Nicolas. He hadn't dared hope for a third-act reunion between the Rafe character and his father, but as of this morning he'd found it necessary to include a character symbolizing David.

That had been the shock of shocks, looking out the window and seeing his son walk up the stairs from the dock. David had been in London; he'd flown down, hired a private boat in Sorrento, come straight to the villa.

Max had wanted David to accompany him to the hospital, to pick up Rafe and bring him home. David said he'd needed to make a business call, he'd see Rafe when he arrived. But Max realized his son had taken time alone to make peace with Christina and with this place. From the kitchen window, Max could see the spot on the lawn where Christina had broken her hip, the fall that had led to her final decline.

Someone had left a bouquet of roses on the spot. White roses, her favorite. And when Max and Rafe entered the house from the hospital, Max saw white petals and torn leaves on the terrace's tile floor, from where David had trimmed the roses' stems of thorns.

The doorbell rang. Perhaps Max should have kept the evening lower key, but he knew Rafe's welcome home needed to include Nicolas. Amanda and Renata, back from Rome, were overjoyed about their moon gate, and wanted to meet Lucy, the young woman who had provided such precise calculations for the arch. And Max couldn't help inviting John, if only so the old gossip would see David and realize what had taken place between him and Rafe.

As twilight settled, the sky turned deep purple. The Bay of Naples sparkled with the lights of boats coming and going. Drinks were served, then dinner. Everyone sat at the long table, eating the delicious meal.

Max toasted his son and grandson and beloved guests, Lucy toasted the Gardiners and thanked them for being so kind to her family, Pell toasted everyone gathered together, Amanda and Renata toasted Lucy's geometry and the moon gate, John toasted secrets of the summer night, and Nicolas toasted the fish. Max waited to hear from David, Rafe, and especially Lyra, but they all stayed quiet.

After dinner, when darkness had completely fallen, the sky blazed with stars. Max had always loved the night sky from this terrace—there were so few house lights around, it sometimes felt as if he could reach out his hand, touch the stars' white fire. Never more than tonight.

Lyra had been sitting beside him. At one point, after coffee, she'd reached over and squeezed his hand. When he looked at her face, he saw her staring up at the sky with such intensity, her eyes bright and distant, he thought something must be wrong. She excused herself, and was gone a few minutes before returning with the white canvas bag she'd brought.

While everyone kept talking, Max watched her reach into the bag, pull out her tripod. She set it up beside the balustrade. Everyone at the table continued their conversations, glancing at Lyra, aware she was doing something. Max was trying not to eavesdrop too blatantly on David and Rafe, seated across the table and a few seats down. John, however, had no such compunctions.

"Well," John said, nodding toward them. "Sounds as if things are going very well."

"Looks that way," Max said.

"David's arrival has given me an idea for the title of your new play," John said. "'The Prodigal Father.'"

As much as Max would have liked to dismiss it, John's title had the ring of truth and wisdom. But looking around the table, at the people who had so recently returned to one another, again he was struck by the danger of limitation, of making his story too small.

The Davis girls sat side by side, watching their mother with such interest and love; Travis seemed rapt with Pell, with the way she was focused on Lyra. Families sometimes went apart. Like ships lost at sea, they sent out mysterious signals and found their ways back to one another.

"Hmm," John said, leaning very obviously toward Rafe and David. "Who's Monica, do you suppose?"

"I have no idea," Max said. "Why?"

"Seems she has called Rafe in New York," John said. "Left several messages. David is giving him the phone number now."

Max leaned over, watched David scrolling through his BlackBerry, saw Rafe scribble the number down on the palm of his hand. Seconds later, Rafe excused himself, went tearing into the villa, obviously to make a call, as if he hadn't just come home from the hospital.

"So?" John asked.

"So, what?"

"My title idea," John said. "What do you think?"

"I like it," Max said. "Very much. But with one small change. 'The Prodigal Family.'"

"Superb," John said. "Much better. Don't forget to mention the inspiration, though."

"Of course not," Max said. And then Lyra clinked her knife against her wineglass. And Max sat up straight, knowing she was finally ready to make her toast.

Twenty-Two

I shivered, but not because the air was cool. It was another warm, lovely, perfect Capri night. Warmth rose from the rocks, along with the scents of verbena, lavender, and lemons. No, the tingle under my skin came from the sight of my mother standing by the tripod, a look of such love in her eyes.

It brought back memories.

Sitting between Lucy and Travis, I felt them lean into me, our arms and shoulders touching, as if propping each other up, or keeping each other tied to earth. I felt I might rise, as if I had wings. I felt as if I might fly up to heaven to find my father, bring him back to earth just for this moment. So he could see us all together.

The strongest memory I was having was of my mother holding me. After she clinked her glass, she pulled the telescope out of her bag, started passing it around the table.

"I have a toast to make," she said. "To my favorite constellation . . ."

People called out their guesses: "Orion!" "The Pleiades!" "Lyra!"

"You're partly right," she said. "But Lyra the star—also known as its Latin name, Vega. Along with Capella and Pollux."

"Lyra, dear," Nicolas said, laughing, "I am an old man of the sea. Many years on many decks, and I've used a sextant all that time, plotting courses by the stars. I do not want to tell you this, but those stars are not in the same constellation."

"They're far apart," I said, suddenly remembering my first days on Capri, when my mother and I were first together. "Vega, Capella, and Pollux . . ." The three stars whose names were engraved on the telescope's brass tube. The telescope came to me, and I felt the letters with my thumb.

"Let me see," Lucy said, and I showed her. Seeing the names, gleaming in candlelight, I shivered again. My mother was holding me; it was winter, and cold. I heard the river rushing beneath our feet, down below the bridge. The night was even clearer than the one right now, so freezing we could see our breath. And we'd looked through the telescope, had it pointing at the sky when my father drove to find us, to rescue us both.

"Why those three stars?" I asked.

"Well, my father showed them to me long ago. I

was a little girl, and we would take star walks, just as I did with my girls. He showed me Lyra, told me that's where my name came from. And with Capella and Pollux: they're us," my mother said.

"Us?" I asked.

"You, me, and Lucy."

And I heard it then, my mother's voice whispering in my ear as we'd stood on that icy bridge over the half-frozen river over half my lifetime ago. **I love you, Capella,** she'd said. **My sweetheart, my star in the sky.**

"Capella," I said now.

"I wanted there to be meaning," she said. "I looked for it that night, in the sky. I should have been looking in your eyes. Yours and Lucy's."

I stood up. I carried the telescope over to my mother. She was crying, and I know she couldn't see well enough to fix it to the tripod. I did it for her, then put my arms around her. The sound of water was everywhere. Instead of an ice-filled river, it was the warm rush of waves breaking on the rocky shore below. The tide was in. I thought of all the starfish, safely covered by the salt water, on black rocks washed by the flow of waves.

"That night is over," I said to her. "We can't erase it, but we've healed it. The ghosts of that night are gone."

"Are you sure?" she asked.

I nodded, and bent to look through the telescope. I wanted her face next to mine, our cheeks pressing together. When I was little, and she'd take me stargazing, we'd look through the scope as if we could see at the same time. We were so close, I'd imagine she could see through my eye and I through hers. In some ways, living so many years apart, I realized that we had done just that.

"Do you have it, Lucy?" I asked.

"I do," she said. "But it's over at Mom's house."

"In your backpack?" Travis asked my sister. She said yes, and he said he'd get it. My football star boyfriend sprinted off Max's terrace, and I heard him running through the yards, over to my mother's house.

Stars swung overhead, down to the horizon. Everyone at the table took a turn looking through the scope, sighing at the strange beauty of our galaxy. Rafe came out of the house, smiling from ear to ear.

"She was home," he said. "Waiting for my call. Somehow I forgot I'd told her I was from New York."

"She's a lucky girl," I said. I had no idea who she was, but I could see that he was happy.

And then Travis was back. He carried Lucy's backpack in both hands, as if it held something breakable, set it down carefully on the wooden table between my sister and me. Lucy unzipped the compartment, pulled out a stiff cardboard file folder. She set it on the rustic surface, and gave me a look. Sticking out of the corner of the file, I saw the point of one gold foil star.

I'd kept this folder in my bureau drawer in Grosse Pointe, took it to Newport after our father died. For a long time after our mother left, Lucy and I would open the file, spread the paper out, and study it with care—as if we might find some clue to where she'd gone, how we could find her. But it had been many years since Lucy and I had looked at it together; the last time, we'd re-glued some of the stars. Since then, I couldn't even remember opening the folder.

Our first moment alone together, here in Capri, Lucy told me she'd brought it with her. At first I was unsure. This trip had had its rocky moments. I'd nearly left to return home. But Lucy explained to me that's exactly why she'd packed it, carried it all this way. **Because** my visit had at times been so hard, **because** reuniting with my mother had had its ups and downs.

I told her I threw it out, I said to Lucy. **And I told her we still had it,** Lucy replied.

And so we did, still have it.

"What is that?" my mother asked.

We didn't answer. Just pulled the old yellowed paper from the cardboard. The sheet had been folded so long, there were tears along the creases. Lucy unfolded it carefully, laid it on the table.

"Our map," my mother said.

"Dorset," I said, looking at the child's colored-in country and ocean. The land mass, drawn with green crayon by my mother, was irregularly shaped, vaguely circular, an island.

Blue water surrounded the island; I remembered leaning over the paper, carefully coloring in the sea, using all the blue crayons in the box. Midnight blue, periwinkle, thistle blue, turquoise, navy blue, cornflower, all blended on the page, my version of the deep blue sea. And there, all around the drawing's border, were the bright foil stars Lucy had stuck on.

"Some of them were loose," Lucy said. "Pell and I glued them back."

The three of us stared at it for a long time. We'd made it during the last days our mother lived with us. Our father had watched us, knowing that she would be leaving soon. Perhaps he had realized, even more than she, how important this map would become to all of us.

"What is it?" Max asked.

"A map," my mother said, wiping her eyes. "Of a place we all dreamed of. The three of us."

"It was a country we made up," I explained. "We called it Dorset, after the road we lived on."

"It looks like Capri," Rafe said, looking over my mother's shoulder.

"It does," Lucy said, and staring at it now, I realized my mother had drawn the shape of Capri. She had known where she was going; it was her way of telling us where she would be. The knowledge pierced my heart; to go back ten years, remembering what our family was about to go through . . . how had she been able to bear it? How had any of us?

"Sometimes," Max said, "when parents and children are far apart, they have to reach for what is there. A map, a telescope . . . even the stars in the sky. It's not perfect, because it's not the person. But it holds their place, until the family can come back together."

"Like us," Lucy said.

"Yes," Max said, smiling at her.

"And us," David said. He had come from the far end of the table to stand by Rafe and look at the map. Everyone turned to look at him. He was angular and handsome, just like his father and son; he'd said very little up to that point. He had a very reserved British manner. But just then, putting his hand on Rafe's shoulder, we all saw his chin wobbling. Rafe nodded.

"Thank you, Dad," Rafe said, and I knew everyone at the table was wondering what objects and symbols—what map, telescope, stars—they'd used to stay connected. Perhaps, of all of us, only Max and I knew for sure, had seen him walking the beach every single day, saving starfish as he had with his father, when he was a little boy.

"I have one more toast to make," my mother said.

We all reached for our glasses, raised them

high. My mother looked straight up, as if to toast the stars.

"Here's to Taylor," she said.

"Dad!" Lucy and I said, gazing up into the Milky Way, sending love and kisses to our wonderful father. Travis stood beside me; we held hands, and I sent a silent prayer to his father too.

"And," my mother continued, still looking heavenward, "to Christina."

"To Christina!" we all said.

And we stood there in a half-circle facing out to sea, looking up at the constellations. Down below, waves rolled in, breaking on the rocks, covering the starfish, reflecting the stars. We were each separate, and we were all together.

We had made such mistakes, over and over again. But somehow, miraculously, with clumsy and heartbreaking effort, we managed to fix them and just keep going. Life and love required advanced skill and we were all, even the oldest among us, just beginners. But standing on Max's terrace overlooking the sea, I knew we'd all keep trying.

Epilogue

Il Faraglioni towered out of the ocean, white rocks sparkling in the morning light, one an arched formation with a keyhole opening that boats could drive through, made from thousands of years of wind and waves. Seagulls, terns, and long-legged waders roosted on flat surfaces, and tufts of grass and flowers took root in every shallow crevice.

"Here we are," Pell called, driving the boat, slowing it down.

Lucy reclined in the stern. Their mother sat beside her, head tilted back as the breeze blew her hair out behind. They all wore bathing suits, knowing that a swim was part of the day's plan. But for now, they stared up at the rocks, austere and eternal.

It was just the three of them. Travis had stayed in Anacapri, to tour the island with Rafe and Max. David had flown back to London. Lucy knew Travis had offered to come and serve as skipper, but Pell had spent many summers on the water, knew her way around boats. She wanted this trip to be just for the girls.

Lucy gazed at the islands. Max had told her that they were home to the **lucertola azzurra,** a rare blue lizard, the only place it existed in the world. When she'd asked Pell if they could explore the islands, Pell had nodded. This was their time—just for the three of them.

Now Pell cut the engine. She signaled for Lucy to drop the anchor. It went over the side with a splash; Lucy watched it speed down to the bottom, sparkling metal shooting through clear water.

Pell reached into the cabinet under the console, pulled out three net bags filled with masks, snorkels, and fins. Rafe had spoken to Nicolas, helped her find a dive shop, and they'd gotten the gear they needed.

"In all the years I've lived here, I've never snorkeled," their mother said.

"Well, you have the garden and sky covered," Pell said. "Time to check out the ocean."

"What will we see?" Lucy asked. "Is it like a coral reef, with angelfish, grouper, eels . . . ?"

"You'll see," Pell said. "Starfish."

Lucy smiled at the nickname. She tugged on her fins, eager to jump over the side. Pell helped her adjust the strap on her mask. Their mother took out her camera, snapped pictures. Lucy was beaming so wide, her cheeks ached. If the trip ended right this minute, she would be the happiest girl on earth.

She gazed at her mother and older sister. They looked so much alike, with identical blue eyes. Lucy leaned over the side, to look at her own reflection in the water and see if she matched up. It was too blurry, but she really didn't care—she already knew. She was one of them, a Davis woman through and through.

They had come together—a mother and her two daughters—and they would go apart again. When Lucy and Pell returned to Newport, their mother would stay on Capri. It wasn't life the way anyone would have dreamed it. But people were who they were.

All of Lucy's 2:01 a.m. sleepless nights had taught her that. She was only fourteen, but she knew things couldn't be forced. Life had unfolded for her family differently than it had for others. There was so much about it that seemed unfair, cruel, beyond belief. She thought back to Grosse Pointe, to the earliest days, when they'd all been together. If someone had told Lucy that her mother would leave, her father be taken by death, Lucy would have thought it was a wicked fairy tale. Such events were too unthinkable to be real.

Life was a tide, spun by forces too great to be questioned, sweeping in and out. It might be easier to build a seawall of sand, circle the castle, protect the ramparts, than try to alter or affect the tide of life. Lucy's mother had to stay on Capri. It's where she gardened, where she lived. Staying here would keep her happy and sane, so she and her daughters could go on. Who knew what the future would bring? Maybe someday they would all live in the same place again.

And maybe not.

Lucy glanced around the boat. Pell was checking the anchor line; their mother was staring at her with such boundless love Lucy thought her own heart might burst. Then her mother looked at Lucy with the same light in her eyes, and Lucy smiled at her. This trip had made them a family.

They might do things differently than other people, but they belonged to one another. They always had, but this summer they'd realized it in a new way. Somewhere in the world it might be 2:01 a.m., but Lucy had a mother. She and Pell had their family back. It was as if Lucy's mother read her mind: she nodded, resolutely, as if nothing could ever shake her from what she felt, what they all had.

And then it was time to go in the water.

"Ready?" Pell asked.

"Ready," Lucy and their mother said.

They stood up on the rail, and one by one jumped in, hit the water with a shock. It felt cold at first, but Lucy got used to it right away. They swam in a line, from the yellow boat toward the eroded arch. Sunlight slanted through the rock opening, turning the turquoise water jade green.

Through her mask, Lucy saw sparkles of gold—as

if particles of the sun had fallen into the sea, drifting downward. No, they were swimming. Tiny fish! So excited, Lucy pointed. She saw bubbles escape Pell's mouth, and through the mask her sister's eyes were smiling.

The three of them swam toward the school of fish. Underwater, Lucy heard her heart beating in her ears; the sound of her breathing was steady. Otherwise the world was silent as they advanced in a line, Lucy between her mother and Pell. They approached the creatures, which were not the fish Lucy had first thought.

"Seahorses!" she said, the word dissolving in laughter and bubbles.

Pell nodded, and their mother stopped swimming. The two girls reached out their hands, and the tiny seahorses swam closer, their fins beating like miniature wings, and they wrapped their long tails around the sisters' fingers. When Lucy turned, to make sure her mother felt the seahorses too, she saw her mother holding back, just watching.

Lucy looked at Pell, and Pell at her mother. It wouldn't do for her to be so far away, so the two girls reached out their hands. The seahorses scattered, and Lyra took her daughters' hands. They held tight for a minute, just treading water. Bubbles drifted up to the surface; maybe into the sky, maybe up to Taylor.

"I love you, I love you, I love you," Lucy said underwater, talking to her father, mother, and sister.

Then Lucy, Pell, and their mother turned seaward. Still holding hands, they swam in a straight line through the blue water, surrounded by glints of gold, by a thousand seahorses. The tide came in, and the family swam.

Acknowledgments

Deep thanks to Nita Taublib, Tracy Devine, and Kerri Buckley, and to everyone at Bantam Books.

Much appreciation to Andrea Cirillo and all at the Jane Rotrosen Agency.

I'm ever so appreciative to Sarah Walker for every single thing.

Continuing and endless gratitude to Twigg Crawford.

Thank you to Sam Ekwurtzel for a year of art.

I am so appreciative to Jim Weikart for taking such good care.

I am grateful to my sister and brother-in-law, Maureen and Olivier Onorato, for their knowledge of seahorses and love of the sea and all marine creatures.

Peace and love to Jason Hancock and Amy Rhilinger, and the earth-loving Cooper.

Thank you to Pat Peter for her wisdom and generosity, and to the inimitable Emily Goodman.

Endless thanks to Proctor II and its wonderful staff, with special thanks to Dr. Cathleen Gould, Dr. Sherry Winternitz, Toby Hartman, Julie Twohig, Nina McCloskey, Rob Peirce, Paula Burley, Maxine Peake, Laura Marble, Erika Skorupski, Deborah Ford, and especially for lending me her guitar, Christina Dafnoulelis.

About the Author

~

LUANNE RICE is the author of twenty-eight novels, most recently **The Geometry of Sisters, Last Kiss, Light of the Moon, What Matters Most, The Edge of Winter, Sandcastles, Summer of Roses, Summer's Child, Silver Bells,** and **Beach Girls**. She lives in New York City and Old Lyme, Connecticut.

www.luannerice.com

LIKE WHAT YOU'VE READ?

If you enjoyed this large print edition of **THE DEEP BLUE SEA FOR BEGINNERS,** here are a few of Luanne Rice's latest bestsellers also available in large print.

THE GEOMETRY OF SISTERS
(paperback)
978-0-7393-2828-6 • 0-7393-2828-X
$25.00$28.00C

LAST KISS
(paperback)
978-0-7393-2789-0 • 0-7393-2789-5 $25.00/$28.00C

LIGHT OF THE MOON
(paperback)
978-0-7393-2773-9 • 0-7393-2773-9
$25.00/$28.00C

WHAT MATTERS MOST
(hardcover)
978-0-7393-2727-2 • 0-7393-2727-5
$26.95/$34.95C

Large print books are available wherever books are sold and at many local libraries.

All prices are subject to change. Check with your local retailer for current pricing and availability. For more information on these and other large print titles, visit www.randomhouse.com/largeprint.